I0662718

Hellmakers & Fearbreakers

Dean Myers

Published 2010 by arima publishing

www.arimapublishing.com

ISBN 978 1 84549 432 2

© Dean Myers 2010

All rights reserved

This book is copyright. Subject to statutory exception and to provisions of relevant collective licensing agreements, no part of this publication may be reproduced, stored in a retrieval system, or transmitted in any form or by any means, without the prior written permission of the author.

Printed and bound in the United Kingdom

Typeset in Garamond 12/14

This book is sold subject to the conditions that it shall not, by way of trade or otherwise, be lent, re-sold, hired out, or otherwise circulated without the publisher's prior consent in any form of binding or cover other than that which it is published and without a similar condition including this condition being imposed on the subsequent purchaser.

In this work of fiction, the characters, places and events are either the product of the author's imagination or they are used entirely fictitiously. The moral rights of the author have been asserted. Any resemblance to actual persons, living or dead, is purely coincidental.

Swirl is an imprint of arima publishing.

arima publishing
ASK House, Northgate Avenue
Bury St Edmunds, Suffolk IP32 6BB
t: (+44) 01284 700321
www.arimapublishing.com

Acknowledgements

The author would like to thank

*Jon Broster for his unlimited patience and dedication in helping me
make this book possible.*
*Rachel Broster for her help and positive support with proof reading
and editing.*
*Christine Rishworth and Anne Smalley for further proof reading
and editing.*
Further thanks to-
Jessmog.
*Richard Pernaski. Nicola Lee. Andrea Bloodworth. Jazz
Richards. Sarah Brookes.*

To Mum for all that she does, and all she has done.
And Dad for his influence, and my Sister for her kindness.

Chapter one

Breaking Point

In the late seventeenth century, far in the North Atlantic Ocean, an old ship sails on the third part of the triangular trade voyage, its cargo of West Africans delivered to The Americas for the dark trade of slavery. Loaded with sugar, tobacco and rum, her course is set for England. From a distant bird's eye view of the ship, the enchanting image betrays its reality, for the many voyages have witnessed the suffering and bloodshed of countless innocent men women and children.

It was not only the slaves that were terrorised, the crew also suffered. Anyone who had the misfortune to sail on the vessel, called Eroda, would have to answer to its merciless captain. The captain's method of keeping order was by way of his cousin, who lived by the name and reputation of Bone Breaker. Breaker stood a head taller than most men and twice as wide at the shoulder. He was a large, heavy, ugly bully of a man who loved the violence. The boards creaked beneath his beat when he patrolled the deck. It was a day much like any other day and Breaker was educating a shipmate in the way of pain.

Cain's head slammed hard onto the deck of the ship. The impact wrecked his senses; he coughed out a burst of blood that flooded from his nose, down into the back of his throat.

A second cough cleared his vision; he watched as channels of his blood flowed between the joints of wood where he lay. A cold rush of fear cut through his stomach driven by the realisation of the attack from Breaker, and the dread of more violence increasingly chilled his blood.

"If I keep still, he'll leave me be......don't move.....don't move!" Cain whispered in a desperate panic.

A combination of fear, pain and tears saturated the child within the young man. The pounding of his heart was so intense he felt it hammering against the deck, and with each beat, the anticipation of Breaker's next move grew.

The creak of big boots on the deck behind him drove out the affirmations of stillness; panic set in, and his instincts now commanded, escape, hide, anything to relieve the terror. Pulling himself up onto his hands and knees, he cautiously crawled away from the foot of his persecutor, desperately hoping to avoid another hard lesson dealt by fists loaded with knuckles like cannon balls. Cain couldn't recall why he had taken the blow to begin with, even though only a few seconds had passed.

Breaker's eyes sharpened with an evil pleasure at the sight of the young man's expression, an expression which exposed his pain, dread and the grip of fear.

A grin formed on Breaker's face which was the ugliest and meanest sight above or below the ocean. The monster of a man looked about, drew a large intake of breath and exploded forwards to deliver a devastating kick into Cain's ribs.

The magnitude of the attack launched Cain from the deck, spinning him before he thudded down onto the boards. Various members of the crew grimaced as Cain began rolling in agony while gasping and trying to cry out; his lungs screamed in spasm as he felt the terror of suffocation. He was in hell. A cough finally released the paralysis and out of pain and disorientation, he fought back the sickness while gulping in as much air as possible.

"I'm going to be killed, I'm going to die." The impact of this realisation hit him a thousand times harder than the ugly giant. A moment passed, fighting with each and every breath Cain felt the presence of death depart as he hung on to his life by a thread.

Breaker loved the power, the rush, the fear that he had created in his victim; he watched Cain roll around the blood stained deck trying to breath and escape. He was satisfied with his work; he turned to patrol the deck hoping some other member of the crew would dare make eye contact.

Still gasping for air, Cain lay gazing up at the cold grey sky through the large sails and rigging, his senses slowly began regenerating out of a swirl of distorted confusion and terror. The sway of the ship rocked his head from side to side on the wooden deck. In the distance he could hear the sound of the ocean, and a little closer he could also hear the footsteps of the crew bouncing off the boards. A wave dipped the ship turning Cain's head to his left shoulder; at the bow of the vessel he could see Breaker's huge frame. "Oh God it's over!" The relief felt like a warm blanket around his soul.

He rolled over and crawled away to try to compose himself. No one would dare help him. Slowly he struggled and sat up to lean his aching, beaten body against the mid mast; he spat out a little blood and desperately gasped for air. The white linen of his shirt flapped in the sea breeze, except for the blood drenched collar, which stuck to his neck with a tacky grip.

His senses grew a little stronger, and he realised that, although the encounter with Breaker had indeed been a violent experience, he was lucky to have survived. The Triangle trade had claimed the lives of many slaves and crew members through long and hard Atlantic crossings; murder, deceit and disease were constant travelling companions for those who dared sail the dark and gruesome voyages.

Cain looked down at his trail of blood. The adrenalin began to fade leaving him trembling with aftershock. He observed his palms quivering uncontrollably; he placed each of them under an armpit to comfort himself and try to recover.

He gazed along the port side; the rear mast on the higher deck was to his left, and the front mast to his right. The sails above him boomed a cracking sound as the wind swept through them and danced around the rigging, the creak of the ropes and movement of timber nursed Cain gently out of his fear. He realized his love of the sea, and although it was a hard life, working as a shipmate on normal trading ships was where he felt most at home.

He tried to stand but a sharp shock from his left lower ribs dropped him back to the deck. Gasping for air and groaning from pain he realised he needed a little more time to try to pull himself together.

Leaning back against the mast he rested his elbows on his knees and his head in his hands. He rubbed his forehead.

"Oww!" A stinging pain from a large cut above his right eyebrow triggered a yelp and a curse. He padded it gently, and wondered with a sigh what other injuries were going to show up. It occurred to him that at the age of twenty four, he would have liked to have kept his looks so he may at least one day attract himself a wife.

"If Breaker doesn't get me, or the disease doesn't cripple me, the beatings will disfigure me," he thought.

"Hey drink this, and stay out of trouble!" A crew member leaned from behind the mast and placed a bowl of water into Cain's lap. Cupping it with trembling hands he peered down to catch his reflection, he could see the damage wrought by the assault. Using the water as a mirror he pulled back his long dark hair and tied it into the nape of his neck.

Blood dripped into the bowl as he padded the cut above his right eyebrow. Cain always felt proud of his features; he stood about five foot ten with a medium body frame and clear brown eyes. He had always hated violence and now even more so, thanks to Breaker.

"Why would anyone have such strong desire to cause such pain to another, and take such pleasure in doing so?" He asked himself as he looked at Breaker and the captain who still stood towards the bow.

"This trade is vile!" he affirmed, and with his words he felt a vibration of strength, an indicator of a true statement.

Cain's mother had taught him to ask God for help or for a sign in times of trouble; he did not believe such help existed, so this was a perfect time to challenge all of her past preaching.

He looked to the horizon, cleared his mind and whispered.

"This trade is vile, poor people are being enslaved and crew members are dying; it sickens me. If any power is out there, show me a sign that it will end, or is true power only for those who can afford it? Are you helping only the rich?"

Cain's words were of pure defiance; he sighed and awaited a sign. But all he could hear was the captain complaining about conflict in the Triangle trade caused by a trouble maker.

"Zachary Macaulay is going to spoil it for all of us, someone should sort him," the captain moaned; Breaker nodded in agreement.

Cain had heard this name mentioned a few times before, Zachary Macaulay was the son of a Scottish minister, and was campaigning to abolish the slave trade.

"Could that be a sign?" he thought as his spine tingled, "Could a sign really come through so fast?"

The sensations felt like a message to him that all would be taken care of, and the Triangle trade might at last come to an end, but Cain's ego awoke and whispered that the conversation he had overheard was mere coincidence, why would he be so worthy of such a sign?

One dark thought seduced another, and a feeling of power began to grow.

He looked across at Breaker and the small captain who often hid behind the giant.

"Hmmm I would like to see you bleed," he muttered in Breaker's direction but not loud enough for anyone to hear, fear was still present. "Always the fear holds me back, this is no life, this feeling of ice in my veins caused by others." Cain was now talking to himself with no concern of who heard him. He gazed at Breaker: "I wonder if you ever feel this fear; I wonder if anyone has ever hurt you? I want to hurt you.....I want to kill you! This is no way to live," he whispered, "Why wait for the attack?" Anger grew deep within his soul, "No more fear!" he vowed to himself.

Cain sat for a moment, he felt powerful, he felt anger, and one hateful thought attracted another, and another, and with it the feeling of more power.

"If there is a power out there, give me strength to overcome the feelings of fear, no matter how much danger I feel, and with this power, I vow to take revenge, to do unto others as they have done to me..... and hurt those who hurt others."

And with the vow, a tremor left his spine. Cain was out of patience, deep resentment finally lit the fuse to a mix of explosive repressed anger.

He pushed his way up the mast to his feet, the anger and adrenalin coursed through his entire being, the pain from his ribs threw fuel on the fire of his growing hostility, as he marched towards Breaker and the captain.

"Next time we must bring more..."

"Excuse me Mr Breaker," Cain's words interrupted the captain. Breaker turned to see his most recent victim.

"The next time we fight I wonder if we might use swords to even things up?" Cain's words were defiant and challenging. The crew froze in disbelief as they awaited another bloodbath. "A brave man such as you, with such honour, would not fear a blade through the heart; we all know that you are not a bully who uses his size and strength against the weak, the hungry and the desperate, we all respect your bravery," Cain added, his voice was cold and clear and heard by all, especially Breaker.

Breaker turned to look at the captain and then to the expressions on the faces of the crew; he was confused; how dare anyone stand and insult him, especially after such a beating?

He felt his heart thump a little faster at the thought of sword play with this man, who no longer seemed to fear him.

What was he up to? Where was the fear? Why was this little man not running scared? What did he know? Breaker's thoughts began to expand their fears within.

An uncomfortable dose of adrenalin created by the fear of confusion and bravery of this little man's challenge seeped into Breakers blood stream.

He had absolutely no desire to cross swords with him for fear that Cain might have skills with such a weapon. But to deny the challenge may expose the coward and bully which deep inside he knew himself to be and, being a bully, he could never accept a challenge on unknown or equal terms.

Cain's fear began to grow again; a cold grip crushed his heart and sank into his stomach like a freezing steel cannon ball, and as the ice began to race around his body, he felt the committed vow which was his driving force and strength, had just vanished and betrayed him, leaving him in a state of weakness.

Fear was back. However, Cain felt the presence of something else, something new, he did not question it, he knew the fear was just as strong as ever before, but his reaction to it had changed.

Hatred and anger had offset the effects of the usual dread he felt in Breaker's presence and he was not going to give the giant any pleasure of seeing how incredibly scared he truly was.

Cain hid his fear well and with enough strength to hold his defiant gaze straight into Breakers eyes.

The natural flow of adrenalin made its presence known as Breaker began to experience trembling in muscles all over his body. He felt cold, and it was then that he made the mistake of not recognizing the difference between the natural effects of adrenalin, and fear. As the discomfort increased, so did the fear of being afraid, and so the cycle continued to grow. His ignorance of what he was experiencing stood against him and it was beginning to show.

The stare-down continued; Cain was intense, focussed on containing himself, he would not turn, run and hide. Distracted, he did not see the blood draining from Breaker's face.

"Breaker," murmured the captain, who also could not believe his eyes, "Breaker!" He repeated with more authority. It was enough to shake the giant into a violent reaction; he exploded forward, grabbing Cain by the throat as he retracted his right arm, loading up for a devastating punch.

"You are mine and I will kill you!" he growled savagely.

"I swear if you hurt me again...somehow... someway...I will take your life". Cain choked. His words carried an ice-cold chill which ran up Breaker's spine and exploded across his shoulder blades. Deep within, Cain vowed to himself, no matter what happened, he would survive this. But his soul-level promise would have to be strong enough to overcome Breaker's attack.

A wrecking-ball fist cracked Cain's head and his unconscious body hit the deck once more.

This time though his bones flashed an intense sharp blue light through his flesh, unseen by the crew, all but one...the ugly one.

The captain gave an order to spare Cain's life and to tie him to the racks; too many crew members had gone missing in the past, and the campaigners against the Triangle trade were looking for evidence such as this to help them abolish it completely.

The captain's intention was to do all he could to keep the trade alive, by whatever means possible.

Chapter two

Priests' View

1977

It was a warm Friday evening at Septembers end.

Jaden sat on his favourite old wooden bench, looking out to sea from the cliffs of England's Whitby coast.

Behind him was the old Saint Mary's church which was shadowed by the ruins of an Abbey. The spirit of the sea breeze whispered through the majestic gravestones standing in the cemetery, and the sun cast many shadows as its warm, orange rays illuminated the ruin.

Summer was coming to an end, it was still warm in the evenings, but the night would bring a mild frost.

Jaden had spent many hours over many visits watching the sun drop seductively behind the town.

Born and raised in central England, twenty five year old Jaden escaped and spent his weekends in Whitby whenever possible. Here he would empty his mind of the weight of heavy thoughts and worries. It was his place of sanctuary from work, past or present lovers, and life in the city.

At the side of the church pathway lay one hundred and ninety nine stone steps leading steeply down into the town and harbour, which had small cobbled streets, little craft shops, cafés and many public houses and inns.

Jaden spread his arms across the back of what he claimed to be his bench. He watched the boats return home to the stone harbour at the mouth of the river Esk. The Esk divided the town and could be crossed via a heavy swing bridge.

Distant laughter and the echoes of various conversations from tourists and locals, along with the smell of restaurants gave presence of the town below.

Jaden breathed in and closed his eyes. He held his breath and let the sun's rays soak through his eyelids, warming his soul.

"Ahhhhh!" he sighed. Every exhalation relieved stresses and tensions from his whole being.

"I love it." he whispered gently to himself. He allowed himself to drift with it all for a while; Priests' View had seduced him again just as always. He remained in this state of tranquillity for an hour or so.

"Why can't it always be this way?" his mind whispered.

A distant chant disturbed his semi meditative state. He opened his eyes and observed a few people to his right walking towards the Abbey ruin. His eyes followed them curiously. He yawned and refocused. A vicar of the church walked past him from his left.

"Where are all those people going?" asked Jaden

The vicar turned,

"Ah it's the Ghost walk, they do it here all the time, there's more people here this evening than usual though. An archaeological dig has uncovered an old unmarked grave".

"A grave?" asked Jaden.

"Well," replied the vicar, "the dig exposed an old skeleton; they think it will bring about an angry ghost, it's a morbid curiosity. You know how people are".

"Yeah, I know how they are, but I don't understand them. Can you see the bones then?" Jaden found himself feeling curious.

"No my son…the actual grave is secure from the public".

Jaden felt himself pulled in the direction of the ghost walkers; he stood up to see the unmarked grave, but the crowd blocked his vision. He drifted towards the edge of the cemetery where the mysterious old bones had recently been discovered. The ghost hunters moved to their next adventure and Jaden could see nothing but what appeared to be a wooden shed. As he came closer he realised it was to secure the grave from tourists.

A warning banner read: KEEP OUT BY ORDER OF EAST YORKSHIRE POLICE.

The lonely grave lay far out from the cemetery towards the edge of the cliffs.

"Hmm, I wonder how you ended up out here by yourself?" Jaden thought.

The last rays of the sun finally dipped, the ghost walkers began to feel the excitement and anticipation of a ghostly appearance or maybe a supernatural experience, but Jaden felt the cold touch of night creeping in, so he headed back to the inn where he was lodging. "The Four Masts" stood at the bottom of the ninety nine steps. As he opened the door, the warmth of the people and the heat from the old clanking radiators welcomed him.

He queued briefly at the old bar, then he sat alone at a corner table near the windows. He sipped his cold beer whilst watching the lights from the shops across the harbour reflecting off the dark water.

"It's not easy to sit all alone in a busy bar!" Jaden thought, observing that all the other customers were either couples, or groups of men and women of all ages.

Jaden wore a smile but he tried to keep it neutral in order to remain unnoticed. He felt that he may appear to be the lonely man of the pub who had no friends. While continuing to drink his beer he observed once again the wooden beams above and the old barrels used for tables, pictures of ships and fishing equipment hanging off the walls, lamps and a sextant high on a shelf, nothing had changed since his last visit two months ago.

Jaden peered over the rim of his beer glass; echoes of his past whispered into his mind. As the alcohol began to relax the tension of being alone, his thoughts filled his soul trying to recreate the feelings from a time which seemed so long ago. He realized he missed the feeling of being in love. The sadness was first amplified by alcohol, and then dampened by it, as he continued to visit the bar.

Chapter three

The Mantra

The following morning Jaden paid the price of alcohol abuse. He awoke with a dizzy, sickening headache. Sitting on the edge of the bed he gazed at his reflection in the cabinet mirror. He allowed a few moments for the room to stop spinning before posing and flexing his biceps, hoping to find a little more size with tension, then grunted as he relaxed and stepped into the shower.

Thirty minutes later he was out, his shoulder length hair still wet but not quite long enough to tie back. He pushed his long fringe out his face so he could see where he was going.

By twelve noon he had walked over the swing bridge, made his way to the edge of the harbour and was now returning back towards the inn near the one hundred and ninety nine steps.

"Café or abbey? Hmmmm tough decision!" he joked to himself.

While contemplating hunger versus sitting on his bench, he came up with the ingenious idea of buying a sandwich so he could take pleasure in both.

Finally, after making the tough decision of the correct filling and salad dressing for his sandwich, he made his way towards the Abbey. His short walk took him past the town hall where he noticed a psychic fare was being held on the following Sunday morning. His curious nature could not let such an opportunity pass him by.

Jaden had a burning interest in all things unexplained and mysterious. He had attended countless workshops and read many books on the esoteric Chinese arts of chi gung, gung fu and meditation.

Despite his fascination, he had always maintained a degree of healthy scepticism regarding anything that he had learned; he filtered it all through his own experience and kept a few blends of this and that which he felt worked for him.

"I'll be in there tomorrow," he said to himself as he made his way up the steps.

"All the books I have bought and read about health and keeping fit, and then I drink gallons of beer and eat fast greasy food; what a hypocrite

I am!" Jaden laughed at his strange behaviour.

He arrived at his bench slightly gasping from the haul up the steps.

"Finally!" he croaked, sitting down to admire the view. His intention now was to try to clear his body of the effects of the previous night's drinking marathon.

He took a quick look around to check who was present.

"Not many," he thought, "good! It's easier to meditate with fewer people around."

With eyes closed he began to focus his thoughts on a sequence of internal organs. The energy tingled but felt weak because of the alcohol still present in his system. He continued, but the sick feeling disturbed his peace.

"Why do I do it?" Jaden muttered, angry with himself for drinking so much. Finally he relaxed and let go. He felt the energy building up stronger causing his headache to diminish.

A subtle whisper of a distant message from long ago manifested as a connection between Jaden's conscious and subconscious mind. He tried to make sense of it but the more he focused, the more it faded. His attempt to get a stronger feel of this strange sensation gave him a little burst of fear, the adrenaline of a fight maybe.

"What is this all about?" he felt the energy of someone who might need him. A cold shock ran down his spine and burst into his kidneys with a jolt.

"It must be the beer!" He concluded.

With a deep sigh Jaden continued his meditation, but his body was tired, sleep seduced him, and with his head propped on his shoulder, much to the amusement of passers-by, he snored away, fast asleep on the bench.

A light breeze with a hint of rain lifted Jaden's awareness, he slowly opened his eyes.

The crisp sea breeze sharpened his senses, he sat for a while feeling his damp hair whipping at his face.

"Afternoon," came a voice from behind him. He turned to see an old black African man edging his way around the bench; he used a wooden walking stick and wore a long brown coat, black scarf and trilby hat.

"Hello, how are you?" asked Jaden as the visitor sat to his right on the bench.

The old man nodded and smiled, resting both hands on his walking stick while he settled on the bench.

After a few moments of silence the old man introduced himself as Delmar, and a conversation began about the weather, Whitby and the latest news. Jaden found him to be very charming; he loved Delmar's accent and his infectious laugh as he shared some old memories. Delmar then mentioned boxing; he had fought as a heavyweight.

Jaden had trained in various martial arts and had always been curious about boxing, he had many questions and their conversation was beginning to feel more like an interview with the older man.

"I have sparred in a few martial arts over the years but I never feel like I have really got anywhere...... with any art," Jaden confessed.

"I train hard, I do all the drills, but it's just the last element I just can't seem to reach," he added.

"Hmmm," Del nodded, he sat back and smiled while looking at Jaden with an analytical expression.

"You're a good man, with a good heart," Delmar spoke clearly, "your problem may be that you think to hit someone makes ya a bad man, not the good man.... that ya know yourself to be; so you have a conflict within ya that ya cannot see".

Jaden felt his jaw drop; old man Delmar's wise words had just solved an ongoing problem that no high ranking black belt could overcome. Their recurring answer was to prescribe more drills and harder physical workouts.

"Ya know there is something inside ya soul to solve cos' ya can feel it," Delmar continued, knowing from Jaden's expression that he had struck a chord with him.

"So how I think affects the outcome?" Jaden asked.

"How ya think, and how ya feel" Delmar whispered. "I can help ya wi' a mantra" he added.

"A mantra?" Jaden was puzzled.

"I will tell it to ya, like someone once told it to me... if you want it" Delmar smiled.

Jaden felt overwhelmed by the ever growing presence and charisma of this old man.

The old man's voice lowered, taking on an otherworldly tone.

Stop and listen to how you feel,
Your inner compass will then reveal,
Your soul's desires the truth of you,
To release resistance anchoring you,

Accept the ghosts which haunt your mind,
They may have led you to this point in time,
Allow their whispers of all your fears,
Focus on joy; the darkness clears.

Delmar had Jaden repeat it back to him. They talked for a couple of hours before Delmar finally wished Jaden all the best and departed to Saint Mary's church.

Chapter four

The Skeleton Key

Jancine sat behind her table in the town hall.

A rainy Sunday morning was dampening the trade of the psychic fare. A gifted medium, she originally hailed from New Zealand. After only giving two readings she smiled to herself at the memory of an old joke, "Psychic fare cancelled due to unforeseen circumstances"

The enchanting sound of pipes and smell of various burning incenses filled the room.

Jancine made her way past the tables to the small kitchen area for a cup of tea. She chatted briefly with a few of the other stall holders, then headed back to her table.

She picked up her book and continued to read her half finished love story.

"Excuse me."

Jancine looked over her book to see the six foot light frame of a pleasant looking man who seemed to have an inquiry.

"Hello" she replied.

"I am interested in a reading, maybe tarot cards."

"Well, it's eight pounds for a straight reading, but I also charge an extra four if you want me to tape it for you." Jancine pointed to a small recorder.

"Ok. I will have the full deal then please," replied the man as he removed his leather jacket and sat down. Jancine removed a blank tape from its wrapping, stuck on a label, and wrote the date.

"What's your name?" she asked.

"Jaden" he replied.

Jancine asked no other questions, not wanting to compromise her reading for him.

She passed Jaden a deck of cards and asked him to shuffle them.

Jaden's nature, normally so fluid when shuffling cards, faded fast; he struggled with his hands and kept dropping the deck. Cards seemed to eject themselves from the pack randomly, he blushed as he picked them

23

up and tried again.

It was no use, the more he attempted a basic shuffle, the more cards he dropped.

Jancine could see his frustration, and she began to sense something strange in the young man's aura.

"Stop! It's ok," she said.

"Sorry I can't seem to..." Jaden felt embarrassed.

"It's fine," Jancine interrupted, "the energy isn't right in this place today," she added to try and comfort him.

"Are you here for the rest of the day?" she asked.

"I am here until Tuesday; I have a few days off work." Jaden answered.

"If you still want a reading, you can come to my home later this evening; it's only down the road in Scarborough, same price."

Jaden paused for a moment, going to Scarborough would mean he would have to drive, he intended to be at the bar for seven in the hope of maybe meeting a nice girl or getting drunk, or both!

"Ok, I'll see you later," he replied.

As Jancine gave him directions, Jaden's ego was screaming at him:

"What, you were supposed to be having fun, why can't you learn to say no, you are so weak sometimes!" Over and over his internal dialogue plaguing him until he finally reached a compromise, planning to get drunk after his reading with Jancine.

Sun light gently faded and Jaden opened his eyes after a long spell of Chi meditation. After focusing his mind on each of his internal organs, his concentration moved to the point just behind his navel where he could store energy. Sometimes he found these practices to be a struggle as a good teacher was hard to find, so he relied on books and seminars for guidance. He felt light headed as his senses gently awoke after staying deep for over an hour. He realised there was a lot more to learn, he could now feel the energy building up and his next step was to try to circulate it around points of his body.

With the aid of a few strong coffees he pulled himself together and headed out towards Scarborough.

Jancine found herself frantically cleaning and tidying her house; she knew that her clients always expected her home to be a peaceful environment with incense burning, Celtic music playing and crystals on every windowsill. She had an untidy nature though, always clean, but lots of clutter. There were always books, shoes and clothes on the floor, and the smell of her boxer dog named Sapphire met you at the door.

She heard Jaden's car pull onto the drive of the small semi-detached house and went to greet him. She invited him in and poured him a cup of tea, noticing that he looked a little out of sorts.

"Are you feeling ok Jaden?"

"I think I have overdone my meditation," he answered as he sat back in a large cane chair. He then began to passionately explain how energy is all around us, this energy may be directed by our thoughts, and science is now proving what ancient mystics have always taught.

As each moment passed a dizzy sickness grew inside of him and began to affect his senses.

"Jaden you don't look well enough for a reading, what's wrong?" Jancine watched as her client grew evermore pale.

"The further I drove from Whitby, the weaker I felt, and now I feel like…" Jaden rubbed his eyes, and tried to pull himself together.

"Would you like some water?" Jancine tied back her long black hair and quickly marched into her small kitchen.

Jaden called to her over the noise of the running tap: "It's the grave!"

Jancine rushed back in to find Jaden passed out on the chair.

"Jaden, wake up! You've fainted. Jaden, Jaden!" She grabbed him by both shoulders and gently shook him.

"The skeleton………..the bones, it is I," he murmured.

Jancine paused.

"The bones at the Abbey, they are mine, from my last lifetime, I must go to the grave!" There was an ethereal quality to Jaden's words.

"I am here to undo the fear…by my own desire."

"Tell me Jaden…what do you mean?" Jancine realised that Jaden was in a deep trance.

"All has come together perfectly, the discovery of the body in the cemetery coinciding with my visit to the Abbey, and if I touch the bones….." Jaden's voice began to fade.

"If you touch the bones…?" Jancine shouted with anticipation, but it was of no use, Jaden lapsed into unconsciousness.

The central heating hummed hypnotically, keeping Jaden in a deep, safe and warm sleep on Jancine's sofa. He had the same feeling when he had the odd nap in his car; the lovely awareness of the soul recharging. An odd snort and movement from Sapphire dreaming about chasing a dog from her garden, or being fed some of her favourite biscuits, added to the harmony of man and dog safely sleeping in a warm sanctuary. A disturbance outside the house faded in and out of Jaden's consciousness as he tried to reclaim his slumber. But it was no use; he turned to lie on his back while rubbing his forehead with a yawn. Sapphire lightly growled at the anticipation of anyone who dared trespass on the property without her kind permission. The darkness began to fade slightly as Jaden began to focus. The dog jumped up onto the sofa, looking for some attention when she realized that her guest had awoken. As Jaden tried to make sense of his present location, the disturbance from outside got closer to the house. He could hear the voices of a man and woman shouting abuse at each other. Sapphire froze, her ears pricked up and she began to growl; her growl becoming a bark. Jaden sat up to listen and comfort her but she darted to the door.

The rattling of keys behind Jaden gave him a fright as he realized someone was about to enter the door of the room where he was sleeping. He vaguely remembered visiting Jancine's house and his mind began to race for further answers. A light flicked on to his right revealing a staircase leading from the bedrooms above into the living room. Jancine raced down just as the door from the outside opened. Jancine's daughter Rebecca marched in, bringing with her the smoky night air. She was muttering and cursing with such anger that she completely missed the sight of Jaden shrinking under the covers on the sofa. Sapphire jumped all over the room with excitement, running over to Jaden for a second then returning to Rebecca. Jancine was trying to gain control and calm down both her daughter and her dog. Eventually peace was restored, and Jancine introduced Jaden and Rebecca to each other. Jaden listened carefully as Jancine explained the trance he was in to Rebecca; he had no recollection of his words regarding the bones at the Abbey being his. This was the first time he had heard it too. The very idea of having a previous life, and his old bones lying exposed at the Abbey was far too incredible for him to believe, so he rationalised it by blaming his own vivid imagination; that combined with too much Chi from the afternoon's over training.

Dawn was breaking and the topic of conversation was mainly revolving around two subjects, Rebecca's fight with her very recent ex-boyfriend and Jaden's trance and possible reincarnation.

With Sapphire sitting on and warming Jaden's toes he felt the urge to show off his knowledge.

"Some far eastern philosophy believes that our memories are stored in an energy field all around us, and they are accessed by the vibrations of our whole body. Our body is our key to access the field of our past thoughts." He paused to check their reaction, and, not feeling like a geek quite yet, he continued.

"Science is also beginning to agree with some old teachings about energy and how it behaves according to our thoughts." Mission accomplished, he now felt like a geek.

"Sorry, I read all sorts of rubbish." he blushed.

"It's very interesting Jaden," Jancine laughed, "You should see some of the things I read. I would have been burnt at the stake a few hundred years ago for my practices!" she added.

Conversation continued and theories of ex-lovers, energy fields and spirituality blended into one seriously passionate debate. Sapphire was now resting her chin on Jaden's knee and gazing at him with her electric blue eyes. Although Jaden was chatting with Rebecca and Jancine, Sapphire was very sure that the new guest was really chatting with her, and she hoped the rest of the pack in her house liked him.

Jancine slipped into the kitchen to make tea for everyone. Jaden felt a little shy and awkward; the silence grew into an eternity.

"Who's that funny looking chap in the photo?" He pointed to a picture hanging on the wall behind the television in front of them.

"That's Uncle Dennis, my mum's brother." Rebecca chuckled.

"Well done mate, good lad, you just called her uncle a funny lookin' chap. Nice start!" Jaden thought to himself.

"We call him Wing Nut, look at those big ears!" Rebecca added.

"And that big wrecking ball size head with a face painted on the front." Jaden replied.

"He is coming over soon, and he is a tough ol' cookie so watch out." Jancine added as she sat back down with three steaming hot mugs of tea.

"Ah he is harmless really." she added

"Unless you upset him, eh mum?" Laughed Rebecca.

All topics covered and yawns all around finally ended a pleasant and unexpected gathering and a new friendship was born. Jaden drove back in the early hours to his lodge at Whitby. Sapphire would have joined him if she could have only made it to the car, but she was spotted trying to escape as he made his exit.

It was Monday evening and Jaden had packed all of his clothes, ready to return home the following day. The dread of working at the power station overshadowed the usual ambience of The Four Masts inn where he sat, once again, with a beer.

He worked in the mechanical maintenance division of the station, he liked to describe some of the work there as heartbreaking, but he was very proud of his skills and ability to use his hands and his brains. Having to constantly solve problems under pressure, and then work psychically hard to fix the faults, he could not relate to any man wanting to work in an office. He did not class their work as a real job, and even the smart ones would probably never be able to climb to the power plant's higher reaches with heavy tools, let alone manage to fix anything.

The *us and them* division was strong in Jaden. He had had many arguments regarding engineering being the backbone of England. He also felt that they were blinded by their own self importance, and that they looked down on him because he wore a boiler suit for work, instead of the three piece suit to the office.

It was a strange time in life for Jaden, his character had developed from that of a teenager who may collapse under peer pressure and laugh at a sick joke, or at the downfall of a poor soul which he did not truly find funny, to that of a man who was at the boundaries of integrity. It was a matter of heart versus mind. He knew that he was generalising about the office workers, and that some of them must be decent, hard working people, but sometimes his ego would outweigh his better reason and anger would displace his usually harmonious instincts. To his credit though Jaden was trying to work on this part of himself; he called it his soul work.

As he delved into the dark recesses of his own mind, he began to realize that it was his own ignorance that was the problem. He also knew that while he stereotyped people, he too was guilty of the hypocrisy that he saw in others.

The night carried Jaden to the inn, he sat with his drink near to the door where he watched people drift in and out through the smoky air. While reflecting upon the events of his visit he laughed as Sapphire bounded into his thoughts. The conversation between himself, Jancine, and Rebecca began to run its dialogue. The topic of reincarnation led him back to his own words regarding the bones in the grave at the Abbey. He gazed at the door of the inn as he held the thought of the skeleton just at the top of the steps.

The door drifted open with a breeze which felt like a cold invitation to step outside into the night and maybe, just maybe, visit the grave.

Jaden shook off the idea with a tremor, but his ego was now making an entrance.

"Scared are you? Daren't even go up the steps in the dark!" The ego communicated a great deal of fear in a one hit feeling.

His soul work had taught him that in the past, fear had often made him do things that he really did not want to do. He now knew that his ego would always try to remind him that he could never do this or that, when he succeeded though, the ego would always take the credit by saying: *"Never doubted you mate, not for one minute!"* The ego always supported whichever team was winning at the time.

Alcohol was slowly drowning any chance of removing the strong disguise of the ego being anything other than the false, empty words of its true nature.

Jaden began to take the challenge seriously. The door opened again at the whim of the ice cold winds.

"What am I going to do if I do visit the grave anyway?" he said to try to regain some sense of the very thought of visiting an old skeleton.

"Just see what happens when you get there!" his ego replied.

"But why?" Jaden protested

"Because those old bones were once yours." echoed the silencing answer.

Jaden felt the need for a strong one; he ordered a double whiskey, drank it in one hard shot and headed for the exit. His room was below the inn, so he had to go outside to walk around and down the back. He paused and breathed in the cold air, to his right were the dark steps up towards the Abbey.

"*Dare ya!*" whispered the inner voice. Jaden sighed and looked down the alleyway towards his room, then he turned and gazed up towards the old dark Abbey. After a few moments' pause, and more abuse from his ego, he made a decision, and with the cold night air upon him, he began his journey up the steps towards the Abbey.

"I can't believe I am actually doing this".

The alcohol had displaced his common sense and reason. The chatter of his mind continued, but as he approached the half way point, the words of his ego became less challenging, more fearful.

"*Why are you doing this? You've proved your point, let's go home now.*"

He paused for a second and tried to slow his heart rate which was pounding in his ears. The wind swirled out of the night and down the steps casting a spine chilling spell deep into Jaden's soul; a warning to turn and go back. The crash of the sea below held him at the halfway point as he breathed deeply to regain composure.

"Come on, come on!" he affirmed and, clinging onto the cold rail, he took another step towards the Abbey. Ten minutes later and he was near the top.

His feet weighed heavy with fear, every cell in his body urging him to turn around and go back to the lovely warm inn.

"Come on Jay!" he said to himself; he took a few more deep breaths, paused and slowly climbed the final few steps, each one dropping from eye level to be replaced by the moon lit ruin of the Abbey.

The place Jaden loved so much had a dark presence. Under normal circumstances he would have loved to be here, but this time things were different, he was in the true grip of fear.

"Come on!" he ordered himself, forcing one fearful, heavy foot slowly in front of the other, and, little by little, Jaden entered the cemetery.

The gravestones cast long shadows in the moonlight, and the sound of the wind breathing through them toyed with his nerves.

The loneliness at the Abbey and cemetery was overwhelming, he took another breath, and the cold night air chilled his bones.

"Nearly there!" he whispered. The frosty ground crunched beneath his feet and he could still hear the cold sea crashing distantly on the rocks below. Slowly, carefully he walked through the old dark cemetery; the icy breeze whispered evermore haunting warnings as it whistled through the stone graves. The Abbey watched and waited in silence. His journey was almost complete; his shadow was upon the makeshift wooden cabin which guarded the exposed grave. Feeling his way around it he found the entrance; the lock on the thin, hard wooden door was cheap. It wasn't really guarding much of value, or so they had thought. Jaden took out his key-ring torch and fumbled away, his hands trembling from the adrenalin.

"Come on, come on!" he repeated frantically. He was in a race against time, time long enough for the reality of what he was doing to kick in and stop him. A few minutes passed, and the lock was off.

The door slowly creaked open, exposing the darkest, most fearful entrance Jaden had ever experienced.

He crossed the threshold, the few steps seeming to take forever. He held his breath, releasing it only when he was engulfed in shadow. Once inside he pressed his back against the timber. He felt sick; slowly with both hands shaking on his key ring torch, Jaden took a breath, swallowed hard, and pointed the beam slowly to his feet. The light exposed the deep grave, the beam probed deeper as slowly Jaden ran the torch outwards. There they lay, the skeletal bones of maybe, just maybe, the remains of a former self. He froze, his heart was punching him in the throat and his veins felt like rods of ice.

"No fear!" Jaden whispered as a mantra. It had no effect; he turned, tore out of the cabin, rounded a corner and slammed his back onto the wooden wall.

"What the hell am I doing?" he sighed, the fear loosening its grip a touch. Taking a few minutes to come together he whispered: "What am I so afraid of....this can't be true." He slid down the timber and crouched.

The cemetery was dark and still.

"It's just some old bones." he said trying to calm down.

"The dead can't hurt ya!" and with that thought, and before fear had a chance to regain its power, Jaden turned, strode straight back into the cabin and jumped into the grave. With one knee bent he carefully reached forwards, his right palm shaking while slowly edging towards the skull. There was a pause, a slow intake of breath, then the final reach. Contact was made. Jaden touched the skull.

"ARGHH!" he exhaled with shock, swallowing hard, trying to catch his breath, the rush driving his heart to the full, but just when he felt he had conquered his fear by jumping into a grave and touching an old skeleton, his attention was snatched away. There could be no denying the energy travelling up his arm. Fear multiplied and dominated him. He realised that he had just unlocked something very powerful. Dead and alive, the skull and Jaden; it gripped his hand with the discharge of micro-cellular memory. His body was reading information stored in the bones and he had no choice in the matter. He tried to let go but the skull would not release him. The fear was destroying him.

"HELP!" he screamed, frantically feeling his palm becoming tighter, the shock travelling up his arm causing his body to spasm.

The bones began to glow, a dull green radiance driving Jaden's panic further still.

"OH MY GOD HELP ME!" he screamed as the skull glowed evermore brightly. A burst of green light exploded from the skull, its searing brilliance engulfing him. A violent shock of pain wrenched through Jaden's chest.

"Oh god...I'm gonna faint...." He tried to resist but failed and lay once again in a grave of his past.

The distant sound of thunder served as a gentle wake up call. As his eyes began to open, the blur faded giving sight of the ocean and its far horizon. The wonderful smell of the fresh open sea breeze filled Cain's lungs, his mind began to clear, and something felt oddly unfamiliar.

He turned his head to see his hands bound and tied to the rack. His tongue ran around the inside of his mouth tasting dry blood, a reminder of his violent clash with Old Ugly.

"I survived!" Cain murmured.

A few moments passed and the gentle swing of the creaking ship massaged his senses, he felt mentally and psychically stronger with each tilt.

"What's happening to me?"

His body felt heavy and powerful, the unfolding energy washing over him, immersing his entire structure. Cain experienced an immediate knowing of skills and perception which far outweighed his current understanding of his world. He hung from the rack feeling the ecstasy of an incredible vibration, which displaced his sense of his original self.

The vibration faded fast, but Cain needed a moment to compose and realign himself, to come to terms with the how and the why of this life changing event.

"I know words....I can read". As this incredible new information began to take shape, he worked on the rope which bound his hands. Before the fight with Breaker, Cain had been uneducated and illiterate, but it now began to dawn on him that he had within his grasp huge, unearned knowledge, but from whence he did not know.

He peered at the ship through the rack, the feeling of fear palpable in the air, and even with his restricted view he could see why. The captain and Breaker were on patrol.

"You can take them out now...you have the skills," Cain's ego whispered as it introduced him to his new fighting ability.

"*Boang sau, woo da yut jee choong kuen,*" his tongue stumbled over the strange Cantonese words, never before spoken, but keenly understood. The power he felt was overwhelming, the passion to be free from the rack drove him forward, gnawing desperately at the ropes that bound him.

As one arm became free and began to work on the other knot, a feeling of peace flooded his soul.

"I can help people, I can teach them to read and write, and maybe make a little bit of money." The thought felt spine tinglingly wonderful.

"I don't need this violence and heartbreaking work, and I don't need to fight Breaker, I can stay out of his way, we are almost home."

"*Are you going to let the Captain and Breaker get away with it all? Feel your strength, use it!* Or are you truly beaten by them?" The ego began its dark reminders of the insecurities and weaknesses which had haunted Cain's past.

"*You vowed to kill them, and now you have the knowledge to do it! No excuses, look at them! What right do they have? Imagine the Captain's face as you step on his ugly cousin's throat right before you choke him to death. How good it would feel!"*

The hatred began its flood to drown the peaceful thoughts and inspirations of changing trades, leaving Cain at the mercy of an inner conflict.

The small, pointed-nosed captain and Breaker were on deck, and, as was their wont, both of them were giving hell to a crewmember.

The captain shouted in the face of a small young man, while old ugly held him high by his hair. The poor boy screamed in pain and terror.

"You are NOTHING, you only eat and when I say you eat!" screamed the captain in the young one's face.

"Please don't throw me overboard sir," sobbed the reply.

'WHACK!' the captain's hand slapped the young face so hard that it could even be heard by some of the crew in the lower decks.

"I didn't give you permission to speak boy."

"HEY SCUM, tell the young one to wait his turn! You've not finished with me yet!"

As one, Breaker and the captain turned to see who had been stupid enough to mutter even a single word while they were on deck, and to actually interrupt with an insult was indeed a death wish. Cain stepped forward.

For a brief moment the Captain and Breaker were crushed by disbelief. They turned to look at each other for confirmation of their senses, the captain shocked by the interruption, Breaker confused because he was sure he had dealt with Cain for the last time. All eyes of the crew focused upon the three men.

Cain stood square on to the captain with a vicious expression, and all on board felt the presence of something dark within his soul. He stepped closer and stared deep into the captain's eyes.

"You are a coward, who hides behind fake authority, and you hide even further behind your brain-dead plant life pet cousin who calls himself Breaker, we all call him Breaker the ugly faker."

The verbal attack was delivered straight into the heart of the captain and Breaker. Cain felt twice as strong, and twice as confident. The captain felt his power over the men fading fast, and as the power faded, fear replaced it.

The crew were beside themselves; all of their heartbeats synchronized as they waited with dread to see what punishment Cain would receive. *Had the previous beating from Old Ugly not been enough?* They all asked themselves.

One of the men in the rigging whispered to his shipmate: "Cain must have had a good smack in his head."

"Or he's been in the sun too long!" came the other's reply.

"So then my boy," the captain began the death sentence, "you seem to know an awful lot. Tell us more of what you know about my fake authority as you call it........ maybe we should have put you in charge eh?" The captain followed his words with laughter, which were soon echoed by a few crewmembers that dared not remain silent during the fake sounds of joy along with the merciless, insecure, angry, little man.

Cain's response was immediate: "You are an ignorant fool with the insight of a dead squid, and when I have finished with Breaker I'm going to smash your weak little skull through the deck of the ship!"

The captain paused for a brief moment to allow validation of the threat to be analysed by his cowardly thought process.

"KILL HIM NOW!" He blasted to his cousin.

As Breaker stepped forward so did Cain; he was ready, and Breaker could see it.

"It won't happen this time," Cain informed Ugly; his words disrupted Breaker's usual confidence; the bully's eyes drove a piercing stare to attempt to break the smaller man's spirit, but Cain gave an expression which radiated confidence and an icy cold aggression.

Although he felt uneasy, Breaker followed his orders and threw his infamous big right fist. Pain exploded through his rear right inner knee joint while his attack was neutralized. His right arm had been deflected straight over his target - Cain's head. Pain and confusion scrambled the brute's tiny mind.

The crew watched in awe as Cain exploded into a simultaneous attack and defence structure, he kicked Breaker's knee while blocking his right punch.

Breaker began to buckle onto his rear knee; a second attack took form in the way of a sickening blast from Cain's left palm erupting between Breaker's eyes.

Breaker was under attack; he felt submerged in pain and disorientation, fear and shock, the last impact left his big head tilted back, his jaw line high and exposed.

"In for the kill!" Cain felt hatred powering his entire being, the aggression drove out any chance of forgiveness towards his enemy. With a large draw of breath, he threw his body forwards so that his fist would carry all of his weight to maximise its damage to the target, and as it connected, Cain squeezed his fist for a split second before relaxing the energy and driving through Breaker's jaw. Cain exhaled with a timely gasp upon impact, the cracking sound of the bigger man's face held the crew in anticipation of its result. Breaker's large frame crumpled into a heap on the boards, he was out cold before his big skull thudded down and bounced, scattering teeth and bloody mess.

The Captain froze, one hand holding the handle of his sword and, although he tried, he dared not draw it; he relied on Breaker to do all of his hands-on dirty work.

Cain stepped towards the coward.

"Scared are ya boy?" Cain recognized the symptoms of terror from the long voyages on the Eroda; he had experienced it himself and witnessed it in the poor slaves and his shipmates.

A wave of peace fluxed into Cain's soul; the bully had been defeated, the Captain had no power over the crew, their fear was fading; Cain began to let it go.

"What......let it go...you have got this far, he deserves to pay!" Cain's ego was back, and he found himself in the vibration of deep hatred. He launched himself forwards, screaming abuse at the Captain.

"No please....... we have to keep order on the ship it's the only......" The captain searched desperately for excuses, but he could see the hatred in Cain's eyes.

The captain dropped to his knees, hoping that his submissive position would aid his salvation, but it was of no use; Cain kicked him hard in the face, leaving the captain straight out on his back. He then sat high on his chest with the full intention of killing him.

The pleading cries for forgiveness from the captain only made Cain's crushing grip around his throat evermore ferocious. Cain looked into the Captain's eyes with a hate-filled gaze.

"Look at me…. You dog; my face will be the last thing you see before you go to hell!" screamed Cain.

Instant darkness shadowed Cain's awareness, his eyes flickered open revealing the blur of Breaker's large frame and the Captain choking and gasping for breath beside him. Somehow Breaker had managed to regain consciousness and had kicked Cain from behind, knocking him almost senseless.

"Take this mutinous wretch aft! Find something heavy… some chains to weigh him down and throw him overboard!" the captain spluttered the order at two crewmates.

Cain was spent of energy from his rage, but his expression of hatred drove fear into the Captain's heart. He felt the shipmates lift him, and as they dragged his tired body towards the back of the ship, he could see the damage he had caused to Breaker's ugly face. Blood was still pouring from his mouth and he walked with a painful limp from the damage of the kick.

Cain realised that the main reason he was about to be thrown overboard was because the Captain and Breaker feared him. This new knowledge empowered him, but he cursed himself for being defeated.

"It's not over. I am not ready. I'm not yet ready to die," he thought.

"HEY FAKER!" Cain shouted; all of the crew stood to attention once again at the sound of the rebel's voice, the Captain and Breaker each wore a slightly smug expression to try and disguise the feelings of defeat and fear which they desperately tried to hide.

Cain spat a glob of blood at Breaker.

"I vowed to kill you both…. and I shall kill you both, in this life and thereafter….for all of eternity."

Cain's vow held all on board in thrall until he had finished his threat.

The words carried such hatred that some of the men were glad they were in neither Breaker's nor the Captain's shoes.

"What are you waiting for?" the captain hurried the men. Cain relaxed as he was dragged aft; night was falling, it was almost dark, and with it came a fog.

An intermittent banging and the sound of rusty old hinges creaking as the door swung in the morning breeze served as an alarm call for Jaden.

Sunrise gave a dim, orange light of dawn which shone into the hut where he lay in the old grave with the skeleton. As his eyes slowly opened, none of the images before him registered, his system was on autopilot and his body gently moved independently of any instruction of the mind which was still scattered.

He felt docile, spiritually drained; his body continued to adjust its position and Jaden found himself sitting upright, his legs crossed as in a yoga position which he sometimes practiced. Little by little his mind began to register his surroundings, overlapping his dreamy images of Breaker and the Captain. Slowly he leaned forwards and reached for the skull, holding it up face to face he looked into the dark empty sockets that had once held eyes.

"Did I......did I once look out to the world from here? Was I once Cain?" He was mesmerised and sat for what seemed like an age attempting to contemplate all possibilities, but he had not the energy to pull himself together and focus. He replaced the skull and climbed to his feet, gracelessly stumbled out of the grave and made his way outside of the wooden shed that housed the ancient bones. Dawn's cold sea breeze cut into him, causing a shudder which awoke his senses, but his physical body was still independent of the direction of the will of the mind. He squinted in the cold light of dawn and gave his farewell to the bones while feeling a certain irony that the essence of Cain was rising from the dead and leaving his grave.

Still feeling very weak and confused, he staggered through the cemetery and sat on his usual bench in an attempt to gain composure.

"That can't have been real," he reasoned.

"Cain... was....ordered to be thrown overboard, so there is no way...if I was once Cain, that my bones would have ended up in a grave at Whitby, I would have been fish food".

Chapter five

Scarborough

Sapphire was leading Rebecca down to Scarborough beach to show off her new collar and play catch with her small rubber tooth-dented ball. Cold waves crashed in the distance and fresh February winds carried sea spray into the nostrils of anyone brave enough to venture the winter beach. Sapphire loved her morning walks; she ran in and out of the sea, barked at the waves, other dogs, sea gulls, her own shadow and any passers by.

"Come here you crazy dog!" Rebecca laughed, but it was no use, Sapphire was far too busy joyfully bounding in and out of the ice cold sea and thundering along the sand.

In the distance a car rolled into a parking area which faced the sea. The owner of the black Fiat 130 coupe was Carl Carlyle, Rebecca's ex-boyfriend. At nineteen, he was already an up and coming criminal; his father was a wealthy landlord who had no idea of the dark dealings of his son's illegal money-making schemes. A large figure stood, patiently waiting for the vehicle to come to a rest. The passenger door opened and in squeezed Carl's friend Krzysztof.

"How heavy are you now? …. I better check the suspension for damage from your big ass." Carl remarked, grinning as Krzysztof struggled with the seat belt.

"I'm back on the juice, it's not my fault you buy these poser cars," answered Krzysztof.

"Not steroids and ice cream again!" laughed Carl as he started the engine.

"There's more to bodybuilding than steroids and ice cream pencil neck. I'd like to see you in the gym any day; you'd be in bed for a week recovering while your mummy wiped your nose, you pipsqueak!" Krzysztof was abrupt. He frowned, craning his huge neck forward.

"Isn't that your ex-girlfriend on the beach down there?" he said, jabbing a thick finger toward Rebecca in the distance.

Carl stepped on the brake pedal and squinted through the windscreen.

"Yeah I think it is, she is lovely, look at her Krys."

"Yes I always said she was way too good for you. Did she want a real man instead of you? She told me that you were hung like a field mouse mate," Krzysztof replied.

"Thanks for that Krys," Carl grunted; he found *Krys* far easier to pronounce than his friend's Polish given name.

"Hey any time mate, and if you ever want any money for a bit of an operation to make it man sized, me and the lads will have a whip round for you!" laughed the big man.

"Shall I go over and talk to her?" Carl was ignoring the sarcasm.

"Leave it mate, she's not worth it, and you were a bit rough with her," Krzysztof's words served as an uncomfortable reminder of a violent night.

"I had a few too many beers and she was talking to that poser with the motorbike," Carl dismissed his bad behaviour.

The car sped off with the screech of burning tyres indicating to Krzysztof that he had once again touched a nerve. Carl had no social skills; he liked to give out the verbal abuse, but would throw a tantrum when he was on the receiving end; a spoilt child had grown into a spoilt man. Krzysztof smiled to himself while feeling his own biceps which were still pumped up from his heavy workout. His large physique was intimidating which was why Carl liked to be seen by his side as a warning to anyone who dared cross him.

The atmosphere in the car was dull while Carl continued to sulk over his loss of Rebecca's love for him. Krzysztof leaned forwards and turned the radio on hoping to distract the soul draining mood emitting from his friend.

"You will find someone else," Krzysztof said while adjusting the tuner in search of a good tune.

"Hmmm," grunted Carl dismissively.

"Ah forget it," Krzysztof thought to himself as he realised his attempts to cheer up Carl were falling on deaf ears. Rock music thundered out of the speakers and Krzysztof smiled to congratulate himself on finding a good channel. He leaned back into the seat with both hands clasped behind his head, feeling the grade one stubble of a short haircut. Carl stared at the road through his sunglasses feeling sorry for himself; he knew that he wasn't going to get his own way on this one. He realized that Rebecca had seen his true colours, so there was no way back to her heart; his jealous and spoilt nature had led to a vile night of violence towards her and her male friend. Deep within he knew his actions were dishonourable, but to admit that to her and himself would open a door of acceptance of a weak spirited, selfish and insecure man. But acceptance of weakness is the beginning of growth, in Carl's case however he preferred the head in the sand approach to life.

Sapphire froze, her body pointing at a distant figure heading towards her, she barked and wagged the stub of her tail.

"Saph what's up?" Rebecca asked, but before she had time to repeat the question her dog bolted and sped towards a man in the distance. He dropped onto one knee to greet her. Rebecca soon recognised him and ran closer towards them.

"Uncle Dennis," Rebecca called out. It was a scramble for attention between the three of them but Sapphire was winning paws down.

Dennis was a tall lean strong New Zealander, his all season's outdoor work on the power grid reflected in the well-weathered face of the thirty-five year old.

"Your bloody beaches are cold, even the bloody fish are wearing coats. I saw a crab earlier doing star jumps to keep warm, or should that be starfish jumps? He pinched my bloody scarf," Dennis joked.

"You will have to wear some thermals around you big old ears then!" Rebecca replied.

"These ears, are reflector shields for women, otherwise I wouldn't be able to keep them all off me!" he replied as he grabbed the rubber ball and threw it hard for Sapphire to retrieve.

The conversation carried them along the cold beach to a converted trailer which sold snacks and hot beverages.

"I think you should get me a tea," Dennis cheekily requested.

"Hang on!" Rebecca replied as she finally wrestled Sapphire back onto her dog lead and dipped into her pocket for some money to buy her Uncle a hot drink.

"Mum will be picking up her old accent now you are around,"

Rebecca joked.

"Well it's about bloody time you both came to see me back at mine. It's only about a twenty four hour flight and now my arse is the same shape as the seats on the plane," replied Dennis while stirring in the three large spoons of sugar he had just poured into his mug of tea.

Sapphire gave them both a hypnotic "*I haven't been fed for weeks*" glassy-eyed begging look. Her manipulation worked very well on Dennis, he quickly purchased a chocolate bar to share with her, while he listened to Rebecca's report of the latest gossip regarding her and her Mum's life and times since his last visit.

"Are you going to take me into town so I can shop for presents to take back home?" Dennis asked, slamming down his empty mug.

"Of course, you can even buy me something if you like!" replied Rebecca.

The banter between them continued as they headed into town for a long day of shopping and further snacking.

Later that day Jancine found herself singing aloud as she made up the spare bed for her brother; she wondered if she could convince Dennis to move to England. He loved life and you never found him down in the mouth; he could put a positive spin on almost anything and had a magical charm which seemed to have a natural cheering effect on anyone he conversed with. He did not, on the other hand, suffer fools gladly, and would square up with anyone stupid enough to cross him.

The door of the little house flew open and in bounded the three of them led by Sapphire, who headed straight for her treat-jar full of biscuits to see if she could try her luck with Jancine. It was mayhem in the little house as Sapphire watched the three of them racing around trying to get out of the damp clothes and settle in, she eventually gave up on the treat-jar and headed to her hot radiator for a nap until her house was once again in order.

Tea was served closely followed by a battle for the bathroom between Rebecca and Dennis; they both liked a drink and wanted to be socializing as soon as possible.

Eight o'clock came and the taxi outside hooted its horn right on time. Dennis and Rebecca had decided to share the fare into town, each gave a quick kiss on Jancine's cheek and out they went into the cold night.

Jancine watched the taxi disappear into the distance, leaving the house peaceful with the smell of aftershave and perfume mixing into the misty steam of two recent hot showers. With a sigh into the silence Jancine turned up the thermostat to warm her little house ready for her meditation.

The rain tapped on the glass and the wind howled through the guttering; it enhanced the cosy, warm feeling of being safe at home. Jancine smiled at the subtle little high pitch moans coming from her dog who was dreaming by the radiator. The patchouli scented candle filled the room adding to the feeling of tranquillity as the flame danced around its wick. She then began to focus gently on her breathing to induce a meditative state, and little by little she faded into a peaceful trance.

The energy felt like a warm wave of bliss massaging her non local soul in the field of awareness in which we all bathe.

Warm currents spiralled through her crown and mid brow. It felt much stronger than usual. Jancine let go of all resistance, simply allowing thoughts to pass through her mind, not attempting to judge or change any of them. The energy flowed freely, *let go and let God* was the vibration that she held.

The awareness of rain maintained the feeling of safety in the conservatory, Jancine's meditative flux flowed deeper still and the presence of loved ones no longer in this life embraced her heart, overflowing her with an instant knowing of their messages of love for her. The power dissolved any sign of sadness or loss; there was no missing the loved ones in this vibration, only the awareness of their presence being stronger then ever. The peace and affirmation of separation being only an illusion lifted Jancine's soul, serving as the highest message one can feel.

The love she felt in her heart affected the field around her, creating a peaceful flux unimaginable to science and critics of the time. Miracles often occur at this level of vibration, and peace may be induced around the radius of the individual of a magnitude relative to the power and experience of the practitioner.

"Prepare to teach!" a gentle signal was received.

Jancine found herself searching for the source of the message, but it was elusive, like trying to catch a shadow, and it was time to come back down as prompted by her soul. Her focus wandered back to the random thoughts of her mind. Her eyes flickered gently and slowly opened; she felt slightly dizzy while the full awareness of the spiritual field gently left her in a state of peace. Jancine smiled as she felt herself slip back into the awareness of the physical world, she realized that the full potential of the vibration she had just experienced could not be felt once consciousness had been regained. But simply knowing where she had just been was wonderfully calming. After a few moments of composure she stretched her arms and stood up with a deep yawn.

Sapphire sensed the passive mood in the air and knew this was a good time to hang around the treat jar and take full advantage of the situation.

Carl sensed he had upset Krzysztof; the meeting with the two Cockneys had gone well, but now they had a near 100 mile journey back to Scarborough. A distant church bell rang prompting Carl to glance at his watch; it was midnight. The pair crunched across the gravel of the car park as they returned to Carl's black Fiat.

"What's up?" He asked

"What's up?.........what's up?" Krzysztof mocked, as they got in the car for the return journey. "I'll tell you what's up! You have just told one of the biggest gangsters in the south that my family in Poland have got a ready supply of weapons!" Krzysztof blasted with increasing volume.

"Think of the money we can…." Carl began to attempt justification but was quickly interrupted.

"**One**….. we are not in their league, if things go wrong, we get killed….**Two**, my family over in Poland, we ain't in their league either, if things go wrong we get killed, either way, we get killed!"

"What could go wrong?" Carl asked feeling nervous at the aggression building in Krzysztof's voice.

"That's the problem with you Carl, you are a wannabe villain, but you don't need the money because your family is already rich. Most villains get into crime 'cos they have to, you are an amateur and the weapons trade boys will spot you a mile off, you are too stupid and dangerous to have inside knowledge, they'll use you then they will kill you, then me, and anyone else who gets in their way, you friggin' idiot."

Krzysztof began removing his seat belt.

"Stop the car!" he ordered.

"Why? What?" Carl slowed down in confusion, but before he could do anything to calm down his big friend, the door was open and Krzysztof was marching into the night.

"Must be 'roid rage!" Carl thought, blaming his friend's use of anabolic steroids and dismissing his own short-sightedness.

Chapter six

Whitby Frost

The cold December of 1979 cast a fine blanket of crisp white snow over Whitby. The town resembled a picture from a Christmas card, and at the Abbey the sounds of choir practice echoed around the cemetery.

Delmar shuffled carefully along the snowy pathway between the gravestones; the crunch of ice under his carefully placed feet popped, leaving a trail all the way from his car which he had parked behind the old ruin.

He paused to catch his breath. It formed a misty cloud as he blew through his clasped palms.

"Nearly there." he smiled to himself, looking towards the bench near the church.

As he approached he could see it was already occupied by a man wearing at least two coats, a hat and scarf and long wellington boots. As Delmar came closer he reached into his pocket for a plastic bag to place onto the seat in order to have a dry place to sit.

"Hello," he said as he dusted off the flaky snow and carefully placed the plastic bag to make a clear seating area.

"Hello again Delmar," came the reply.

"Ah Jaden." smiled Delmar; each was flattered by the other having remembered his name.

"You have got a black eye Jaden," Delmar observed with a hint of curiosity.

"After our last conversation, you inspired me, and I have started boxing, not to compete, but for self-defence." Jaden was excited and could not get his words out fast enough.

"Self-defence?" Delmar asked.

"Yes, it was a real eye-opener for me, the depth of the art, the fitness and the courage required to get in the ring, and the lack of politics is so refreshing," Jaden became more and more excited as he explained his feelings.

"Politics?" Delmar was curious.

"I have trained in various martial arts, there is so much arguing over the best methods, they don't inspire anyone who walks through the door who may need to learn self-defence, in fact, most of the instructors only seem interested in demonstrating their own skills and showing off, rather than truly helping anyone. But boxing's different; there's no room for theory, I turn up to train, I spar, which soon highlights what works and what's useless. I don't feel like I have failed to block if I get hit; I know how it feels to take a punch and hit back, and to continue when I am afraid or hurt or both, it's just such an incredible art!"

"The art…" Delmar began to give some advice, but Jaden was too busy explaining and interrupted him.

"I have never quite understood martial arts. I know traditional artists who have defeated non traditional artists, and vice versa, and people who have never trained who have beat up black belts in a bar room brawl."

Delmar listened to Jaden and allowed him to get all of his discoveries off his chest.

"How did you feel when you got in the ring for the first time?" Delmar asked while he reached into his large coat pocket.

"I was terrified!" he answered.

"Good lad. I respect that Jaden," Delmar started unscrewing the lid off the hip flask which he had pulled from his pocket.

"Respect that I was scared but continued?" Jaden thought he had worked out the answers regarding facing his fear.

"Yes, but mainly for admitting to me that you were afraid; most people are so ashamed of their fear, but it's a natural feeling…….the ones who are frozen by the fear, are those who fight against it." Delmar offered Jaden a drink from his flask.

The younger man took a small sip, "WOW!" he coughed, "What the hell is that? Neat Heat?"

Delmar's laughter invited Jaden to join in.

"Neat Heat, I like that!" said Delmar, pleased with the new name for his secret winter warmer.

"What do you mean fight against it?" Jaden could not let the wisdom of Delmar pass him by. He felt a strong admiration and respect for the old fighter.

Delmar held up the flask.

"Imagine this flask is fear!" he said.

"Ok."

"Some people only see the flask, the fear, but look all around us, the whole coast, the church, the Abbey. The flask is only part of the whole picture. Now Jaden, the more you look and concentrate on the flask, the closer it becomes, until you can hold it and feel it; if you keep looking and talking about the flask, we both end up looking at it, and miss our view from the Abbey, but if we accept it, then I may just take a sip from it, use it for its purpose, then pop it back into my pocket and enjoy the day."

Jaden loved analogies and asked: "So, don't do anything about the fear, just allow it to be in contrast with the whole picture?"

"Just realize fear is a natural part of the picture," Delmar added.

"All the lads in the gym think I am soft!" laughed Jaden, "I rescued a drowning spider out of the loo in the changing room, they laughed at me, I suppose they're right!"

"Well maybe one day a spider will return the favour and save you," Delmar answered.

"Well I don't see how!" Jaden smiled but Delmar remained silent while he sipped a little more of his winter warmer.

"Intention is the key to being a damn good boxer, and of course you can apply it to any art, including how you live your life," Delmar nodded confirming the strength he felt from his own words.

"If you love what you do, whatever it is, boxing, cooking, rock climbing, then it's worth it. If you train to hurt someone for the sake of the ego, eventually you will fail, but if you train for the love of the hard work of any art, then you have already succeeded."

Jaden felt like he was in the presence of a mysterious old Zen master or priest from another time.

"Thank you Delmar, for your advice." It was becoming clear to Jaden that Delmar was not just some old ex-fighter, but a man with great depth and spiritual experience.

"When receiving advice Jaden, keep your own council, and when giving advice don't worry too much about choosing the right or wrong words; we don't always know all of the answers, but we can always have the right intention, which should always be, to help others find peace." Delmar spoke with a clear, edifying tone; his words carried great compassion, touching Jaden's very soul.

Conversation continued on Jaden's bench of wisdom, Delmar sipped his Neat Heat, while Jaden interviewed him on an unusual mix of both spirituality and the strategies and tactics of boxing.

On Whitby beach Sapphire was exploring for any hidden sticks or even food if she was lucky. She sped along near the sea but found the water to be uncomfortably cold, so ventured only paw deep.

A familiar figure in the distance caught her eye; she stopped to focus and gave a quick bark to attract his attention. The stranger gave no reaction, so she decided that the best way to confirm his identity would be to pick up his scent. She galloped with Rebecca's voice in the distance calling her back to heel.

Jaden froze at the sight of the huge boxer dog thundering towards him at light speed, but he soon recognised Jancine's dog Sapphire.

"Calm down Saph! You gonna paw me to death," Jaden laughed with relief at surviving the impact from a four legged missile. Sapphire checked his scent, she barked with excitement and Jaden was flattered that she remembered him after such a long time; he looked along the beach to see if he could locate Jancine.

Sapphire froze at the disturbing energy she sensed in the direction of Rebecca.

"Gruff!" she barked at two strangers in the distance who stood too close to one of the members of her pack.

"I'm not interested Carl, will you please leave me alone, it's been over a year now just move on!" Rebecca protested.

"Come on mate, let's go; I'm freezing to death, why anyone would want to be on a beach in December I will never know." Krzysztof pulled up the collar of his big winter coat; he had truly lost interest in Carl's undying obsession with Rebecca.

"Have you been drinking? I can smell it on your breath!" Rebecca shouted in response to Carl's aggressive manner.

Sapphire bounded up, most displeased at the loud and threatening manner of the man towards Rebecca, she explained this to him with a nipping bite into his groin area which caused him to yelp with pain and fall onto the cold wet snowy sand.

After a short pause, Krzysztof reacted as would any true friend in his situation, bursting out into hysterical laughter, closely followed by Rebecca and Jaden who had witnessed the event, arriving just as Carl fell.

"You asked for that mate!" Krzysztof roared with laughter.

"Have you met my new boyfriend?" Rebecca said and grabbed Jaden by the arm, pulling him close.

"Come on Jaden, let's go to the café," she added as she led him and Sapphire off the beach towards the town. It soon dawned on Jaden that Rebecca was using him as a decoy boyfriend, and once the initial embarrassment of it wore off, he found himself to be rather enjoying walking hand in hand with her.

"I'm sorry about that," she said, as she put the lead on Sapphire at the exit steps.

"Do you fancy a cup of tea…?" Jaden began mumbling, "If you are busy maybe we can do it another time… but if…"

"Yes that would be lovely," smiled Rebecca, interrupting him mid-flow. The three of them headed into the busy little town, and as they walked, snow began to gently fall burying their footsteps behind them.

The little café was full of shoppers trying to avoid the snow outside. Sounds of clanking cups and saucers, chairs sliding along wooden floors and a mass of conversation interrupted any chance of a quiet moment to reflect. Jaden was ordered to sit with Sapphire and hold her lead whilst Rebecca bought the hot beverages and biscuits; he gazed out of the little square windows which gathered snow in the corners of their wooden frames. Condensation misted along the inside of the glass from the steam which carried the smell of coffee.

"There we go Jaden, a nice hot mug of tea." Rebecca sat down across from him delivering a tray full of goodies. Sapphire's nose twitched to detect any signs of biscuits for her, and of course, as ever, a few snacks came her way. Rebecca looked across at Jaden and began to laugh.

"What?" He enquired but it was no use; the more Rebecca tried to explain the reasons for her giggling, the more it grew into uncontrollable laughter. Jaden found himself laughing along with her, even though he was not sure what was so amusing. She finally contained her hysterics and gasped for air.

"Did you see Sapphire bite Carl…. right in his nuts? The look on his face, oh it was so funny."

Jaden began to join in with Rebecca's eye-watering laughter, while Sapphire watched them as they struggled to control themselves. But he still found himself closely monitoring his dialogue with her to give the best impression possible; he found her confidence slightly overwhelming. Two hours quickly passed by, leaving just the pair of them engrossed in conversation. Rebecca informed Jaden that both her mother Jancine and Uncle Dennis had gone back to New Zealand for a long family visit. Rebecca was now living in her mother's house in Scarborough with Sapphire. Jaden was talking about his work at the power plant and boxing, he also enquired if Rebecca knew of Delmar who seemed to be a regular visitor at the Abbey.

"Well I'd better be getting back," Rebecca said softly.

"Ok, well errrr," Jaden began to mumble as usual.

"What?" she asked.

"May I walk you back to you car?" asked Jaden,

"*As if she is going to want to be escorted by you!*" his inner voice immediately began taunting him.

"That would be lovely, a gentleman at last!" Rebecca replied.

"*Never doubted you for a moment, you see it was worth asking her!*" The ego, as usual, quickly turned around to take credit.

"A gentleman….where?" Jaden joked.

Rebecca's curvy figure attracted Jaden's eyes like a moth to a flame; she led Sapphire out of the shop, and his expression was noted by the tea lady behind the counter who smiled at him just as he noticed he had been caught looking. He coughed to try and hide his blush and quickly closed the door behind him.

Finally, they arrived at Rebecca's old rust-bucket of a car which was barely roadworthy, the passenger door ground open and Sapphire shot in like a hairy bullet.

"Have you got my mum's phone number?" Rebecca asked.

"Err yes…I mean… no," Jaden was at it again.

Rebecca fumbled around the car glove box for an old business card with Jancine's phone number, which she had used to give to clients who wanted private readings.

"Give me a call if you want a chat again!" she said handing him the tatty, old card.

"What really? I mean....oh ok thanks I will."

Rebecca got into the car while Jaden carefully placed the precious phone number into his wallet for safe keeping. The old engine turned over, belching out a blast of black smoke; Jaden coughed from the fumes while waving goodbye to Rebecca and Sapphire as she steadily drove out of the car park and faded into the town's traffic.

"Destination: The Four Masts pub." Jaden thought to himself, and as he walked, he reflected upon his day with Delmar and Rebecca. The headlights of the cars in the snowy fog resembled ghosts crossing before him, and although the conditions of winter would normally feel unpleasant, Jaden felt warm with happiness and anticipation of maybe meeting Rebecca again; if he dared make the call.

Chapter seven

You Create That Which You Most Dread

Krzysztof admired himself in the mirror, tensing up his bulky triceps as he worked his way through a range of poses at his local spit and sawdust gym. He had been building up his already large frame with a combination of heavy weight training, anabolic steroids and a high calorie complex diet. Summer was just around the corner and he had begun to consider altering his training schedule in order to reduce his body fat and improve his muscular definition.

"Krys...you've got a phone call!" a voice echoed from across the training room.

"I'll be right there!" Krzysztof replied as he strode towards the counter. "Hello who is it?" the big man enquired.

"Hiya mate, it's me Carl, I've just seen Rebecca in Whitby with that freaky lookin' dude we saw on the beach."

"Hang on, let me guess; you want me to have a bit of a word with him, explain to him that she belongs to you". Krzysztof's answer was heavy with sarcasm.

"Yeah, if you don't mind!" Carl was so blinded by jealousy that he did not even realise that Krzysztof's words had been intended to drive home a point.

"Ok, pick me up from home in an hour," Krzysztof replied with dread.

An hour and a half later Krzysztof found himself gazing out of the passenger window of his friend's sleek looking Fiat as the pair toured the streets of Whitby in search of his ex and Jaden. He pretended to show interest in finding the couple, but in truth he was finding the whole plan tedious. His thoughts drifted back to bodybuilding; he was being encouraged by the gym owner to compete and maybe turn professional.

"I wonder if decline bench press will hit my lower chest better than dips," he thought to himself as his routine ran through his mind

"There they are! Right then!" shouted Carl triumphantly as he pointed out two figures walking up the steps towards the abbey.

"We got 'em now Krys. I'll drive to the abbey and catch them at the top." Carl tore up the hill, oblivious to the blowing horns and swearing left in his wake. Carl's Fiat screeched into the Abbey's little car park flinging gravel aside as he skidded to a halt. The pair jumped out, Krzysztof obliging his jealous little friend, marching behind him as his minder. As he approached the couple he could see by Rebecca's expression that she had already worked out exactly what Carl had in mind for Jaden.

Carl's mouth had already begun to spew forth a torrent of abuse; expletives full of disgusting accusations and character assassination. Krzysztof stared at Jaden, curling his upper lip into a snarl fully designed to instil fear into the smaller man.

"Hang on a moment!" Jaden shouted in order to defuse the situation before it became physical. "We are just friends, we have only seen each three times. I live miles away and I only visit on the odd weekend," he added, nodding towards Rebecca.

Krzysztof's cold stare remained steely while Carl continued to shout abuse and ask lewd personal questions regarding his ex-girlfriend's intentions of courtship.

The two aggressors opened up a door deep within Jaden's memory, a door which he would have preferred to remain forever sealed. The presence of Breaker and the captain seemed to have reappeared to haunt him once again.

"That didn't really happen! It was a dream, it was the alcohol," Jaden affirmed and quickly began to pull himself together. A dark, unrecognizable energy began to crack open within his soul, filling him with a strange and hateful power. The atmosphere around him began to change; he dropped his chin and stared into the eyes of the bodybuilder.

"A long time ago a man of your size crossed me; he did not survive and I promise you that your fate shall be the same, you may know how to lift weights, but do you really know how to fight against someone with an absolute desire to kill you." Jaden's words had an immediate effect upon Krzysztof's bravado; he mistook his own adrenalin for fear, it served as a dark reminder of things long forgotten, of something terrifying.

Carl was disturbed by the lack of panic from Rebecca's man, it made him feel powerless, and he so longed to be feared.

"Smash him Krys!" Carl whimpered, and the giant dutifully stepped forwards. Jaden had a feeling that the giant man's confidence was powered purely by his size, so he instantly interrupted this by words designed to unsteady him, and plant the seeds of doubt.

"I have been knocked out, choked out, by men bigger than you'll ever be, and I have returned the favour, every time." Jaden warned with the coldest expression. "I'll show you violence, do you think your size stops your teeth being smashed out, or feeling the pain of me biting your throat out while I stick my fingers in your eyes. Your biceps won't save you!" he added, then slowly turned to look at Carl, "And you, you spineless little freak, I will dance on your grave boy."

The potential fight began draining out of Krzysztof's heart, he watched as Jaden stepped and put his arm around Rebecca.

"We are just friends at the moment, but if we become lovers I shall make sure that you two are the first to know," Jaden informed his would-be attackers as an act of defiance.

Krzysztof observed Jaden's physicality; his trapezius muscles gave the appearance of leaving a coat hanger in the jacket, he also noticed tiny scars around one eye – a sure indication of a fighter of some description. He felt uneasy, and it was most unexpected.

Jaden let go of the rising hatred and kept in mind the principles of his training along with the philosophy of Delmar. His intention was simply to get Rebecca home safely, and with this in mind, and his understanding of the nature of the ego, he gave Krzysztof a psychological exit.

"You are a big man and a worthy opponent, I respect your art, and I do not wish to fight you, but I will if I have to. Now I am asking you as a man to show some respect by not displaying violence and bloodshed in front of a woman." he said to Krzysztof.

"No problem," answered Krzysztof with a stern tone, hiding his relief at being able to walk away without losing face.

Jaden turned, took Rebecca by the hand and led her gently away from them.

"Wow, wow, what just happened?" she gasped.

"I really ain't so sure; it's something I am trying to forget," Jaden answered vaguely. Little did he realize how the standing of his ground complied with Rebecca's taste in men, and how impressed she was with this dark horse. Rebecca began to rant about the situation with anger and disbelief regarding Carl's disrespectful behaviour. Jaden however had mixed feelings about his diffusion of a potential attack. Upon reflection on the application of Delmar's philosophy along with the boxing and martial arts training, he realised that he had come a long way. In the past, his misunderstanding of the effects of fear would have made him fight just to prove to himself that he could overcome them by engaging in violence. Fear had once made him do things that in his heart, he really did not want to do. He could now walk away knowing that feeling the affects of adrenalin, and being afraid, does not make him a coward.

It was at this point that he realised why in the past that a given situation would haunt him if the fear had dictated his decisions. It would mean that fear could be used against him and control him.

The experience of feeling such a strong hatred made Jaden uncomfortable, as did the reminder of Breaker and the captain. Rebecca was so consumed with her own anger that she did not notice that Jaden was alone with his thoughts, and, before either of them knew it, they were back at the bottom of the steps which they had just climbed.

The cycle of thoughts continued to run their course in Jaden's mind. But he applied Delmar's philosophy, not attempting to change the uncomfortable images in any way; he simply added good thoughts into the mix and gave no attention to the results. He did not realise how powerfully this system could affect every aspect of his life. It was this underestimation which could lead to an unfortunate path.

"Shall we visit the aquarium?" Rebecca broke into Jaden's thoughts.

"Absolutely.....no way....... I can't, I have a phobia, silly I know but." Jaden was shaking his head trying to dispel the combination of both embarrassment and fearful thoughts of the images cast by the creatures in the sea life centre.

"So tell me, what is it you are afraid of?"

"Squids, they have suckers with teeth, and a beak, the beak injects venom ya know, and they can get through a gap the same size as their eye. Some of them are huge. Imagine being attacked with all those suckers and teeth ripping into you, and then you have got the beak to look forward to!" Jaden expressed his fear with an almost anatomical precision.

He continued relating the discovery of his phobia; watching a science fiction adventure as a child, and how he had suffered nightmares ever since. Their chat took them into the town and along the cobbled streets near the craft shops.

"Hang on Jaden, I have to pop in here; this is where I work, my mum owns part of the business."

Jaden looked at the sign above which read "The Magical Mantelpiece". He followed Rebecca through the entrance and immediately felt in harmony with the ambience of the little shop. It certainly had Jancine's touch; aromatic smells and Indian music hypnotised the senses, and wind chimes tinkled as customers tapped them. The shelves were full with all manner of spiritual gifts: Buddha statues and ornaments, candles and holders, incense sticks and oils, books, cards, rings and charms, Indian jewellery and clothes. Jaden was fascinated; he explored the shop while Rebecca engaged in business matters with a member of staff behind the counter.

"Such interesting books!" Jaden was suffering optional anxiety. The range of topics could have been sub-headed, "Jaden's selection." Life after death, meditation, chakra's, visualization; he did not know where to begin. He gazed over at Rebecca who continued chatting.

"Must be fantastic to have a job here!" Jaden thought to himself, "But that would be like employing Count Dracula in a blood bank!" he whispered with a smile. Twenty minutes later and he was engrossed in a large book which taught various methods and effects of positive visualisation.

Rebecca interrupted his reading by flicking the front cover.

"I have to stay behind and lock up; there is a slight problem I have to take care of. If you want you can wait for me in the stockroom upstairs; we'll be closed in half an hour."

"I'll wait for you then, but can I take this book with me?"

"Yes, of course!" Rebecca answered. She led Jaden to the far end of the shop, unlocked a creaky wooden door hidden in the corner, and pointed up an old wooden staircase.

"There's a kettle and tea and coffee up there. I'll come up when I've finished." Rebecca smiled with an expression which Jaden had not seen before.

It was an old building and the walls probably had many stories to tell. Jaden carefully climbed the staircase and entered the stockroom. It was full of colourful boxes of all shapes and sizes, and at the far end was a tiny cobweb covered window. As he searched for something to sit on, he realised he was in the attic.

Muffled voices of customers from the shop below rumbled through the dusty old floorboards. In the corner to the left of the window was a sink, a small kettle and a fridge, a few crates and a rocking chair.

"Perfect," he said, heading straight over to make a cup of tea. Five minutes later Jaden was swaying back and forth in the rocking chair, the hot beverage in one hand and the book in the other. He was transfixed by the weighty volume, and as the pages turned time ran away. The voices from the shop below had grown silent, leaving just the sound of the wind whispering through the attic. Jaden switched on a corner lamp as light from the tiny window behind him began to fade. From just beyond the edges of his concentration he was aware of Rebecca's presence as he heard doors opening and closing, locks turning and footsteps approaching.

"Jaden!" she called to him softly, but the book held his focus.

"Jaden!" she repeated closer to him.

Her tone caught his attention and he lowered the book and gasped at the beautiful, naked, curvaceous Rebecca standing right in front of him. Adrenaline exploded into his bloodstream as he simultaneously dropped his book and his jaw. Rebecca had caught Jaden completely off guard; he had played out many scenarios of how one romantic night would lead to another and end in seduction at the side of a big open fire in a grand hotel somewhere. He should have known that that only ever happened on the big screen. Rebecca giggled at Jaden's expression as he clutched the side of the rocking chair. She stepped towards him, ran her fingers through his hair and pulled him into her body. Jaden could hear his own heart responding to the feel of her body as he explored her with his hands and mouth. Rebecca lifted her left leg and placed her foot on the chair to allow Jaden to explore further; she gently took the lead and placed his head on her inside thigh and slowly guided his kisses inwards.

A strong current fired through Jaden's bloodstream, never had a lover taken the lead in this way; her confidence charged his passion and swept away his inhibitions. He slid forwards off of the chair and onto his knees, lifting her leg onto his shoulder; from here he could love her more deeply, and she pulled him tight as the heat of ecstasy branded them together. Rebecca drew a long breath through her teeth, she paused, pulled Jaden even tighter, and finally exhaled with a trembling gasp of pleasure.

"I needed that!" she said breathing heavily, releasing Jaden's head.

"I can tell," he laughed sitting back in the rocking chair.

"Get those clothes off!" she said.

"What?" Jaden asked, but he had a clear enough idea of what she had said, his question was reflex action in response to his nervousness.

"I said *get those clothes off.*" she repeated, as she leaned forward and unbuckled his belt and jeans.

His ego threw up a few insecurities to consider regarding what underwear he had on, and what she would think of his naked body. But there was no time to worry, because in the blink of an eye Rebecca had him naked and was driving him wild with teasing kisses. His head was spinning from the intensity of her seduction; he was pushed back into the rocking chair by the tension of his thighs. Rebecca was now kneeling and Jaden could hardly believe his eyes at the erotic curvaceous image of her body casting shadows on the wall from the lamp light, her long dark hair spread over his pelvis hiding the foreplay adding to the teasing image of passionate embrace.

"Stop....stop I'm almost," Jaden moaned, and Rebecca again giggled at her power over him, she stood up and Jaden followed her lead by also standing.

"No, no!" she whispered pushing him back down, she then threaded her legs through the arms of the chair and gently lowered herself down. They each released a sigh in unison, Jaden felt incredible warmth, her body temperature seemed higher than any previous lover, and he was beginning to lose control. Rebecca began to rock gently, intensifying the radiance; he tried to distract himself by thinking of plant rooms at the power station where he worked, and wondering if he had ordered the correct type of grease for some large fan bearings. The moment passed and the point of no return was not induced by Rebecca's increasing hip grind. He clasped her hips with both hands to help their rhythm, their breathing and momentum intensified, deeper, faster, and harder, until the point of simultaneous critical overflow erupted. Passers-by in the street below heard the blast of explicit, sexual climaxing screams which were undeniable and unmistakable, causing one or two smiles and nudges.

Rebecca slid off Jaden's lap and collapsed in a heap on the floor, smiling and blowing the hair out of her face.

"Where on earth did that come from?" he asked.

"Well, this afternoon at the abbey, you turned me on."

"Really, how so?" Jaden was clueless.

"It was the way you stood up to Carl and his bulldog Krys, it was incredible. I can still see the looks on their faces, I bet they expected you to be scared of them, but your tone of voice was evil, I was scared, and I was on your side!" she laughed.

"Well... I was scared" answered Jaden.

"I'm starving, let's find somewhere nice to eat," Rebecca suggested as she dressed.

"You took the words right out of my mouth," replied Jaden, as he pulled on his trousers.

Five minutes later and they were out of the shop door, searching Whitby for a hot tasty meal; their explosive sexual encounter had certainly burned a lot of calories and left them both ravenous.

The March winds howled through the cobbled streets and the sound of the sea crashed in the distance.

"There is a nice little Italian place just around this corner," Rebecca pointed. But Jaden was heading to the window of an art shop. He gazed with a blank expression at a large painting of an old galleon with its lights reflecting off the dark water, and shadows cast by the masts from the moonlight.

"There's just something about old ships."

"Jaden, c'mon, I'm starving and freezing." Rebecca pulled him in the direction of the restaurant.

"OK," he said trying to ignore strong currents of the memories from the skeleton experience. He looked up towards the abbey and sighed; the bones had been relocated to somewhere unknown to him, and it brought him relief that he could no longer touch them to find out if his travels on the Eroda had in fact happened.

Later that evening at Jancine's house, Sapphire ears pricked up at the sound of keys turning in the lock of her front door. Rebecca and Jaden burst in, falling over each other in hysterics. Sapphire rushed over to greet them both; she checked Jaden's scent, then tilted her head and glanced at Rebecca. A knowing expression formed on Sapphire's face, and after a slight pause she turned and trotted back to her basket.

"She knows what we've been up to." Rebecca teased.

"Yes, we've been rumbled!" Jaden nodded.

Chapter eight

The Process

Fourteen months passed by, and in that time Jaden and Rebecca had fallen in love, and although the honeymoon period had long passed, they were still a very passionate couple. Jaden had begun to realise that he was burning the candle at both ends; he sometimes worked long hours during the week, trained hard in various fighting arts, and travelled to Whitby on most weekends. Carl and Krzysztof seemed to have faded out of sight and Jancine had returned home from New Zealand.

It was a Friday evening and Jaden was having private instruction from his boxing trainer Richard; Jaden both respected and feared the old fighter, he had a history of violence which included debt collecting, bare knuckle fighting and coaching.

A rough old converted lemonade factory behind his house had lots of well used punch bags hanging from wooden beams which creaked under their swing. Weights, medicine balls and a few well worn skipping ropes were scattered about the place. It had the smell of sweat and blood and the atmosphere of gruelling, character building workouts.

"There's no chandeliers in my place!" Richard often joked to any new comers.

"Always fight off ya guards, and if I see your chin up again, I'm gonna knock you straight out!"

"Ok Rich, ok," Jaden gasped.

"Now remember the scales we worked on last week: top-bottom-top, top-top-bottom, hit two-miss one. Well we are going to work em, but always keep returning to your guards." Richard sternly expressed the structure of the hands and elbows as he explained the drills.

"Ok," Jaden repeated with a nod.

"And stop that flapping with your arms that you've learned in martial arts, remember if I see that chin........... even for a second!"

"Ok Rich."

It was an intense but educating thirty minutes for Jaden; he moved around the small ring under instruction, and under fire from Richard.

And when time was finally called, Jaden's boxing gloves felt like two huge stones pulling his arms out of their sockets.

It was interview time in the sauna; Jaden was asking about the power developed in boxing straight punches, and how to avoid breaking the knuckles in the midst of a street fight. Richard informed him of the difference between driving a "shot" and throwing the shot using bodyweight.

"Sometimes just push his head back with an open hand to lift his chin, then throw the shot, slaps can be just as dangerous leading to a big shot," he explained, "and of course you can use other things," he added and popped out of the sauna, he returned a moment later and gave Jaden and shiny metal object.

"A knuckle duster!" Jaden said, slipping it on.

"Yes...... sometimes, all you need, is a weapon," Richard said in a deep voice.

Jaden sensed that the time for questions was over. He sat back and sweated it out in the sauna.

The following morning Jaden rose early and began loading a few tools into the boot of his car in order to do a few little jobs for Jancine at her shop, *The Magical Mantelpiece*. He was looking forward to seeing them again and the anticipation of a passionate night with Rebecca always made his journey across the Yorkshire Moors so much more fun.

She did not know he was visiting her this weekend; he should have been working, but a last minute cancellation had allowed him to plan a surprise trip to see her. He had spoken to Jancine and asked her not to tell Rebecca about him coming. He wanted to surprise her.

He planned on working for Jancine during the day; her shop was temporarily closed for refurbishment; then he intended to drive over with a small gift, and take Rebecca out.

After a full English breakfast and coffee top ups from greasy cafes along the way, Jaden was finally alone in the basement of The Magical Mantelpiece. Jancine had let him in and given him the keys to lock up when he had finished. He had to run a few power cables under the shop floor and put some plug sockets in for some new cabinet displays.

Two hours later the job was going according to plan, the radio was on, cables were in; just a few terminations and the job would be complete.

"The caffeine meter is low," Jaden said to himself, deciding he deserved a cup of hot tea out of his loyal flask. He sat down to make a drink whilst listening to the radio, intermittently singing along with the tune and humming the melody to fill the gaps where he had forgotten the words.

He pulled out an old crate from a tiny alcove to sit on and enjoy his break. Gazing around the basement with a smile from the satisfaction of almost completing the job, a cold and uneasy chill settled upon his shoulders; the thought of the skeleton ambushed him once again, and his smile was replaced by a frown.

"It can't have been real, it was the beer," Jaden repeated to himself once again; it was becoming a mantra to keep his nightmares at bay. And before the thoughts could get a hold of him, he decided to get on and finish the work which would also help distract him from the confusion.

He began to push the crate back, but it ground to a halt midway, he tried again, but it was stuck fast.

"What now?" he muttered, leaning over to investigate. The floor appeared to have a tiny ridge keeping the crate from being pushed back; he leaned closer and cleared the dust with his hands.

"A trapdoor!" he was confused, he thought that he was already in the basement of the building and could get no lower.

"Where on earth does this go?" he asked himself.

"Why don't we find out?" he answered. He pulled the crate all the way back out and began forcing a screwdriver into the wooden frame of the trapdoor. It was hard work; he scraped the dirt out of the groove which had sealed the wood in the many years since it was last slammed shut.

Finally, he managed to work two flat bladed screwdrivers beneath the old door and prise enough of a gap to wedge in the handle of an adjustable spanner and prevent it re-closing. He knelt at the edge and squeezed in both hands palms up. Gritting his teeth and tugging hard, he began to move it, inch by inch, and with a grind of old hinges, the trapdoor finally opened.

Jaden was intrigued; he pulled the rubber-coated torch out from his tool box and shone the beam down the dark, square hole.

"Hmmm, an old cellar." The tiny steps invited him down for further investigation, and before long he was deep within the dark foundations of the building. He ran the beam along the cold stone floor and brick walls; it appeared to be empty, there was just the occasional drip and a few cracks expanding from the building above. He continued to drift the beam in various positions in search of something interesting, when it fell across an old wooden box in one corner. Jaden's heart jumped with excitement; he trod carefully in the darkness and bent down to closely examine what appeared to be a one foot by two foot chest. It looked old; there were three hinges at the back, and no front lock. It was held together by thick rope bound all the way around it. The battered corners and scars gave evidence of long hard journeys. Jaden respectfully wiped and blew the thick dust from its top to inspect it further. Suddenly he was disturbed by a creak and a thump on the old floorboards above. He held his breath; the pounding of his heart pulsing loud in his ears. He swallowed hard and listened carefully; there was nothing but the wind breathing through the cellar.

"Get a grip Jaden!" he ordered himself as he placed his torch on the ground, shining at the box. He gently released the knot and unravelled the rope; his anticipation grew as he guessed at its hidden contents,

"What's the secret in the box?" he thought as he slowly lifted the lid against the resistance of stiff hinges. But he was disturbed again by distant and muffled laughter from somewhere above. With a drive from adrenalin he grabbed his torch and jumped to his feet to make a dash up the cellar steps and peer into the basement. Once again he was met by silence; he tilted his head and with bated breath, attentively listened.

"I bet it's the voices from people in the street. Now what's in the box?" He turned back to the cellar, determined to see if he had found anything of value. He trapped the torch between his cheek and hunched shoulder, and carefully opened the lid.

The light revealed a large brown sack sealed fully by stitches. Jaden reached in and removed it from the old chest and carried it up out of the cellar, all the way out of the basement, and onto the well lit shop floor.

It felt like an old coat or some kind of clothing; he slipped out the blade of his pen knife and slit the bag.

He was correct; a thick black garment tumbled out and landed at his feet.

"Won't be retiring just yet then." Disappointedly he unrolled the garment to reveal a hooded cloak. He spread it out on the floor with the back facing him and kneeled down to try to smooth it out with his hands. On closer inspection, a triangle with seven small circles at each point faded into the black of the cloth.

"That's interesting." He gazed around the shop, just over his left shoulder he found what he was looking for, a large mirror.

He threw the large cloak over his shoulders and winced as something thudded into his collar bone. On closer inspection he discovered a large, triangular clasp with strange patterns embossed in the centre.

"Interesting." he repeated as he laced through the old frayed cord and fastened it firmly with the clasp. He pulled the hood over his head and stepped towards the mirror, a dark, brooding figure stared back from beyond the silvered pane.

"The Zen master is here," he laughed "or should it be the reaper?"

He turned to his right and posed; he liked the feeling of the mysterious cloth which draped over his body. He stretched out into a long martial art stance and then into his boxing guards; the flap of the cape snapped in sharp transition from one fighting discipline to the next.

The combat demonstrations quickly raised his body temperature, so he assumed a static chi kung position, holding out both arms as if supporting a large round ball in front of his chest. His fingers soon tingled with the flow of energy, and the cloak began to charge as it drew essence from Jaden's aura field. He blinked and a blur flashed across his sight, as if he had been staring at a light bulb or the sun for far too long; the more he tried to bring it into focus, the more the blue light escaped him. Within this flux, the image of a strange key shaped object appeared, again Jaden attempted to work out the details of the elusive object, but the harder he tried, the further it slipped away.

His concentration was broken by an outburst of distant laughter from above the shop.

He cast about himself and quickly grabbed a claw hammer from his tool box, before stealing quietly onto the shop floor, and then towards the attic stairs to investigate the voices from above.

Step by step he trod carefully, certain there was someone in the attic. As he drew nearer the door, the muffled voices grew ever closer. Jaden paused for a moment to catch his breath, he had the distinct feeling that he was about to disturb some thieves, he clenched his fist tightly around the hammer, ready to use it as a makeshift weapon. Slowly he pushed the door, just enough to peer through.

Shock, cold sweat and immediate sickness savagely ambushed Jaden; he could not believe his eyes or his ears. A second look into the attic for confirmation served as heart crushing pain and outright confusion; he dropped the hammer and slid back down the staircase sideways with his back against the wall for support. His life had just changed, and the shock was beginning to settle itself into pain. There seemed to be no air in the shop. He opened the door and began drifting through the streets of Whitby without any thought of any destination. The arguments began to churn over in his mind as he attempted to search for reason and justification, the feeling of being lost, used and worthless was uncontrollably destroying his confidence. Words of inadequacy led to soul-draining mental battles which Jaden was losing.

He found himself sitting on his bench at the Abbey, the cloak flapping in the wind as it draped over the back, absorbing power from the charging field of the nearby church.

"You alright Jaden?" A familiar voice of concern from his left caused Jaden to fight against crying in public.

"Hello Del, are you well?" Jaden could not look at the old man, he was still searching for composure.

"Jaden, you look devastated."

"I have just.....I have just.... seen, my girlfriend with Krys the bodybuilder, naked in the rocking chair. I thought that was just for us, I just can't..." Jaden began to choke on his words.

"Oh, I am so sorry to hear that my friend," Delmar replied. The giggling laughter of two teenage girls from a bench close by caused Jaden to pull himself together; they seemed to be nudging each other as they glanced in his direction.

"I always said to people if I caught my girl with anyone, that I would beat the life out of them, but I was so hurt, you could've knocked me down with a feather," confessed Jaden.

"This may be part of a process Jaden," Delmar was hoping to find words of comfort.

"If you have been visualizing being with someone who loves you, and you love them, then maybe this girl is not the one for you, maybe she likes more violent men, bad men, and you are not....well, not the violent man that she took you to be. Your visualization may be working Jaden, and you have exposed this girl for what she really is, and now you can allow for your true love to come forth," he added.

"What, so this is my fault? How did you know about my visualizations? Part of a process?" Jaden felt betrayed by Delmar's words, and the giggling from the teenagers began to irritate him.

"I am tired of this spiritual path, always trying to do the right thing, think the right thoughts, what's the point in it all anyway? The villain won, he got my girl, he even betrayed his own friend Carl in the process. Rebecca has had all three of us now."

Jaden stood up, and looked at Delmar.

"I have to go Del. I need to get out of this place, I don't think I will ever return, so thank you for all your advice, and I wish you all the best"

Jaden walked past the giggling girls.

"Do you always talk to yourself weirdo?" one of them shouted. She turned to her friend and nodded at Jaden, "*Nice coat!*" she sniggered.

He turned towards them wearing a dirty expression, ready to gently suggest that they mind their own business, only to find an empty bench where he expected Delmar to be smiling out to sea.

"Where the…?" He was nowhere to be seen, not near the church, or the Abbey; the girls continued to laugh at Jaden's confused expression.

"I am losing my mind?" he said as he headed back down the steps towards the car park.

Chapter nine

Altered States Open Dangerous Gates

After a tearful drive through the Yorkshire moors, Jaden finally pulled over and sat on the bonnet of his British Leyland mini-van. He stared over a rusty gate leading to a field of grazing horses. He longed to hear Rebecca's voice; if only he could find a way to justify her actions, to make it all alright. His mind was full of agonising questions. How long she had been secretly seeing Krys? Why? Was the bodybuilder a better lover? How could she do that in their rocking chair?

Then there was the process which Delmar had mentioned; how did he know about the visualisations? And where had he gone?

He realised that Rebecca was unaware that he knew that she had been unfaithful, and with this knowledge, he vowed that he would never see or speak to her again. His days of visiting Whitby were well and truly over.

"I'll disappear out of her life, and never tell her why; she doesn't deserve an explanation."

Jaden was in the stream of the unseen process that Delmar had described, but the energy of a distant vow still pursued him, shadowing him, awaiting the moment when it would manifest itself and although the cloak protected him, it was not over, not yet.

"I have to return the key, and get my tools; I've got to go back." Jaden realized.

He felt weak, as though the carpet of security had been snatched from beneath his feet. Reluctantly he got back into his mini and wound down the window. A chestnut coloured horse appeared at the gate and held Jaden's eyes in its gaze; he felt an association, as if the horse recognised his heartache.

"What am I gonna do now?" But the horse just held its gaze. In the distance, the sun touched the edge of the hills, spilling orange light across the moors. The beautiful evening seemed to add cruelty to Jaden's loss; serving as a reminder that he should have been spending it with Rebecca, not talking to a big old horse.

"Come on, one last run, and you can get out for good." Jaden muttered in a last effort to pull himself together.

The engine turned over and he headed back to The Magic Mantelpiece to collect his things and drop off the keys.

It was a painful exercise stepping back into the shop, and just as before, he could not breathe.

"Rebecca!" he shouted up the old stairs, ensuring that it was empty before gathering his tools and loading them into his mini-van. Tears rolled down his cheeks as he closed the shop door and posted the key; it was over.

The cloak flapped in the breeze swirling down the empty cobbled street.

"I can't believe I'm still wearing this." he croaked, looking down at the ancient cloth. He removed it carefully and wiped his tears on the strange triangle pattern. It struck him that he could not return it because he had just locked up and posted the keys, so he rolled it up and placed it neatly on his passenger seat.

It faded gently and completely vanished into a blue mist, which drifted through the door seal and through the door, back towards the cellar in the shop.

"One last drink, just one…. to steady your nerves." an inner voice whispered.

"I can't drink and drive!" he answered.

"I thought you were tired of doing the right thing all of the time! Just one, for the road." his ego whispered.

And feeling vulnerable, Jaden agreed that just one drink would not hurt.

Ten minuets later he found himself in a small public house peering into the bottom of a glass tumbler. His life lay in ruins, and his empty stomach churned as it soaked up the lonely whisky; the dizzying effects from the lack of food grew stronger, and, although hungry, there was no way that he could face eating anything.

The alcohol opened a gate that allowed dark thoughts to displace the original self disciplined structures of Jaden's mind.

"All that training! Are you going to let the steroid freak get away with that? Are you a man? I bet they laughed at you! It's not too late to make them pay. Make them pay!"

"There's no point. I am sure that it will come back to them; what goes around comes around." Jaden silenced his ego, slammed down the tumbler, and left the public inn.

The mini-van left the car park and began edging out of town. He decided to drive out of Whitby, taking the route past the harbour for one last look. Although the whisper of temptation to take revenge lay as a seed in the depth of his mind, he contained himself, but the dark energy of a vow still followed him, taunting him and influencing his direction with intention of drawing more power.

BANG.

A car on the opposite side of the road skidded sideways and bounced off the corner of Jaden's bonnet. He pushed hard on the steering wheel as a reflex which aided his seat belt to brace him in position.

The other vehicle had not been travelling fast, but the impact had still had enough force to knock out the windscreen.

Jaden squinted through the hole in his car but steam hissed from the cracked radiator fogging his vision. Finally it cleared.

"You have got to be kiddin' me!" he shouted as he recognized Krys the bodybuilder's big ugly face peering back at him from behind the steering wheel of the dented car in front.

A sly and smug grin formed on the other man's face as he looked Jaden straight in the eye.

"NO WAY!" Jaden shouted. He had tried so hard to walk away; he looked out to the edge of the harbour which seemed to be so close to the exit roads leading to his escape.

Krys began waving at Jaden to antagonize him.

BANG, Jaden slammed his hands hard onto his steering wheel in frustration; the glove box fell open from the impact across the dashboard revealing a shiny metal object.

Heartache and betrayal began to convert into empowering chemicals which suffocated his tolerance of those with no integrity.

"He had my girl, but there's no need to rub it in my face. He has no right, I tried to walk away, I tried to leave it..........but look at him, laughin'......laughin' at me, scum!"

Jaden's temperament was that of a damp forest, hard to light, but once burning, a serious issue. Hatred began to course through his veins, along with whispers from the ego which was tinged with just enough alcohol to overpower his normal reasoning.

He held up his right hand in view of Krys and smiled as he slipped on the bright, silver knuckle duster and returned the wave; it was worth it to see the change of expression on the bodybuilder's face, and the power which Jaden felt from the panic stricken scum caused his resistance to inflicting revenge to evaporate. He got out of the Mini and watched as Krys reached and began to turn the key in the ignition to try and escape. The engine was dead, so he quickly removed the seatbelt and began to climb out of his car.

Jaden was burning up; he was aching to hurt Rebecca's secret lover. He rushed over and kicked the door with every fibre of every single hate-filled cell in his body. It smashed into Krys' face; blood exploded, splattering the window and he fell back into the car, his legs hanging out of the door. Jaden tore open the door and slammed into it again; the giant screamed as his shins shattered and bone ripped through his skin.

"Not smiling now are ya? Ya fucking fairy!" Jaden yelled, in the face of his victim.

Krys sat up in reaction to the intense pain searing from his broken shins, but he was met by a knuckle duster exploding into his face. The fear and adrenalin did not aid his pain, a pitiful moaning plead for mercy fell on deaf ears as Jaden dragged him out of the car and threw him onto the ground so that he could really work on him.

A gathering crowd watched in horror at the fountains of blood spewing from Krys' head and face. Jaden was relentless, he sat on the bodybuilder's massive chest and delivered a vicious barrage of punches from his knuckle dusting right hand.

"ARGHH!" The crowd winced at yet another scream, but this time it came from Jaden. An intense jabbing pain from his left rib cage drove him to his feet.

He gasped in disbelief at the sight of a knife protruding from his body, the pain tripled with every second.

Jaden's adrenalin helped him to maintain his stance; the crowd watched with morbid fascination as he began to pull out the weapon.

"Arghhh, arghhh!" Out squelched the long blade; warm blood trickled through his fingers as he compressed the deep wound, the crowd gasped along with Jaden as the heavy cold steel clanked onto the road.

Jaden's eyes scoured the crowd. They found a fearful expression on a familiar face which gave away the identity of the cowardly knife attacker. Carl had run in from behind and plunged in the blade in hope of saving his friend Krys.

"YOU!" Jaden shouted.

"I'll kill you, I swear, I will. I'll kill you both." Dark forces whispered as the vow was almost complete.

"Krzysztof......Krys help." Carl desperately shouted the Polish given name and the English short version in hope of awakening his bodyguard, but it was no use; the bodybuilder lay still in the ever increasing pool of blood flooding from the multitude of gaping cuts from is face and head.

Jaden picked up the knife and staggered towards Carl, his expression radiating hatred. The crowd split and ran in all directions with an outburst of panicked screaming, Carl stumbled as he tried to turn and run away, but the intense fear of Jaden and the knife spurred him back to his feet and he sprinted into the welcoming darkness of the harbour.

"That's a mistake." Jaden whispered. Carl would have nowhere to go, the harbour ended at the rough bone crushing waves of the unforgiving cold North Sea.

The night wind that hurled waves against the stone walls accompanied Jaden as he hunted in the early darkness. Blood continued to pour from him, leaving behind him a telltale trail of his passing as he pursued Carl. His anger began to ebb as the pain from his gaping wound demanded attention.

He stopped to lean against the foot of the harbour's large stone lighthouse. His breathing was laboured; desperately he gulped down the cold air.

A familiar voice called to him from the distance, he listened carefully with hope and anticipation.

"Jaden ...Jaden, stop!" a distant cry from Rebecca immediately ended the hunt; her voice cut and hurt him much more deeply than the knife wound ever could.

Rebecca rushed out of the darkness, her face wet with tears at the sight of her bloodstained man.

He turned, slumping against the lighthouse wall as his eyes met her. As he sank to the ground, he left a sticky trail that betrayed the severity of his injuries. He felt sick; the combination of heartbreak and the loss of blood was taking its toll. He stared into her eyes as she bundled him up in her arms.

"Jaden, you're bleeding, look at you, it's everywhere," she gasped.

"You don't say," he replied sarcastically.

Jaden dropped his head in sorrow and gazed silently at the floor. Rebecca was finally beginning to realize the magnitude of the damage caused; she felt his pain, exposed by his lost expression.

"What have I done?......I'm sorry Jaden, I'm so sorry," she cried.

"I saw you.....with him," Jaden answered quickly in order to focus on withholding back the tears.

"I know, we saw you leave the shop, it was a stupid mistake. I was drunk, one thing led to another, it meant nothing I swear. I've been looking for you all day." Rebecca drowned Jaden's face in the kisses of regret.

"I don't know what to say, I don't feel so good," Jaden began to tremble from the after shock of spent adrenalin. He climbed back to his feet with Rebecca's aid, and, arm in arm, they began to stagger back towards his wrecked Mini van.

The distant sound of police and ambulance sirens echoed through the small streets on route towards them, in the distance Jaden could see Krzysztof and Carl who must have sneaked past them to be reunited with his only friend.

The power of a distant vow influenced and interrupted Jaden's aura field.

"That looks like Breaker, and the captain, from the Eroda," Jaden said, his tone confused, but angry.

"Who?" Rebecca asked.

Jaden's heart throbbed in protest; he felt the warning: "*Let it go!*" and the feeling of "*Last chance saloon*" tried to hold him steady, but the tiny amount of alcohol still present in his system had just enough power to amplify his ego; he could not simply walk on by.

"I hate them; I almost killed one of them, but I failed, I won't fail this time though." Jaden was given another heartfelt warning; his words felt heavy, vile vibrations rattled through his bones.

Krzysztof sat up, leaning his back against the blood stained car door, pure white and writhing in the agony of his broken shins as he begged for assistance; Carl helpless beside him.

Jaden made his way through the crowd to observe. The fight was over; he had won, but a distant curse blinded him, and in the place of Krzysztof and Carl, he perceived Breaker and the Captain.

Against the warning given from a soul level, Jaden silenced the crowd with a promise,

"Its not over, I will kill you, both of you, I swear!"

Jaden felt a raging power depart from his spine leaving a cold trace of ice in the blood; he staggered back onto the edge of the harbour with Rebecca trying to hold him up.

"Jaden what's wrong?" she cried as he fell to one knee.

He was growing weaker with every breath, and the mistake of not listening to his heart was becoming evident, something precious had just been cast away.

"No, please, not like this, no!" the coldest realization was upon his soul, death was drawing in. He fought hard to regain his feet, but it was of no use, even with Rebecca's help, he could not fight it off, he fell back onto the cold floor with tears again glazing his eyes.

"I've just thrown it all away Rebecca," he whispered.

"No Jaden, don't say that, no, stay with me," Rebecca cried hysterically.

Jaden squinted as her image began to dim and fade out, and the echo of oncoming sirens drowned her desperate cries.

"I'm gonna miss you the most of all." His last breath was given, to the love of his life.

Chapter ten

The Essence of Process

Euphoria spilled into Jaden's consciousness.

A realigning charge of healing, blissful, pure, loving energy gently released his physical vibration; spiritual flux and the joyful remembrance of the true nature of creative self served as the greatest of any possible relief.

This is home; it was the time on earth which was the altered state of experience.

Jaden was an icicle in the divine ocean, releasing form to melt back into the loving current of the sacred sea.

But the soul felt a disturbing energy.

Immediate knowing of process cast a dark shadow.

The nature of creative process was revealed.

His visualization of a life and love with Rebecca had created the potential to realise that very outcome. Her love for Jaden had been disguised to her, but his departure, caused by her betrayal, had revealed to her the depth of her feelings towards him. Only now she had felt loss, did the weight of it dawn on her.

Krzysztof was a skinny child who had suffered at the hands of bullies at school.

Although he used the name Krys to try and fit in with the children, his surname - Dombrowski - was enough to fuel the mindset of bullies, enough difference to justify their attacks. Later in life Krzysztof had taken up bodybuilding in hope of prevent the abuse, but his large stature never drowned the deep fears which still haunted him. His display of defiance in the wave through the windscreen served only as a lie to himself, but Jaden's violent attack reminded him of the dread of the school playground, and his large size did not serve as a deterrent.

The soul of Jaden drowned in sorrow from an image of its physical aggressive onslaught to Krzysztof. And the hypocrisy of feeling the justification of such an attack, when he would have condemned such a sight, had he been an onlooker from the crowd.

Jaden ignored the heartfelt warnings; if he had followed his feelings, the creative visualization process could have taken form, but now the hatred had changed the potential. Krzysztof and Carl's friendship had been fading, and their life of crime had also begun to diminish into none existence. But Carl now had the power which he had always craved. The crowd had witnessed him stab Jaden, and now feared him, and Krzysztof felt in debt for his life, so their bond would once again become strong.

The consequences of a hateful vow ran deeper still. Jaden's consciousness became aware of the power of creative energy of which we are all either blessed or cursed, depending on choice or perception. His passion to kill his enemies both as Jaden and as Cain had finally caused his soul to divide, leaving just its darkest side to take revenge.

The little soul revisited the physical plane to gain more experience of the consequence of the process; it felt the life-draining darkness of hatred as it watched itself replay Jaden sitting on his victim's chest and exploding into a violent onslaught of attacks with a weapon.

And the promise of the taking of their lives, made with such passion, finally released vital creative energy. The power of the soul's ability to divide was revealed as Jaden split into three distinct and unbalanced energies, one of which was charged with hateful desires of revenge. And a weaker fragment of conscious energy left to find its path.

This loss of power caused his death at the harbour; the soul could no longer contain his physical structure. But there was also an awareness of a far distant vow, to which Jaden had fallen victim.

As the little soul once again let go of its presence in the physical world, the returning bliss of healing love and light was interrupted by its desire to return as Jaden.

Creative energy, still active in the spiritual flux, began to take shape, and a warning of a lack of power was given.

But the little soul surrendered its blissful transition, so it could once again take form, and as Jaden began to feel the cold chill from the concrete floor through his bones, the euphoria of spiritual awareness evaporated.

Silence, darkness, and an uneasy shadow of fear cast upon Jaden's senses as he opened his eyes to find himself alone. But this was not Whitby; there was no Abbey in the distance, no land in sight, just the cold ragged harbour with the long standing lighthouse at the north end.

He rolled onto all fours and paused to regain clarity. His vision was blurred and the unfamiliarity overwhelmed him. He shook his head and crawled to peer over the edge at the sea, but the sight of an ocean of dark red blood struck a terrifying feeling of dread as he struggled to gasp for air.

In the distance, the sinister tip of some large sea-creature's head bobbed up through a thick red wave and caught sight of Jaden.

"Where the hell am I?" he cried as drops of warm sickly blood fell like rain from the closely swirling dense black clouds above.

Chapter eleven

Priests and Predators

May 2004, Northern Poland

A small and lonely church sits overlooking its cemetery on a dark and dreadful rainy night.

Within the old stone walls a priest closes the large battered bible to retire for the night. One by one he blows out the candles, each carefully positioned to assist the dimming bulbs from the voltage drop of the swinging power lines.

THUD THUD THUD BANG BANG

A rapid fire of knocks from outside the thick wooden door startled the old man.

BANG BANG it continued.

He paused for a moment, then approached and shouted through the door.

"Czesc, kto tam?" ("Hello, who's that?")

"Help me please, help, open the door!" came an urgent reply.

BANG BANG; the desperate hammering cries for sanctuary induced a slight panic as the old man fumbled in his pocket to find the key; it clanked on the cold floor.

"Hurry please ...c'mon let me in."

"I drop the key...wait please.........ok, I have it."

He cranked open the rusty old lock and unlatched the bolts.

The doors burst wide open, and the storm threw in its cold hard rain and a pale stranger through the archway.

"Hide me! Lock the doors, hide me please," he gasped.

"Slow down.....my English not so good, what is happen to you?" the old man asked as he began to help the stranger to his feet, but the newcomer scrabbled urgently to slam the door and turn the key with cold and wet shaking hands.

"Is someone after you?"

"Someone.....something... do you have somewhere I can hide?"

replied the pale and panic-stricken man. "Do you have a phone?"

"Follow me!"

Half way down the small aisle a flash from outside illuminated the floor of the chapel through the old sacred stained glass windows, then faded leaving both of them in almost complete darkness.

"The storm has cut off the power again," explained the priest "Wait here!"

A single candle still burning served as a flickering beacon in the rear of the church. As the old man shuffled and finally reached out to grab it, he screamed from an intense and powerful burning impact which shocked through his body and hammered him hard onto the ground.

"Arghhhh!" sharp, excruciating pain intensified and crushed his left shoulder, he rolled in agony trying to compress the injury with his right hand, but warm blood spilled between his fingers, drenching his wrist watch.

"I've been shot!" realisation struck him as he writhed on the floor in search of pain relief.

"Please, please, don't kill me, no, I have a family!" the stranger's voice screamed for mercy from out of the darkness.

"Silence!" a dark and sinister voice commanded.

There was a third presence in the darkness in the church.

"I need answers, I need names, and I will ask you only once!"

The priest held still, whispering words of prayer for his pain and confusion to pass. He squinted into the darkness; shadows of the unseen disappeared as he tried focus on them, and voices continued to echo through the old rafters.

Pain seared through him as he crawled in search of the candle, its light now extinguished.

The pleading and threats grew more intense, but the old man only had a basic understanding of the English language and much was lost on him; he heard mention of England's east coast, something of guns and the name Carl Carlyle.

The cold contact of the floor eased his injury as he lay on his back to stretch out and remove a cigarette lighter from his pocket to help him find the candle. As he sparked up a flame to light his way, a simultaneous flash and the clinking of two spent rounds bouncing on the church floor gave horrific hints of a cold assassination close by.

He held still for a moment, praying desperately. His left arm was useless; the pain from his shoulder was too intense to allow him to move any further. His lighter revealed the candle resting on the floor. He transferred the flame to the wick, it gently grew, giving rise to unholy looking shadows throughout church.

"Who's there?" his voice echoed; the slam of the heavy, old storm-battered door was the only answer.

The priest struggled to his feet with a gasp and carefully trod back down the aisle in search of the poor stranger, but his instincts filled him with dread. The darkness drained his soul, there seemed to be no air. He swallowed hard and gasped as he felt evil eyes upon him.

"Who's there?" he repeated. Black silence

He was suddenly struck powerfully from behind.

"Arghhhhh!" he screamed upon meeting the cold floor once again; a heavy boot pinning him, crushing his spine.

Desperately he reached for the candle; as it rolled down the aisle it felt like a cold desertion as the light shone through his fingertips and faded into the distance.

The priest watched in horror as the wick remained lit and continued to burn as the candle rolled on the cold floor and into the empty wide open skull of the dead stranger. The shadows gave a gruesome expression of death as the fading light illuminated the eye sockets just as the blood dampened and extinguished the flame.

"Urrgh!" grunted the priest as the crushing pressure of the boot increased; the cold click of a pistol loading broke the silence.

"Damn you, damn you, how dare you....... this is a house of God!" he coughed under the pinning weight of the killer.

Time stood still as the poor man awaited his death.

"Damn me you say? Send me to hell? Maybe I have been there already, maybe, just maybe.......... I am still in hell," the dark voice carried the hint of a Russian accent, although, unbeknown to the vicar, the accent was in fact, fake.

"So answer my question father, if this church has so much...power, how is it that I could kill this scum? Why was I not struck down?" he added.

"Why did you have to kill him, and in here, whatever he had done, could you not forgive him?" gasped the priest as the pressure increased further still.

"Don't weep for this scum! He was a killer, an assassin, and he never forgave anyone!"

"Are you not the same?"

"No, I don't kill for a price, but I do kill those who do, and you have just judged and cursed me, and you would gladly send me to hell." The killer reached forwards and pressed the silencer hard into the back of the priest's neck. "You better test your faith my friend," he added

"Please...... please, forgive....... This man o lord, he is lost, and before I die, please....let my life be the last one that he takes. Help him!"

"You pray for me under the weight of your own death?"

The old man gave no answer, the pain from his wounded shoulder faded under the anticipation of drawing last breath, he closed his eyes, sighed, and let go.

Bang................................the heavy door slammed shut.

Light shone through his eyelids; he slowly opened them, but there were no angels to greet him. The lights flickered back on revealing the corpse before him, and an empty church. The killer was gone, and the priest realised that his prayer of salvation for another, had robbed a grave of a victim, that victim being himself.

Chapter twelve

Cold Astril

Brunon Dombrowski stood at the foot of his brother's grave; the mourners returned to the funeral cars leaving him to gather his thoughts as he gazed wide eyed at the large polished wooden coffin.

Never would he have dreamed that someone would dare assassinate his brother. The fear associated with the family name was more than enough to prevent even the smallest of challenges. He wondered if he had become complacent; dealing arms in the underground weapons trade was an incredibly dangerous place to allow even the slightest fall of the guard.

He stood alone for a moment in the small Polish cemetery, pausing to fight against the feelings that he had in common with the innumerable families of victims that he had put to death over the many years.

The returns did not sit too well in his gut, and the feeling of being at the receiving end was not welcome.

With a deep sigh he turned to walk away and looked for his security, each posted at a corner of the cemetery, only to find them lying still on the ground.

The headstone to his right exploded, smashing into a million pieces.

"What the…?"

A bullet erupted through his bladder folding him, dropping his agonised body at the edge of his brother's open grave.

Beyond the cemetery walls stood a stretched black funeral car full of lawyers, crooked police chiefs and various hangers-on, its occupants oblivious to the stealth attack upon Brunon and his men. They competed in their displays of grief, each crying louder and shedding more tears than the next; they remained unaware of the large black van reversing up beside them.

Astril scrambled from the driver's seat into the back of the large van. He pulled on thick Teflon plated biker wear and a helmet, the protection was required for the rapid ejection of discharge shells from the three rotary six-barrel machines-guns mounted on the "A" frame near the back doors. His veins felt like power lines from the intense flow of adrenaline, he had mastered the unsteadiness brought on by the cold rush of chemicals which quickened the blood, a fully matured killer, who could pull a trigger as naturally as he could blink. The rear double doors of the van slowly opened revealing the target.

The driver of the limo was the first to realise that he was about to die; he choked at the exposure of the eighteen barrel tips of three mini guns protruding from the darkness of the van. Silence fell in the vehicle as Astril gave them a second to anticipate their fate.

His heart was at maximum contraction flooding his system with blood rich mixtures which almost displaced the reality of what he was about to commit.

He squeezed the common trigger and the three barrels of each gun began to pour out six-thousand rounds of seven point six millimetre depleted uranium ammunition per minute, giving a total of eighteen thousand rounds ripping through the car and its passengers.

"ARGHH!" he adored the kick from the awesome power of the weapons as the car disintegrated under the thousands of rounds ripping through the metal, pulverising all those within; glass, blood and bone spewed out of the wreckage as it rocked and sparked from the onslaught of rapid fire. The screams fell silent but the attack continued until there was nothing left.

The smoking barrels purred down to a standstill, leaving the sound of dogs barking in the distance along with distant cries of witnesses making good their escape.

Astril lifted the visor from the helmet to survey the damage he had wrought.

"Killed with your own weapons!" he whispered victoriously. This kill had been a last minute decision; originally Brunon had been his only target, but the information gleaned from his victim in the church had led to him stealing the van with the three mini guns.

As the smoke cleared, the remains of the car and all those within came into view, all were dead, and as far as Astril was concerned, anyone with the villains, was probably being fed by the money extracted from their many repressed victims; as for the lawyers, killing them was a pleasure.

He dropped down a plank of wood and wheeled a large v max motor bike down onto the grass; he kicked out the stand and disappeared back into the van to grab a back pack and a pistol. He quickly threw a few smoke bombs to obscure the vision of possible witnesses, and, after throwing a tiny petrol bomb into the back of the van, ran into the cemetery.

Just behind Brunon, a young man, a grave digger, was hiding behind a large headstone; he watched as Astril appeared from out of the smoke, jogging towards his victim who lay writhing on the ground, blood and urine spilling from the entry wounds of Astril's earlier shot.

The young boy was overwhelmed by the dark presence of the figure standing above one of the region's most feared men.

"What kind of assassin are you?" Brunon cried in pain and anger as Astril bent down removing his bike helmet.

"I am no assassin…….. I seek revenge…….. I take pleasure in your death!"

"You won't get away with it; do you know who I am?" Brunon gave his last desperate attempt at salvation using fear.

"I know exactly what you are," Astril whispered "You can't threaten me, for I am already dead, I have nothing, I have no one, you made that so when killed my family when I was a child. And know, before you die, that I shall spare none of yours!"

Astril removed his back pack and took out a battery powered drill and a small syringe.

"Your amateur hit men were very inaccurate with their shots!" Astril squeezed the trigger of the battery drill, the motor engaged with a high pitch squeal of meshing gears that only hinted at what was to come.

"My brother suffered before he died……………so guess what!"

And the thirst for revenge was quenched, witnessed by the poor, young grave digger, who, for two months, could neither speak of nor describe the sights and sounds of the torment inflicted upon Brunon.

Eight hours later and Astril was suffering the after effects of the saturation of his blood with stress hormones.

The shakes from the physical comedown felt like ice cold demon snakes tapping at his spine and hissing poison through his veins.

"No turning back now, you did it, all of them, you killed all of them." His ego whispered as it repeated the cries for mercy from Brunon, and replayed

the images of the impact that the three guns had made on the car full of victims.

His heart remained silent under the damp fog of dark energy born of a distant vow.

A bellowing gust of wind rocked the campervan on its old chassis, nudging him back to his senses.

Cold, black coffee laced with vodka and a cigarette kept him company as his thumb flicked the loading chamber of an old revolver.

The stimulants served as a cheap reward for a dangerous and successful execution.

He gazed outside at a burning bin full of his biker wear; the smell of smoke filled his nostrils.

Another cigarette fired its nicotine into his blood as he reclined, blowing the smoke across a large letter "A" tattooed on his chest.

"A few more. Only a few more to deal with, then its over!" he thought.

No date, no time, and in no place....

Jaden screamed for answers as he ran around the lighthouse avoiding the constantly reaching tentacles of a hidden creature in the blood ocean below.

"If I am dead, why do I still have a body?" he cried, "Why even have gravity?"

Chapter thirteen

Hellmakers' mirror

July 2004

An urgent meeting was required. Carl Carlyle arrived at East Midlands Airport. He had spent the morning in a business meeting regarding pistol ammunitions with a dangerous client in the city of Nottingham. Krzysztof Dombrowski threw his small leather and well-travelled bag into the boot of Carl's Aston Martin Vantage and then squeezed into the passenger seat.

There was a cold silence between them; Carl pulled out of the airport and began to drive towards the motorway.

"I'm sorry mate but you've flown up here for nothin'. I've only had the one meetin', the second one's cancelled. We'll head to London from here, you could have flown straight there!" Carl muttered. He had a burning question, but dared not ask for fear of the answer, but Krzysztof's pale expression had given indication of bad news. It would have been easier to ask him over the phone, but unfortunately that was a security risk.

"Poland?" Carl asked while staring hard at the road.

"You had better pull over, so we can talk," Krzysztof replied.

The six large cooling towers of the nearby power station overlooked the small lay-by where the Aston Martin rolled in.

"Well?" Carl looked at Krzysztof who stared into the foot-well, "Krys?"

"I warned you years ago about getting into the weapons trade, do you remember? And I knew this day would come," Krzysztof spoke in a slow monotone.

"What...what day, what?"

"Its over Carl, we're finished!"

"Finished, why, tell me what happened?"

"What happened! I'll tell you what happened, most of my family in

Poland have been killed, murdered, they are all dead. So you have no supplier, and I have no family, not anymore!"

"You what? What the hell am I gonna do? I need the guns!" Carl was as considerate as Krzysztof had expected.

"Ah, you spineless little maggot," Krys shouted, spit hitting the dashboard, "That's the good news; the assassin may yet be coming for us. Whoever he is, he has managed to kill most of my family and connections."

"Let him come, bring him on, I'll sort him!" Carl was suffering his usual delusions of grandeur.

Krzysztof shook his head while laughing sarcastically under his breath. "As I said, that was the good news, now here my little friend….is the bad news. There was an eye witness; he was about thirteen, a grave digger".

"Yes…..and what did…?

"Listen!" Krzysztof interrupted, "There are police involved so it took a while to get the info' but he did not kill him straight away, he hurt my uncle Brunon, made him suffer."

The car remained silent for almost a minute.

"What did he do to him?" Carl's throat was suddenly very dry.

Krzysztof glared straight ahead through the windscreen as he spoke: "He shot him in the bladder, and returned after killing everyone. He beat him badly, then drilled a tiny hole into his skull, right between the eyes and injected acid into his brain with a syringe. He let him suffer a while before throwing him on top of my other dead uncle's coffin, and then threw a petrol bomb into the grave, I guess as a mark of disrespect. And he may well be on his way over here, coming after us. Do you still fancy your chances in toy town Crooksville?"

Carl reached forward and fumbled to start the engine. Blood drained from his face as he rolled out of the junction heading to the motorway that led them back to the seeming safety of London where they both now lived.

Krzysztof stared wide eyed at the blur of lines dividing the three lanes of the motorway. Neither of them spoke, the junctions shot past as they sped towards the capital.

Krzysztof's thoughts drifted to Scarborough; he missed the coast, and he was often plagued with thoughts of "*what could have been*" if only he had stayed there and maybe opened a health club. The life of a villain, a gangster, was not without sacrifice. He felt he was indebted to Carl, who may have saved him from Jaden's assault many years ago in Whitby. In the years since, he had half-heartedly followed Carl into the arms trade, using his own family to supply their weapons from Eastern Europe. Their clients were of the dark and unforgiving underworld; now some unknown soulless creature, even darker than the most ruthless of them, was drawing near.

Carl was concentrating on business. The straight run of the motorway allowed him to both cruise, and contemplate.

"Bounty hunters, mercenaries! That's it! We'll get the best, and double our security!" he blurted.

"*More money than sense!*" thought Krzysztof; an accurate conclusion, as Carl was becoming very a wealthy villain.

"The Killer might not be after us! It could've been something that went down in Poland, a local thing, a revenge hit!" Carl continued.

"Maybe, maybe not, but I have lost a lot of family. I know we weren't close, but we have no supplier now, and it all seems …."

"Seems what?" Carl asked.

"All seems a bit real, I have always said we are out of our depth here."

Carl shook his head: "No way Krys, we have been in it for too long. Look at how far we have come; we'll just have to find some other way of getting supplies. Leave it with me, I'll sort it," Carl continued.

Krzysztof's heart weighed heavy as the city's tower blocks rose from the horizon. He folded his arms and tucked his knuckles tight under his hard biceps. Carl continued to babble, loving the sound of his own voice; Krzysztof however, remained silent as the words remained impenetrable.

The speeding car rocked him gently, and one yawn lead to another, leaving him with rapid-blinking glazed eyes. His bones weighed like lead, and caffeine from the many beverages could no longer sustain alertness. The toil from the trip to Poland, along with news of the murders and bloodshed of his family, finally caught up with him. He faded into a deep sleep.

An old ship…. a woman in a black cloak, a witch, or a magician perhaps, whispering to him, messages of *try to save your friend, but also save yourself, make things right.* It came to him not as words, but knowings, feelings.

Ah, the sound of the sea, the sway of the old ship, the smell of salt water; it feels so good to be back, especially without the captain.

The brakes hammered down jolting Krzysztof back to consciousness.

"Wakey, wakey! We're home," Carl sneered, "Shall I bring a blanket to cover you next time? You are knockin' on a bit you ol' bastard."

Krzysztof yawned and stretched out with a growl. He removed the seatbelt and squeezed out of the car and without a word, grabbed his large bag and slammed the passenger door closed.

He watched as Carl sped away down the street.

"You are older than I am; you will be fifty soon!" he answered the fading car, and while fumbling around his pockets for his door keys, Krzysztof was unaware of the seed which now lay in his heart; planted there from the distant past, perhaps to save this life.

Chapter fourteen

Other Sides

Jaden witnessed the cry of a million dreadful screams. Over and over they wailed from below the ocean.

"No...I am sorry...please...no!" he begged, but his voice drowned into the many agonising torments surrounding him. He was sick, lonely and terrified. He wept, intermittently screaming for help, but it was useless, he was alone, damned.

With his back pressing hard against the stone lighthouse, he endured the smell of thick dark red blood as the vicious waves crashed over his body.

Though his hands clutched his head, his nightmare revealed itself through his fingertips, as the black creature, which had been stalking him, desperately pulled itself onto the edge of what little remained of the harbour as it sought its delicacy.

The bladder sucking sound emanating from the massive nightmarish thing shocked Jaden; making him retch until he covered himself in vomit. Small squid in fish tanks had been known to induce him to faint; this was the worst situation that he could ever possibly imagine.

The creature began to slide towards him, its tentacles slowly dragging it forward, and although it made no sense to Jaden why he still felt alive, and with it, the physical traits of his humanity, the terror of the creature and the environment displaced any concept of being dead already and with it, the fear of dying again.

It all felt unquestionably real.

He scanned for a way out, he knew that if he jumped into the Blood Sea, the creature would follow him, and be sure to finish him.

The lighthouse had many deep cracks running through its old stonework; he stretched up, fed his fingers into them and pulled his body up, powered by the energy of pure fear.

Frantically he scrambled; his fingers and forearms screamed with the strain of a narrow grip desperately supporting his body weight.

He turned his head to look down and gasped at the sight of waving tentacles laden with hooks and thousands of suction glands frighteningly, and desperately reaching for him.

"No…no," he whimpered, his grip was weakening, but he knew that if he slipped now he would be in the beak of the hungry creature.

He focused his eyes on the top of the tower and began to climb; struggling desperately he finally made it to the top. A vibration of climbing to safety burst from his core and entered the ether.

He jumped over the rail and collapsed on the ledge, lungs bursting, gasping for air or whatever it was that he was breathing.

The glass panels of the lighthouse's rotunda had been bricked up, perhaps no ships would ever dare sail this way, perhaps it was designed to cause shipwrecks, or even to prevent access to the old lighthouse.

The metal bars vibrated from the heavy impact of a hook of a tentacle as it wrapped around the frame.

"No, no, no way!" Jaden screamed as he realised the creature was pulling itself towards the top of the lighthouse.

He crawled around to the opposite side of the ledge and discovered an old iron door which was ajar. He slid his fingers around the edge and pulled hard, but the hinges had decayed and the door held fast.

"ARGHHH COME ON!" he screamed as his attempts to gain entry became ever more desperate. The door creaked open a few inches causing Jaden to lose his grip and slip, his inertia almost throwing him off the edge.

The creature's head rose to the level of the railing and their eyes met, pupils shrinking simultaneously.

"Squids such as this do not exist!" Jaden confirmed, it didn't seem fair; how could a sea creature pursue him on land, and up a tower?

The fear of stealthy tentacles from behind drove him to his feet and back to prizing at the door with white knuckle tension.

He posted his left foot on the wall to aid his pull; the fear of being crushed in the creature's stinking maw numbed the pain of his bleeding palms compressed against the sharp edge of the rusty old door.

With a jolt the door cracked open another two inches. The sickly bladder sucking sound drew near, but he dared not look behind himself.

Jaden forced himself through the seemingly impassable gap, almost breaking his ribs in order to escape this manifestation of his nightmares. He fell inside onto a dark ledge.

The aggressive hammering at the door gave warning that the hunt was still on, and it was only a matter a time before the hungry predator would be inside the tower.

Jaden peered through the gap and remembered the thing that he hated most of all about invertebrates: they could squeeze through a hole as small as their eye.

The dark spiral stairwell was singularly uninviting, but unfortunately the only route available; there was a tiny ladder up to the lamp room, but that would leave him exposed to the creature. The demonic sounds from the hungry mutant forced his decision. His wounded left palm guided him via the cold wall, and step by heart deafening step, he disappeared down into the blackness.

The luxury of tears would have brought even the slightest of relief to Jaden's torment confusion and pain, but he had left all of his tears on the harbour, weeping in-between the screams for forgiveness, and cries for help.

The steps seemed endless, he realised that he must be well below the level of the Blood Sea by now. The pitch black loneliness pulled the light from the depths of his soul.

The edge of a cold stone step cracked into his back as he collapsed from complete exhaustion.

"I...I... give up, I'm beaten. I surrender!" Jaden closed his eyes and let go.

Down into the darkness he fell, holding onto the thoughts of the love of his family, and the last one to hold him, Rebecca.

Jaden opened his eyes; nothing but darkness and cold silence were embedded in what was left of his soul.

He had reached the bottom of the spiral steps and lay at the pit of the lighthouse.

"Where am I?" he moaned, distraught, lost, and alone.

The seed of fear recreated by the increasingly vile and horrific sounds emanating from the darkness forced him gracelessly to his feet.

Tears streamed down his cheeks leaving the salty taste of dread on his lips.

"Why is this happening to me?" he sobbed.

A candle flickered into life with a damp *hissssss*; its flame on the circular wall behind him revealing a passageway hidden in the darkness. As ghostly shadows toyed and twisted Jaden's torment, the light of the candle reflected in the dark blood pouring down the stone steps and washing over his feet.

The pain and dread were unending anticipation brought unlimited sickness, confusion and terror.

Vomit splattered into the blood, his gut wrenching, expelling a toxic body chemistry that was eating through his stomach. He coughed, choking from the acidic aftertaste.

He tore half the sleeve from the remains of his shredded sweatshirt to wipe his face and dry his eyes. His screaming demanding inquiry of "where, why, where, why?" furiously and repetitively plagued him. The material of his sleeved sopped, it brought comfort as he continued to clean himself up and attempt to gain some semblance of composure.

There was a silence; his mind halted for a moment as he dropped the sleeve into the blood that continually flowed down the steps. It sailed down into the passage way almost beckoning him to follow, and it did seem that there was nowhere else for him to go; he trudged to peer down the dark passage.

"Hello!" he croaked, but the only answer was his own echo. "Hello!" he repeated as he edged forwards.

He paused for a moment, but was soon disturbed; a clinking echo from the steps above gave warning of something on its way down. A dreadful hiss followed by distant and desperate screams faded leaving the sound of whispering moans growing ever louder, and closer.

He reached out and grabbed the candle to light his way, and with one palm trembling to feel the cold walls either side of him, he crouched to venture down the passageway, inch by painfully trodden inch.

His feet splashed through blood which now reached his ankles, filling his shoes; he froze in horror as the candle flame flickered.

"Don't go out, don't go out, please.......stay lit!" he implored, but to his horror the flame spluttered and died, leaving a fading glow upon the smoking wick.

A dim motion of shadows in the distant structure of an archway hinted at an exit from the passage.

"Please let this be the light at the end of the tunnel," he prayed.

The candle splashed into the pooling blood, giving Jaden both hands to support himself along the walls as he hastened down the corridor towards the light.

As the exit drew near he stalled to catch his breath, he then stepped out into the archway. The structure before him resembled the inside of a well, the circular wall disappearing high into the darkness, like a chimney from the bowels of hell reaching into a void of emptiness. Blood flowed past his ankles, pouring down into a black hole of nothingness. The curved wall was dotted with candles, their dim light falling on a narrow ledge that ringed the inside of the structure.

Jaden stepped up out of the stream of blood and onto the ledge. The stone felt cold and wet as he tilted his head back to rest. He peered with fear as anticipation once again grew at the mercy of unending whispers of dread.

"What was that?" He thought he saw something, "There it is again!"

In the darkness, in the centre of the well and level with Jaden's eyes, a small sphere began to intermittently flash and glow.

He immediately recognised the image as the same one that he had tried to grasp when wearing the cloak in the shop, The Magic Mantelpiece.

He held himself still, unsure of what it may bring, as the slam of his heart hammered beats of warning hard on his eardrums, the sphere of light remained peacefully still.

"Who's there?" The rise of a cold feeling of being watched chilled his spine and iced his shoulder blades.

He pinned his aching body hard against the wall.

"I...I can't take anymore of this, help me please....please anyone, I don't deserve this suffering!" His fear peaked and Jaden slid down the wall as he surrendered his soul.

"This must be because of the bones, the skeleton. I am being punished for what I did on the ship, and for what I did to Rebecca's lover."

As Jaden wept into his palms, the sphere remained out of reach in the open void of the dark chamber.

"Help me make this right, whatever it takes, whatever I have done, please help me!" Jaden pleaded to the light.

A silence fell, and the current of blood which spilled from the passageway into the emptiness, immediately ceased its flow. The whispers which had continually plagued him were hushed, leaving a deafening silence.

Jaden pushed his way up the wall back onto his feet; the sphere before him began to strobe a flicker of brilliant white light throughout the chamber causing him to squint and raise his left hand to shield the intense radiance now bursting forth. The light cast a field of energy throughout the chamber which enveloped him.

"Arghhhhhh!" He buried his head in the crook of his arm and sank onto one knee.

He tried to peer into the light but it blinded him, something touched his shoulder, then his hands, and then his back.

"Who's there? What's that? Leave me alone!" he pleaded while frantically waving his arms in panic. The radiance burned through his tightly clasped eyelids, stinging his eyes and locking in tears which demanded an explosive exit.

"If I am dead...why do I have a body? Why are you doing this to me? Help me please!"

And as the echo of his ongoing pleas faded, silence and darkness fell immediately upon him.

The gasping rise and fall of his breath began to steady, and he realised that, once again, he was alone.

He opened his eyes and gave way to floods of tears which he had held in for an eternity; a candle flickered on the far wall of the well. The silence remained with him, but he dared not move, not yet. The cold ledge where he lay drove a deep chill into his ribs causing him to finally sit up, and it was only then that he realised the mysterious light had left something with him.

To his left lay a large black cloth garment emitting spirals of sweet smelling mist. He gazed in stillness for a short time before leaning over to quickly prod and smell the vapour still rising from the fabric. He pawed it cautiously. It seemed familiar to him.

"The cloak...from the shop, it's the cloak!" he whispered. It felt warm to the touch, and to the soul. While gently unfolding and scrutinizing the cloth, he decided not to question its arrival for fear of losing something familiar to him; it was only a cloak, but any link back home served as hope for him.

Its weight hugged his trapezius and shoulders as he slung it over his back. His knees quivered causing him to sink and sit cross legged.

"Oh!" He released a discharge of anxious breath as terror loosened its grip, and the cloak which now wrapped him, began to charge stored energy, back into Jaden's aura field.

Chapter fifteen

Krzysztof's Awakening

Krzysztof stared deep into his own eyes reflecting from the bathroom mirror as he shaved his jaw line. It was 6.00am, and his thoughts left him exhausted from their constant, soul-draining torments. The more he tried to solve them, the more they continued to spiral. *Plop.* The razor dropped into the water; he placed both hands palms down in the sink and leaned his weight forward with a sigh. "Come on Krzys, pull yourself together!"

He dried his face and threw the towel into the wash basket. He squeezed into a black sweatshirt and jeans and headed to his kitchen for breakfast.

Although in his mid-forties, Krzysztof had kept up the training; he had a large muscular frame and carried very little body fat. His size was subconsciously amplifying a problem that he had yet to solve deep within his own psychology, a demon to conquer; its strength was its elusive nature.

He sat down crunching his oats with a feeling of dread joining his breakfast in the pit of his stomach. Carl was coming over to talk business, and that probably meant more dark deals in London.

"Why don't you just tell him you wanna leave 'n' go back home?" Krzysztof's inner voice repeated its ongoing mantra of inquiry.

"Because, I can't, I just can't!" he answered.

"Why? Why not?"

The constant mental chatter over many months of sleepless nights had finally taken its toll, and for the first time, Krzysztof reacted with frustration leading to anger.

"Arghhhh.... It's cos I am scared...a pussy, a coward!" he threw the bowl of food at the wall; it shattered, leaving a trail of sharp splinters over the wooden floor. "Arghhhhhh!" he continued with destructive rage, trying to overcome the shame of what he had finally admitted to himself. He ripped the large flat screen TV from its stand and with a scream launched it into his impressive music system. *BANG,* the electrical circuitry shorted to earth, tripping the breaker and cutting the power to his flat.

When there was nothing left to break, Krzysztof collapsed in a heap, tears of exhausted relief bursting from his eyes. The sharp glass from the smashed screen cut into his right thigh, but he did not realise that he had sustained a wound until the blood ran into the channels between the fingers of his flat palm posted on the floor to support his weight. Endorphins, the body's natural pain killer, released the many tight knots in his muscles leaving him in an entranced state of lesser enlightenment.

"I am bigger and stronger than Carl, but I'm afraid, afraid to break free!"

Krzysztof did not know the cause of his fear, but just having enough courage to admit this to himself brought peace. Deep within, the shame of being so large, yet still afraid, was summoning up a torrent of energy to resist this truth, and the reason was simple; he had originally thought that size was the answer, but as Jaden had demonstrated several years before, size is nothing. It meant that at some point he had reached the wrong conclusion, and fear of not finding the answers was the true nature of his nightmares, now the he felt the refreshing freedom of having to re-evaluate, and discover the relative truth of who he really was.

"What the hell?" Carl had let himself in and was studying the remains of the television.

"I couldn't find the remote, so I had a bit of a scout around..... have you seen it?" Krzys replied.

"What?"

"It's not easy not having a sense of humour is it Carl?"

"Looks like roid rage t' me!"

Krzysztof climbed to his feet, "Roid rage, I'm tired of hearing that. It ain't me who slaps my women and kids is it Carl? Tell me, have you ever actually hit a man?"

"You ain't got no woman have you Krzys?" Carl sneered.

"By choice you weak freak!"

"Maybe all the steroids have took the lead out of your pencil!"

Krzysztof stepped forward "I'll tell you about gear shall I you babbling hypocrite. I do it twelve weeks a year and I'm careful, I don't drink, I watch what I eat, and I train. Now then, what do you do other than talk about things you know nothing about?"

"What… well."

"Shut up, I ain't finished! You drink, and smoke all year round, you're unfit, you eat crap, spend all ya money on drugs, then have a pop at me who takes less risks than you, with the vile garbage you put in your body. I take a bit of a risk, twice a year," he paused, "And I look after myself all year round. You're like all the know nothing mummies' boys who prop the bar up and scoff at someone when you are taking the worst drugs of them all, beer n' fags, you faggot!"

"Krzys calm down! All I'm sayin' is…"

"Carl, go home, get drunk, and beat up your woman!" Krzysztof pulled out the splinter of glass from his leg without a flinch while maintaining the cold stare at Carl.

"I come here to talk business, and that's all the thanks I get! I've found a supplier…"

"Stop…..stop, Carl, its over for me, I have had enough, I am going to head back up north, back home!" Krzysztof finally confessed and the truth did set him free.

"Question is, what you gonna do back in Scarborough? We live down here now, why you…"

"I'm sick of it, the watching my back, for cops and clients, we've made enough money to get out, I'll open a gym or something, why don't you come with me? Leave this life and enjoy things while we still can?"

"They won't let you just walk away, y' can't! They'll take you out, they will, they bloody well will." Carl was desperate, and thought fear could be applied as the usual tool of persuasion.

"Take me out? Kill me you mean? Ah Carl, well although my family are dead, I still have connections with some lovely characters in Poland, so whoever you send had better be ready for some comebacks." Krzysztof growled while tending to the cut from the remains of his TV.

"I can't believe you are doing this, think about it, go on, sleep on it, we…"

"Carl, I'm goin' I have had it, why don't you join me, before you get killed, we've both made enough money, we've been lucky to get this far, believe me. Come on, let's go and open a bar, or something."

"You really are serious aren't you? I don't know what to say, I don't want to go back north, I like this life, and I like the crew we run with." Carl was shaking his head as he backed out of the door.

"You even try to sound like em', *crew we run with* who talks like that?"

"I'm out of here. I'll talk later when you've come to your senses. I always knew the steroids would wreck your brain."

Krzysztof rolled his eyes in disbelief at Carl's repetitive statements regarding anabolic steroids.

"Just go mate, if you ever need to get out of this life, I'll see you back north."

"No, you won't be seeing me! I don't need you, I've got a new supplier, I can get anything me!"

Confirmation swept over Krzysztof, washing him clean of all regret.

"There you go!" his heart whispered, and the big man realized, it had been a paperweight friendship all along, but the truth had only become clear to him when he accepted the truth of his feelings, and had the good intention of rescuing Carl from a dangerous lifestyle.

Carl screeched down the road, and out of sight.

Two hours later Krzysztof joined the motorway heading north out of the capital. He had left all of his belongings, paid the landlord and departed with nothing more than his Jeep and the clothes on his back.

As the open road unfolded in his large windscreen, their final argument played over and over in his mind. Even though he knew he had made the correct decision, the chatter continued to plague him: *"Why didn't you say more? He used you, he knows nothing of steroids, he drinks worse drugs, the taxable drugs are ok then are they? All the smoking and crack it's ok then is it? Can get weapons can he? New supplier? They'll soon learn what Carl's like, then see where he ends up."*

Krzysztof suffered the onslaught of chatter. As each question fell he would silently answer it, only for another to take its place, or an old one previously solved, would be repeated.

"Yorkshire… already!" Krzysztof's mental turmoil had displaced his focus from the present moment on the road, "How did I get here so soon?"

Amazed at the auto-pilot of his mind, he couldn't recall driving through the East Midlands, nor the seeing the steel plants and the power station's massive cooling towers that he knew so well.

He turned right, heading east towards York. Emptiness swallowed his heart, he was alone, he had nothing and no one, and no idea of what he was going to do with his life now.

The chatter continued deep into the Yorkshire moors, but despite all of its taunts, he knew he had made the right decision, and a spark of excitement mixed with his fear of an unknown future.

A road sign appeared in the left, it read –'APRIL'S CAFÉ AND RAILWAY INN'.

Krzysztof indicated and pulled over for some food. The tyres popped on the gravel as he entered the car park of the old converted railway station, the brakes squeaked as the jeep pulled to a stop, he turned off the engine and removed the seatbelt.

"Aaaaawww," he stretched out with a yawn and sat for a moment to compose himself after the relatively long and spur-of-the-moment drive to the north east coast, which had followed the life-changing decision he had made. The contraction of the engine ticked away from behind the dashboard, but the sun shone through his windscreen causing expansion pops and cracking sounds from the interior.

To the left of the small building where old railway sleepers hid under the long grass, a few old carriages rested in their retirement. He followed the track with his eyes as far as he could; the old railway lines faded into the greenness of the Yorkshire moors.

Stepping out of his Jeep he groaned once more with a bone cracking stretch to relieve the embedded shape of the car seat from his spine. Music drifted from the old station building and the smell of food tinted the air.

He checked his pocket to locate his wallet and limped up the five steps into the entrance. The chime tinkled for a second time as he closed the door behind him and looked around.

"Empty!" he smiled to himself, sitting down at a small wooden circular table.

"Won't be a moment!" called a female voice from the small kitchen behind the counter.

"Ok… thank you!" Krzysztof replied. He scanned the small laminated menu standing in a grooved, wooden block.

Thud, thud, thud a pair of fast paced shoes clattered toward him.

"Hello….now what can I get for you?" Krzysztof glanced up at the very blonde but plain, twenty-something waitress holding a pad and pen.

"Can I have the scrambled eggs on toast, but brown toast if you have it, and spread the butter thin for me please?" Krzysztof was looking for a complex carbohydrate and protein meal.

"Anything to drink? Tea, coffee?"

"Just water thanks," Krzysztof replied.

"Thank you!" she turned and clumped back into the kitchen.

Krzysztof gazed around the old converted station while he awaited his lunch, he imagined the passengers from the past, shuffling to and fro, reminiscent of some old black and white classic film. Maybe a steam engine was reuniting distant lovers on the small platform, or taking tourists to visit the coast for their holidays. The chatter of voices filled the room as he watched the old heavy leather suitcases drag along the floor as the passengers pulled them towards the ticket office.

"A penny for them!" the waitress clanked the plate of food on the table.

Krzysztof looked up, startled: "What?"

"Your thoughts, a penny for your thoughts!" she added.

He laughed, "I was somewhere else then!"

"So I noticed!"

"Are you from Oxford or somewhere down that way?" Krzysztof inquired, he was very good at locating a complete stranger's origin from their accent.

"Yes. How did you know? Do I sound that posh?" she smiled.

"Yes you do! So how did you end up, up here in the north?"

"Hang on let me turn the radio down so I can hear you; this radio presenter is irritating me anyway!" she clumped behind the kitchen and switched off her radio, "There that's better, I can hear you now!"

Krzysztof laughed, "What's wrong with the DJ, why don't you like him?"

"He is rude, a coward and a bully!" she replied with urgency. "He's nasty to his guests, and proud of his put downs; you should only be proud if you make someone feel better, not worse!"

Krzysztof nodded while simultaneously chewing his food.

"But he is only rude to certain guests. When he interviewed some cocky guitarist a couple of weeks ago he was such a creep, it was utterly nauseating; he's such a bully, he only insults people who pose him no threat!" she added passionately.

"Yeah, you're right. I've heard him myself, and when he gets pulled up for it, he hides behind it by saying it was all a big joke," Krzysztof added, "If it was me I'd say to him, *well if you want to hurt me with insults, why stop there, lets go outside and you can try to hurt me properly.* Maybe when he gets to puberty and his voice finally breaks – the fat freak!"

The waitress laughed in nervous agreement. "Anyway, you did ask me how I ended up in the north. I sold a business in Oxford to buy this one; I want to convert it to a place of novelty, where guests can sleep in those old converted sleeper cars outside on the tracks, and from here go rambling in the Yorkshire moors."

"How's business going for you?" Krzysztof asked.

"Sorry about the little outburst, but my business is going fine, so fine in fact that a property developer wants to buy me out. He keeps saying he will make an offer I can't refuse, he is a bully too, that's what made me react the way I did, sorry!"

"An offer you can't refuse eh, I hope you don't wake up with a horse's head on your pillow!" Krzysztof grinned.

They looked at each other for a moment and then both of them burst into laughter.

"My name is April by the way, nice to meet you; what is it that you do may I ask?"

"I'm Krzysztof!" he replied. "Nice to meet you too, I have just left a big part of my life to start over again, up here, and I always feel drawn to old ships, so I will take time to look at what I can work with when I get settled, in Whitby maybe, or Scarborough."

"Sounds interesting," April replied as she continued working behind the counter, "If you need any business advice I have an MBA."

"Thanks, and if you need help with the bullying property developer, I have a degree in persuasion!" he replied.

Krzysztof's tormenting mental chatter had faded into the shadows of his mind in the light of good conversation shared with April. They exchanged numbers and he limped back to his jeep to continue his journey to the coast in search of a new life.

Chapter Sixteen

Death

Jaden breathed in strength as the cloak shielded him from the soul draining torment.

A feeling lifted from his heart, it condensed into an immediate knowing, giving the instruction - *Listen to your feelings, influence your thoughts.*

Still perched on the ledge of the dark circular chamber he released all resistance and allowed his fears to do their worst.

The inner voice began: *"You won't survive! This is your fault! You're vile, a hypocrite, a looser, a fake. You deserve to be here, to suffer, it's going to get bad, really bad, worse. Unlovable, who's going to save you? Who would want to? Worthless, how stupid, to think Rebecca could ever love you, or anyone could for that matter, and you think you can fight! You can't fight, you're a coward, look at you, crying. It's over; you should never have been born. You are going to suffer! Something's coming for you, something evil, to hurt you and no one is going help, why would they? Scum, you are scum, ugly, disgusting, a reject, a loser, a two-faced creep, a maggot, a little filth eating maggot. You are filth, rotting, stinking filth. Your parents hate you. You are a disappointment, a failure, a nothing, a nobody, you are spineless. Your death will be good news, people will laugh, celebrate, glad to be rid of you, glad of never having to set eyes on your foul little face again".*

Jaden answered the inner voice of his mind: "I agree, I am a loser, and I have failed, and I deserve all of this, and in the end, when I die, you shall die with me!"

After a short silence the slightly confused ego continued its quest for energy.

"Your fault, this is all your doing, you have lost everything!"

"Yes you are right, you are always right," Jaden interrupted, and continued to agree with every invitation to engage that his mind threw at him. Desperately searching for any vulnerable angle, tirelessly the dark chatter continued, but Jaden accepted that this may be the end for him, and fought only against temptation to contest the onslaught of negativity.

"Maybe you are one of God's rejects, one of his mistakes!"

"Does an all-powerful creator make mistakes?" Jaden answered.

"Well, maybe he did with you. Looks like you failed your test, that's why you are

down here!"

"What test?"

"The free will test, you have made some bad choices to end up here!"

"So an unlimited power needs to test me, to see what choices I will make, to see if I am worthy. So this unlimited creator, has no foresight and no foresight means that the creator is limited, not such a powerful creator after all then it seems, and not so loving, if the creator loved me, why create the parameters to allow such punishment for a wrong choice which may lead to such suffering?"

"How dare you question?"

"I question with the inquisitive nature given to me by my creator, don't give me a kite, and winds for me to fly it, then ask me what I am doing."

Jaden realised then that the mind had successfully engaged him into his usual internal dialogue of conflicting thoughts.

"What is this voice of the mind that we all hear, when we talk within ourselves, where does it come from, and who answers these thoughts? Am I the voice, or the answer?"

Just watch- the feeling affirmed.

Jaden remembered the last part of Delmar's mantra: *Accept the ghosts which haunt your mind, they may have led you to this point in time, allow their whispers of all your fears, focus on joy, the darkness clears.*

He began to focus on feelings of peace, rather than crave it and dwell upon its absence.

"Imagine it now, feel it now, generate it now, and allow the dark thoughts to continue without resistance. Is this the difference between focus and awareness which Del spoke of? Did Del know that I would end up here, if so, how? And the cloak, where has it come from, and what is its power?" he muttered to himself.

A violent tremor shook the chamber; a release of dark energy from the displeased Hellmakers rocked the massive structure. Jaden held his breath, and after a short time, the disturbance subsided.

His mind continued its quest for attention, but Jaden called this awareness, and continued to focus on feelings of peace.

The darkness lifted very slightly, Jaden edged to peer down into the depth of the chamber; dark water revealed shady images as it lapped the cold stone structure like a well leading to hell itself.

He could see intermittent images of the Eroda on a stormy night; it felt real to him, almost as if he was there. Jump- a feeling came from the cloak.

"I know I have been visualizing undoing the vow, but surely, I can't go back. Back from where? I still don't know where I am," he said to himself also addressing the cloak.

"DO YOU THINK THAT WE SHALL RELEASE YOU? YOU MADE A VOW TO KILL, AND WE SHALL SEE TO IT THAT THE VOW IS KEPT.

JUMP IN.............. WE DARE YOU."

Jaden froze, the voice from the shadows far below spoke with evil raptures, exploding every cell in his blood. He dared not ask: "Who's there?" The presence was all around him, its voices were many. Whatever it was, it hated him; he could feel the harm it desired to unleash towards him. His knees buckled under the weight of dread and he dropped like a stone onto the ledge. The Eroda continued to sail, a reflection in the dark waters below.

"You cannot kill me; I know now my consciousness survives death, my creator made me eternal!" Jaden cried, but the certain knowledge that his words were true did little to abate the terror within him. He gazed towards the depths of the chamber.

Jump –it's a crossing, a passage way through time and dimensions. The cloak revealed through immediate knowing into his heart energy.

"WHAT MAKES YOU BELIEVE THAT YOU CAN CROSS DIMENSION AND TIME? YOU WILL FAIL. YOU ALWAYS FAIL". This time the words whispered with a vile hiss emanating from all around him.

Jaden paused, "I have crossed dimensions many times, when I was born, and when I die and return," he answered.

Jump the cloak continued.

"YES, JUMP.........WE INVITE YOU TO."

Jaden realized that the dark spirits could also hear the cloak's communication. He crawled to the edge of the ledge and stared into the reflections in the dark lapping water.

"Don't do it, it's a trick, stay here, hide!" Jaden's mind began to chatter.

Jump.

"IF YOU DARE."

"You will die, stay, run, hide!"

Jump

"Arghhhhhh!" he screamed as the three elements repeated over and over, ripping at what was left of his fragile sanity.

The chatter continued as he climbed back to his feet with the aid of the wall behind him.

Jaden paused for a moment, somewhere deep within, he realised that he had partly created the pain and conditions from which he was presently suffering, and its torments were only compounded by his resistance to it all.

Inspiration came to him and he released judgment of himself, and of his situation as neither good, nor bad, but instead, simply a matter of leaning; he was simply acting and creating from all which he knew at that moment in time.

From this inspiration, which was the result of previously praying for help, he learned the value of forgiveness, forgiveness of the self, which led him to further accept the creation of this dark experience of the now.

He felt great relief knowing that he was not being punished, he was experiencing that which he had focused on, and he now knew, where he had focused he had co-created.

He chose to accept his responsibility, and all that went with it, realizing it may become worse before getting better; to deny the creation of darker things is to halt the possibility of creating and attracting joyful outcomes.

He shuffled forwards, inch by inch, and looked down.

Sorrow condensed forming a single tear which ran down his cheek and fell into the blackness of the well.

Despite his distant feelings of the eternal nature of his soul, seeing and feeling the present horrific dimension led to a conflict of faith. Masters are disciplined to be unaffected by what they see with their eyes, to create from within from what they form in their mind. Jaden however had much to learn and, like most, could be easily influenced to believe that he was powerless. The Hellmakers desired this lie to be fixed in the hearts of the masses, to be affected by the external, rather than to affect the external illusion.

Another tear fell, this time though it was followed by Jaden, as he let himself go, stepping from the safety of the ledge, and out into the darkness.

As he crashed into the cold dark water memories, of his every nightmare washed over him. It seemed as if he sank to an incredible depth. The pressure of the water about him crushed his bones, forcing the air from his lungs.

As he thrashed around in the cold blackness, Jaden soon realized that he may have crossed worlds in some way; he felt himself rising and the pressure began to ease slightly.

Disorientation faded, the cloak pulled him upwards and he began to kick his feet to catch some air as he desperately sought to break through the surface.

Air exploded into his aching lungs as he burst through a majestic rising wave rolling in the moonlit sea. The rush of cold air and crashing sound of waves quickened his blood as the strong current of the waters carried him.

"There's someone in the water!" came a distant voice, "Over there look!"

A large wave lifted Jaden giving him sight of the Eroda's shadow cast upon the churning waters.

He gasped with urgency and fought against the currents with all that he had left.

"C'mon, c'mon!" he spurred himself on as he spat out the salty water that drenched his mouth and lungs.

Although soaking wet, the cloak flapped in the wind, lifting itself high like a black flag. The sailors began to call to each other and point, urging him to swim.

"What's that?" came a cry from high in the rigging, "There's something huge in the water. Move yourself, come on man get out!"

Through stinging eyes, Jaden could see the lights on board. He thrashed harder than ever; gasping and fighting the hypothermia that slowly seized his muscles.

The cloak tore, ripping free and into the winds. It rolled across the ocean towards the Eroda.

Each and every sharp intake of breath felt like razor blades slicing up his heart and lungs. He slowed his pace a touch to ease the pain, but the desperation of trying to reach the ship was as strong as ever. Realisation soon began to dawn on him that he was no longer swimming towards the vessel, but simply fighting to stay still.

"No... please help!" he cried. His body was becoming numb and leaden. The ship began to fade into the darkness of the night as Jaden struggled just to remain afloat.

Cold waves of water and of fear broke over him as he slowly began to sink into the depths of the ocean.

A stream of tears traced his path from the surface to his descent into the unknown.

He drifted helplessly down.

A shadow of something slipped passed him in the darkness. He sensed that he was not alone, but his limbs could not respond to the torture of terror that he felt upon his soul. The presence grew closer, and currents of water changed around his body as the shadowy figure drew nearer.

The pressure of the salt water stung his eyes and crushed his ears, but through the pain he could make out an immense black motion close to his face.

Time stood still; Jaden frowned from the evil radiance burning into his face as giant eye lids slid open revealing the pupils of a vile creature ravenous for him. The hunt was over; the mutant squid had him in its grasp.

His body was snatched and enveloped by the rapid whip of tentacles which pierced his body with the razor sharp hooks hidden within the vast suckers. His right leg was crushed, his knee joint hyper extending as it bent backwards with a snap from the power of the beast's compression.

His pelvis cracked and buckled and his ribs popped exploding splinters of bone into his organs.

Blood spewed from his wrecked body as the squid continued to compact him ready for its feed.

Through the horrific pain Jaden realized that the torn cloak had crossed dimensions, but as it left his body, so did its power, leaving him behind, unprotected, to face the manifestation of his most feared nightmares.

The crush and cracking of ribs and spine continued as the tentacles began to twist his joints into splinters.

The monster released all but one of its deadly tentacles from Jaden's broken body. His limbs swayed in the current as he was lifted to eye level.

The vile creature stared into his bleeding eyes to let him know that he was a victim at its very mercy.

Although in pure torment, Jaden sensed this related more to the fear and repression of his soul than to the natural feeding processes of invertebrates.

He remembered Cain's stare-down against Breaker on the ship, and his defiance.

His eyes mirrored the Squids aggression, and he gave warning with a slight shake of the head.

"If you are doing this for pleasure, I shall destroy you! I will find a way!" he projected the thought into the dark eye of the predator.

The creature held him in its evil stare for a short while before slowly lowering Jaden; he peered helplessly with absolute dread into the giant snapping black beak coming into view.

His smashed and crushed body began to spasm as the broken limbs reacted to his brain's fear-driven message of escape. But it was no use.

Deafening crunching of bones mixed in with Jaden's inner screams as the mutant squid fed on him.

The beak sliced and tore him into pieces, sucking the very life from him, pulling him deeper into some inner organ which shredded him still further into unrecognisable pieces of flesh and bone.

A vile smell of blood and rot made Jaden aware that he was still somehow conscious, and waiting for the acid to dissolve him.

Chapter seventeen

Quantum Connections

March 2005.

In the dead of night, an old farm building near Hastings holds conference to Carl Carlyle's latest band of villains. Four men stood outside. Armed assassins, employed as security to protect these men of the darker trades.

Nearby, in a field of wild and long grass, lying very low under a black sheet, Astril blended perfectly into the dark land.

His night-vision scope was left slightly uncovered to catch the light from the stars.

He flicked open the lens cap, and the killer began to survey other killers.

Out of view as he was, he could see the targets and remain unseen by them; he enjoyed a long-range kill. He swept the gun from left to right as he observed each target.

He wanted to waste the pros first.

He counted them: "One, two, three; now where did the other one go?... Ah, there!"

He smiled at the amateur, who lit a cigarette, giving away both his geographical position, and his mental one - complacency.

None of the men appeared to be wearing headsets; none had used a radio or a phone within the last hour of his observations of them.

"No sign of routines of contact!" he thought, "Good!"

The fourth man was alone, so he was going to be first, Astril checked that the silencer was tight, then loosened his shoulders, and clicked off the safety catch. He locked his cross hairs between the target's shoulder blades, lined upon the victim's vertebral column.

With a slight surge from the adrenal glands, but without hesitation or remorse, Astril gently squeezed the trigger to fire a silent and deadly shot.

The bullet served as an extension of his hatred. It smashed into the target's spine between his shoulder blades, before opening up and expanding through his body devastating him internally. The fragments of bullet smashed out of his chest, ripping shredded heart and lungs with it.

Astril watched the target spin and fall silently onto the grass.

Shifting swiftly back to the other three men, he observed that they were unaware of the assassination. He clicked back the safety lever, collected the spent shell and began to crawl slightly closer, frequently pausing to observe their position.

He settled once again at a new angle, the remaining three had gathered together and were leaning in conversation against an old and battered Range Rover.

A cat disturbed the motion sensors of the security lamps at the farm's side entrance, the beam painted the men in bright, white light.

The rifle was switched to automatic; Astril squeezed the trigger with extreme prejudice and let out a fast flurry of bullets.

All were dead before they hit the ground, blissfully unaware of what had befallen them.

Astril held his breath and scanned the area as he set the rifle back to semi-automatic. He targeted the flood lights in turn, shattering each with a single shot.

He knew Carl was now just inside the building, and relatively unprotected. Revenge could be served at last; and he was going to suffer dearly before termination.

He gathered the shells to remove any evidence of his presence, rolled them into the blanket and bundled it into his backpack.

A minute later and Astril was at the Range Rover, he searched the dead to steal their weapons, a few automatic pistols and ammunition added to the contents of his pack. He then prepared himself to enter the farm house.

Through the hatred and high level adrenalin, and deep breaths of readiness, a feeling cascaded into his soul which gripped his lungs to a dead stop.

Something felt wrong.

He paused for confirmation; his heart exploding blood through his neck, his mouth felt sandy, dry.

The feeling grew stronger, and Astril's strength was his obedience to his guidance system.

He posted up on one knee and scanned through the scope. In the distance he observed crawling figures in black heading towards the farm.

He turned sharply and saw the same behind him; he zoomed in closer. "Police!"

He cursed heavily and rolled back into the long grass. So close to the kill, the time served stalking and gathering information, all the planning and risks, all for nothing.

For a moment he had considered storming the farm to kill anything that moved, but Carl was not the final target, there was another.

He cursed again at his misfortune in choosing to raid Carl's hideout on the same evening as the police.

A helicopter's blades boomed high in the night sky, the pilot reported a smashing sound as the spotlight exploded from a bullet.

The heat signature camera also malfunctioned from the impact of a piercing round, but the crew were still unaware that they had been shot at.

Astril observed the path of the oncoming force, and carefully cut between them.

He knew the roads would be guarded, so he made it cross country.

Four hours later an old barn sheltered him from the early morning rain. His body ached from the low-level crawling and intermittent sprints to avoid capture.

In the light of dawn he stripped down the rifle.

"I will have you yet!" he said while contemplating just how close he had finally come to killing Carl.

The adrenalin had subsided, leaving the familiar shakes and psychological lows.

The sound of the windswept storm outside grew stronger; Astril cloaked himself in the blanket from his backpack and sighed deeply. He watched as raindrops washed along the roof finding holes and dripping off the old beams.

Depression and loneliness crept in to his nightmares as he faded helplessly into a restless and tormented sleep.

July 2005

Krzysztof ducked the beams below deck of his ship, *The Sea Dog*, anchored off Whitby coast. It was a replica of a small galleon that had originally been built for films. The investment had not been cheap, but he intended to recoup the money by renting the vessel for themed weddings and small cruises, or even private executive meetings. His plan had been running for six months and business had just begun to get off the ground. He hired a skipper, small crew, and was learning the ropes. Although she could sail by natural means, below deck were two large diesel engines, and she was also fitted with a satellite navigation system.

Krzysztof made his way past the swinging hammocks, hung there for the sake of authenticity, and climbed the stairs that led up to the deck.

The Abbey watched them from the distant cliffs, catching Krzysztof's eye as he leaned on the wooden portside rail.

His crew worked the deck, testing the rigging and generally looking busy for their boss.

"All's well son!" a rough voice came from behind. Krzysztof turned to see the black bearded skipper Adrian Lord. He was in his late forties, a well rounded captain, moulded by the sea; large, thick, grey woolly polo neck sweater and oil stained denim jeans.

"Good, and we have calm waters, I hope not too many punters are seasick this time, I may have to warn them, they can't have their money back if they are seasick!" Krzysztof joked.

"You've took to the waters well son!" Adrian remarked.

"It doesn't feel like my first time!" came the reply, "We still need a cook, if we are going to look after the crew, even if it is for small coastal cruises. The last one couldn't handle the small galley, we'll need to hurry up with that!" he added.

The midday sun shone through the rigging, the ropes and timbers creaked with each gentle tilt of the vessel.

"*I should have done this years ago!*" Krzysztof thought while following the coastline; he grabbed his small binoculars from his pocket to observe closer.

"There is someone in the lighthouse. I thought it was closed!" he said, pointing it out to the skipper.

"Ah, the old haunted lighthouse son, yes it's open to public now!"

Krzysztof turned to look at Adrian: "Haunted?"

"Surely you heard of Aden's ghost?"

"Aden?"

"Aden, Jaden, something like that, a kid saw it, all of his friends saw it and ran out, but he kept his head and spoke to it, so they say!"

"What did it look like?" Krzysztof was curious.

"They all said it was like a rotting skull and bones dressed in a black cloak!" Adrian attempted his spooky ghost story voice and spoke with a slow and lowered tone.

"So why was the kid not scared?"

"He was a special child, mental problems, so I heard!"

"I see. Ah well I guess I won't be going in the lighthouse then; I'll stay here where it's safe!" Krzysztof laughed

"Hmmmm never say never son!" replied the skipper as he turned and walked across the deck.

Krzysztof refocused on the lighthouse through his binoculars, "Hmm Jaden, there's a name from the past." he whispered to himself. His thoughts prompted fearful feelings and memories of violence in his heart, which carried into an energy field beyond relative time, to a dark and lonely void.

The void of nothing held captive the remains of a vibrating consciousness which once knew life in the physical three dimensional plain of life on earth. But now there was nothing, but nothing, but nothing.

Abiding by quantum spiritual law, to think of someone energetically connects with them, and Krzysztof's feeling entered the stream which connects all things everywhere forever.

To know fear again would be a pleasure the lost soul acknowledged. Fear lays a path, and any path is traceable, and can lead back to where the journey began.

The consciousness searched for self validation.

Krzysztof patrolled his deck. The sun relaxed on the horizon and the seagulls interrupted the waves rushing towards the edge of the coast finally to break over the deadly rocks.

"Time to sail her back to harbour son!" shouted Adrian.

Krzysztof nodded and sat near the forecastle to enjoy his short voyage back. Within moments he was lost in his thoughts as he reflected on the last six months. Despite feeling euphoric he was concerned about approaching the age of fifty. His thoughts entered the ether as watched by a few gentle spirits who found charm in his false worries, simply caused by temporary lapse of the knowledge of the eternal nature of the soul.

A few lost lovers danced through his memories causing a sigh. Loneliness stepped in for attention, but he nudged it with thoughts and anticipation of his new life back home on the coast.

The Seadog entered the harbour powered by the heavy horsepower diesel engines. The crew worked as one, navigating a safe return.

An hour later Krzysztof found himself driving back towards his little flat in Robin Hood's Bay, just south of Whitby. Tired from a long day, he arrived home and locked the door behind him, threw the keys on the side cabinet, and flopped into his large comfortable leather chair.

He noticed a flash on the screen of his mobile which he had left behind on the coffee table.

"Ah, a missed call I bet!" leaning forwards with a groan he scanned fifteen missed calls all from the same number.

"Oh God no! Not the beacon of stupidity!" he shouted as he recognised the number which belonged to the phone of Carl Carlyle. "What the hell does he want after all this time?" he continued as he threw the device onto the floor.

Krzysztof suffered the contrast of a hot and sticky night mixing with cold cloak of fear settling upon his shoulders. He sensed trouble, but for now he decided to ignore it, hoping that it might just go away, whatever it was.

He reached once again for his mobile phone and switched it off. The television was his aid of distraction as he flicked randomly through the channels.

Within a timeless void of antimatter, of dread, of fear, of defeat, of soulless and empty nothingness, of hopelessness, the farthest end of the spectrum from love and joy; a conscious energy was condensing and coming together.

An awareness of something, something of the relative self.

Something about feeling about…….. being.

Awareness of existence.

A cry for help vibrated throughout the blackness.

The illusion of time and movement, and three dimensional state, limitations, love and loss was remembered as the little soul shone its light of glowing awareness.

The void repelled the orb unable to withstand its vibrations. The Hellmakers suffered rage as they sensed the escape.

The orb drifted in wonder of itself, unaware of its source, with no concept of time or physical dimensions.

A spark of intuition allowed the soul to read its closest memory path stored within the quantum universal field. Something about a Jaden, a lowered vibrational form.

The orb vanished.

A skull was ejected from the beak of the giant squid. It bounced as it drifted on the bed of the Blood Sea. Slowly it began to surface, then spin in the currents of a violent angry inter-dimensional storm. The giant waves tossed and threw the remains back onto the stone harbour where Jaden had begun his journey. It landed near the lighthouse which cut into the high winds creating an evil, howling cry. The torn cape blew out of the waves and across the sea, it captured the skull and wrapped around the bone flapping and snapping in the blood saturated gusts.

The remains of Jaden began to reform little by little. As his skeletal structure took shape, the organs began to grow, along with a nervous system and memory. Great physical torment was his first experience, closely followed by nightmarish memories, and above all, he knew that he was painfully lonely.

Dimensionally close and yet so far……

Krzysztof stepped out of the Body Machine gym, his chest aching and pumped. The Scarborough August morning sun burned through the thin clouds.

"It's gonna be hot!"

The door clicked shut on his new silver Audi; he adjusted the seat ready for a drive to Whitby. The dashboard rattled indicating a call from the vibrating mobile phone locked in the glove compartment.

He quickly answered without observing the screen to see who may be calling.

"Krzy....don't hang up, it's me...Carl!"

"For God's sake, what do you want Carl!" Krzysztof replied.

"I really need your help!"

"Surprise, surprise, you call when you need something!"

"We know you have a ship, we are on the run, we need to hide out, somewhere safe, we thought off coast!"

"What, wait, what do you mean on the run, and why are you using an open line to talk about this, do you never learn?" Krzysztof interrupted. He felt immediate rage boiling his blood.

"Krzysztof.... We are on the run from a killer, I need your help!" Carl pleaded.

"A killer?"

"The law raided a meetin' we were havin' at Rundles Farm. Turns out, a killer was right outside, but the coppers must have disturbed him, he wasted our bodyguards, he even took a pop at the rossers' helicopter!"

"Why is a hit man after you? Who ordered the hit?" Krzysztof asked impatiently.

"We dunno, could be anyone. We need a safe hideout, off the coast, on your ship. Krzy we will pay the goin' rate, whatever it is. We need to lie low, where no one can reach us, wont be for long, I plan on leaving the country soon!"

"Why don't you just get out now...straight away, why hide?"

"I have some money comin' my way, from a job, worth waitin' for, soon as I get it, I'm out!"

"You better get over here then ain't ya, I'll see what I can do!" Krzysztof replied.

"We'll be up in a day or two. I'll be in touch!"

The dark dealings of the past whipped its cold chain around his throat as he realised this may be the same assassin who had killed his family in Poland.

His gut instinct whispered feelings of revenge, and he was more than likely also on the hit list.

Chapter eighteen

Soul Division

The newly reformed black cape flapped in the bloody storm of a dark illusionary world.

Nestled under its hood sat Jaden, crossed legged and meditating.

His heart was generating feelings of love, and signalling for the help for which he had pleaded again and again.

The squid would surface now and then, angry, hungry for the one that had got away.

"Help cannot be yours. It cannot come. You have no right. This is your doing!"

The cold voices of many sounded close to Jaden. But he remained still, eyes closed and focused.

"No one listens to you!"

"You seem to!" whispered Jaden.

"Your prayers go unheard!"

"I hear them, and they are for me to hear, for the creator is within me already, and need not listen, for it knows just what I will say before I ever do, the creator is part of the doer and sayer within me!"

Jaden experienced the answers flowing through him from another source; he watched with a feeling of separation of himself. The words though uttered by him, were not his own.

"You have no right to ask for help! This is your doing; take responsibility for your vows of death!" The tormenting voices had intensified in hatred and numbers.

"I have a right to ask for help of my creator. That which gave me life understands me. There and in that power, I shall seek guidance!"

An immediate silence fell, the winds became still, and Jaden felt the presence of hatred.

"There is no connection to your creator here!" This time, a single voice whispered in his right ear.

Jaden opened his eyes slowly. Nothing, no light, just the cold harbour rested beneath him.

The immediate knowing of answers flowed as a stream of energy into his mind

"There is no connection, because there never was any separation from the creative power. The separation is an illusion, and the true connection is my reawakening and awareness of the light within all.......even in you. That is why I must accept the light or its absence in myself, and in others!" Jaden removed his hood; the answers continued to flow.

He stood up in the darkness as the Hellmakers' power was revealed to him through vibrational energy messages.

Energy concentrates where the mind focuses. Thoughts weave energy, energy becomes things.

Lack of faith in self and faith of the guiding compass of feelings allow Hellmakers to influence the mind which can, in turn, lead to creation of negative focus, and creation of negative outcomes; justifications of murder, war and division. Division being the greatest illusion leading to destruction.

Divide from man and creator, and divide from all things.

The Hellmakers on the earth's plane are those who know of the creative power of the soul. They are also aware of the true unlimited source of wealth, health, and joy available to every soul, but they attempt to keep the knowledge secret, driven by the illusion of class and money.

Hellmakers can also be found in the mindset of those who distort love, and put the fear of God into people to convert them to their ways. They use violence, pain and suffering as a tool to force their self-righteous will on others. Most of them are afraid to acknowledge or admit their own blood-stained histories of hypocrisies and violent insecurities, and are even more fearful to allow others their divine given freedom.

They are influenced and feed on the darker energies that will see man fail, and help resist the spiritual evolution on the earth dimension.

A light shone from the distant horizon, Jaden shuffled back and slid down the lighthouse wall as more messages entered his soul.

He knew that the squid, the Blood Sea, the harbour, and his body were not as real, or as condensed as on the earth plane. On earth, thoughts affect energy and the outcome at a slower rate than this dark place he haunted.

It was an interpretation of creative energy taking form, and vibrating into the language of the illusion of a three dimensional plane; a decoding of energy through memory of life on earth, darkness translating into images of his worst fears.

Jaden closed his eyes and looked within.

He saw the vow made by Cain, his former self, to kill Breaker and the captain, *"In this life and thereafter....for all of eternity."*

He saw the consequence of how his heartfelt vow attracted dark power of the Hellmakers who influenced time and space to keep this vow. A dark promise of violence is like a raging fire, self-perpetuating and igniting others to constantly fuel the flames as revenge breeds those seeking further revenge, a growing destructive cycle.

He realised that Krzysztof and Carl Carlyle were Breaker and the Captain re- incarnated, and they were being hunted by Astril, a soul-divided energy flux, which Jaden had left behind at the harbour with his renewed vow to kill them both. The loss of power from the division was why Jaden's soul had been unable to sustain life in the plane once energy had left his body.

Furthermore, he could sense a loving energy around the Eroda, a psychic vibration which promised to help save the future soul of Cain, as he had saved her from captivity and a death sentence. It was Neasa, a gypsy, a prisoner hidden in the depths of the ship, reborn in Astril's time frame, sent to bring love into his heart, and maybe save him.

He could also see the conflicts of positive visualisations regarding Rebecca. He questioned why his images of love took him down the seemingly opposite path of heartbreak only to attract and to discover her unfaithfulness with Krzysztof. He learned that to reach a positive outcome; sometimes you must be shown your own anchors, or the conflicting anchors of others, needed to be exposed from the hidden depth before you can set sail.

You cannot attract health if you subconsciously hate those who love their bodies.

Jaden wept for a moment, the relief lifted him, but there was concern about the momentum of the vow still active, and penetrating Astril's hatred of Carl and Krzysztof.

Jaden focused for a moment, he located the energy field of Astril and held thoughts of peace, much like the vibration he had felt when sitting on the bench at the Abbey.

A moment passed and Jaden finally accepted that he may spend forever searching for a way out of this cold and lost dimension.

The energy messages finally ceased, leaving Jaden exasperated in the illusion of the blood stained harbour.

The tormenting voices of the Hellmakers were silent.

He continued to hold the meditative posture, weak and tortured by ice-blade winds and blood mist off the ocean.

"Be alright….. I'll be alright!" he whispered realising his consciousness had survived the realisation of his worst fears.

At his feet lay a triangular key, the one he had seen in the shop where he had first discovered the cloak. He was too weak to reach forward and pick it up, but knowing it was there brought him comfort, even though he had no idea of its use.

<u>June 2005</u>

Just outside Whitby, deep in the Yorkshire moors, sunrise saw April opening up her café ready for business.

Washing the windows of the entrance door with frantic distraction; April had awoken with a dark feeling in her soul. In the past, she had experienced many predictions through her dreams and she often instinctively knew of things to come. Her mother had noticed this gift and wanted her to develop it further and perhaps to help people in some special way. But April's father had insisted that she develop a mind for business in order to *survive in this world.*

She raced around her kitchen; the plastic mop bucket popped as it was crushed by a frantic slam of the small utility room door.

It was 7.30am and only half an hour to opening time; she continued her high speed morning preparation.

SMASH. A large coffee mug shattered on the floor.

The compressed mop bucket ejected and slid along the tiles as April flung open the door in search of the dustpan and brush.

She collected the fragments carefully on bent knee behind the counter near the cash till.

The door chime tinkled indicating an entrance, a moment later it repeated.

"Just a moment!" she shouted

The silence provoked dark feelings of foreboding to arise within her; this time however, it was tenfold.

She swallowed hard and slowly stood up to see who was there. In the shadows in the corner sat a man glaring over the table; she could sense a menacing violent darkness around him. Just to the left of the till beside her was Gary Stevenson, the wealthy property developer who had been hinting at underhanded tactics with regard to the purchase of April's business.

"What....what do you want?" her voice suffered tremors which combined with a sudden dryness in her mouth. Gary was a suited and booted, self-impressed wannabe *bad boy*. The fear which he detected in the young woman's voice fed his ego like nectar. He glanced over at the man in the shadows, still glaring from the corner, then turned back to grin at April.

"Last chance saloon, we are concerned that a woman out here all alone could have an accident, so we are prepared to offer a good price to take it off your hands, by the end of the month, you know the price...... sleep on the offer while you still can!"

April swallowed hard as he turned and walked out, adjusting the collar of his double breasted suit jacket.

As the door closed behind him, the dark-looking character stood up and slowly approached the counter.

His presence was unmistakably violent, radiating hatred which filled the cafe. As he drew near she sensed that he had hurt a lot of people in the darkest of ways. She stepped back, dreading what she was about to suffer at the hands of what must be one of Gary Steven's henchmen.

A surge of pressure flooded her carotid artery and her knees buckled as the man leapt over the counter.

Her eyes twitched and slowly flickered open; disoriented for a moment she stared at the chest of a man who appeared to be holding her as she lay on the cold floor of the kitchen.

His black shirt was open at the top which revealed the large ink point of a tattoo rising from his chest.

"Don't hurt me!" she whimpered as the memory crashed back into her mind.

The man look puzzled.

"You fainted, I caught you.....so you would not bang your head!" he spoke gently.

"I.... I thought, you were one of Gary's ......ah so you did not jump over the counter to beat me then!"

"No!" laughed the man, "I could see you were becoming faint, I tried to catch you, almost missed you!"

April stood up slowly "Ah, my knees have gone!"

The stranger escorted her into the dining area, sat her down, then filled a mug from the tea urn.

"I have never been served in my own café before.............thank you!"

"So ... What happened?" asked the man.

"The man who was speaking to me, he was threatening me, he wants this business and I thought that you were one of his henchmen. Looks like I am going to have to sell it to him after all!"

"Hmmm that's unfortunate, I was hoping to rent the sleeper car, and stay here a few months!"

"Well maybe you still can.... I mean if you want to!" April's business drive immediately overshadowed her fear; she reeled off the price list without a stutter.

The deal was done, the man handed over a large roll of bank notes, which prompted the dark feeling that she originally felt around him.

His demeanour emitted an uneasy presence, which betrayed true darkness - a far cry from that of Steven's façade of toughness. The newcomer's aura was one of unrelenting, cold intent and had none of the other man's posturing; with no need to prove itself through threats and bullying.

As they walked to the converted sleeper car resting on the rusty tracks, she enquired his details.

"Astril, my name is Astril, no surname, just Astril!"

His goal was to achieve stealth, blend in and give nothing away. However, April's gift lifted his veil slightly, and she sensed a disrupted mindset.

Chapter nineteen

Shadowed

7:00A.M, August 2005

A dark soul spread its arms across Jaden's bench and gazed out to sea. Reflecting upon the conditioning required in order to shadow dangerous targets and learn their habits and routines, he realised that the blade of his soul was well and truly tempered.

"I have paid my dues," he whispered to himself.

The Abbey watched silently over Astril as the winter breeze carried fresh raindrops lightly over his forehead.

He pulled up the collar of his long dark coat and relaxed back into the bench.

Whitby was a perfect town to hide out in while he lined up his target in the nearby town of Scarborough.

He felt a hint of familiarity about the place, he wondered if maybe his mother had brought him here as a child; she had married a Russian man and travelled far and wide through England and Europe.

His hatred left him for a short while, the holy ground dissolved it completely, and his thoughts drifted to the family that he had lost,such a long time ago, and yet, it seemed only yesterday.

His father had been an eye witness to a violent crime committed by the illegal arms dealers, but the Dombrowski hit men had got to the family first, thanks to information on their location from a young Carl Carlyle. Krzysztof remained unaware of the tip off and even now Carl kept this dark secret from his friend.

Young Astril, originally named Brandon Vershinina, had survived thanks to a visit to his mother's sister, Aunt Jessica, who lived in the Irish Republic.

His death, together with that of his whole family, had been widely reported and following his funeral he had been given a new identity by the special branch and had disappeared without a trace.

A security officer, Miles Chambers, had been assigned to watch over Brandon, and he had taken a shine to the young boy. Upon retirement, he had taken Brandon under his wing and had eventually adopted him.

They had settled in Canada, and it was here where Miles had broken the S.A.S. code and taught Brandon how to hunt and kill, both with and without weapons.

On his death bed three years ago whilst under the influence of morphine, Miles had revealed his knowledge of the Dombrowski organisation, and their evil deeds to Brandon's original family. Brandon missed them, especially his mother, and now he had the details of those who took them away from him.

Sorrow and loss and the many years of heartbreak had transformed into anger, hatred, and an insatiable thirst for revenge.

He had left Canada and following his mentor's teachings, had slipped into Europe a faceless ghost. He referred to himself as Astril, one name, one dark agenda. The toil of the last three years had indeed taken its toll; Astril had become unrecognisable to himself, from his nature through to his physicality, the considerate child of yesteryear was lost in a hell-bent mindset of hate and revenge.

The old steps to the left of the bench invited him into the town below, just as they used to, maybe in a dream, or a childhood memory, but for now, the view was soothing, the sound of the ancient sea crashing on the rocks below inducing his thoughts into a peaceful rhythm.

He was unaware of the dark field that surrounded him and warded off passers by, he tried to blend in with the public, but the vengeful bloody deeds in which he had engaged had tainted his soul. No one dared approach him, be it ticket touts or beggars of spare coins.

His skill was the ability to channel raging hatred into a cold and calculating patience, check, check, and check again; that combined with the acceptance and mindset of being "already dead." Unknown, with no one and nothing to lose, his enemies had very little to bargain or threaten him with. Although he had taken his time with Brunon, and the killer in the church, Astril's assassinations were usually of a split second stealthy blur, then he was out and on his way, but the fulfilment and thirst quenching satisfaction that he felt while torturing Brunon, had attracted ever darker and colder forces to his spiritual legion.

Jaden had a right of passage into the depths of Astril's heart energy field from his prison in the Hellmakers dimension; a place created by the energy of fear, fear influenced and co-created by human, and non human consciousness.

It felt like- *let it go Astril.*

He felt an overwhelming peace as he glanced towards the horizon, the same direction where Jaden had discovered the bones years before.

The idea lay as a seed in his heart, and if left alone might be able to flourish.

The Hellmakers' vow had lost its tight grip......something had to be done.

Astril had lost track of Carl, and he was now hunting Krzysztof, whom he had originally intended to kill last. He was already hot on his trail, scanning, planning, calculating.

He seemed to blend into the crowd naturally with his average height and short dark hair cut, but his eyes betrayed his intentions, unforgiving, with absolutely zero tolerance. Although in his mid-twenties, the hard life and toxins from stress, along with the chemical fallout of endless thoughts of anger, had taken its toll, he looked older, edging mid-thirties; a man of no laughter lines, with no traces of a smile.

Dark visualization regarding his enemies' outcome had served him well, as taught to him by a Philippine martial arts weapons guru associate of Miles. Astril was disciplined, regularly employing obscure, esoteric meditation poses. He used the secret process for tracking, killing and escape.

He ventured through the streets and over the swing bridge, then finally out towards the harbour.

Chapter Twenty

Sad When Not Angry

Astril, the dark splintered fragment of Jaden's soul lay sleeping, dreaming of the blood he would draw and the lives he would soon end, his targets being the reincarnated souls of Breaker and the captain of the Eroda. The hateful vow made by Cain to *"kill them in this life and thereafter"* as well as Jaden's reinforcement of the dark promise had caused soul division, leaving behind a heartless creature, easily influenced by the energy vacuum of the Hellmakers. Astril knew his family had been murdered so this was his revenge, but Jaden's hatred at the harbour where he had cursed Krzysztof and Carl, had sent a splinter of his soul to be born to a family that would later become a victim of Carl's trade in weapons, leaving a young assassin in the right place at the right time.

Division had weakened the soul, leaving it easily influenced by the low-end spectrum consciousness.

Jaden haunted a dimension where his thoughts could be influenced, and his fears could be transformed into experiences vibrating and taking distorted forms similar to life on earth, but with a horrific twist.

September was rolling to an end. The creak of the bed springs woke Astril as he turned away from dawn's orange light as it cut through the small blinds.

The old converted railway carriage had become his little sanctuary; hidden, practical, and with no other guests. He could either cook a hot meal on the small gas stove, or buy good food from April in her café.

He yawned which amplified the sound in his ears of April's radio throwing its tunes out of the open doors where she was sweeping the steps ready for opening time. The long yawn continued while he sat up to peer through his blind and observe the little busybody making ready for her customers.

"Right on time!" he whispered.

From within his obsession began to trigger the habitual dark thoughts of revenge against Krzysztof, and then Carl, who had eluded him, thanks to the police raid.

The carriage revealed its cold ambience as he folded back the bed sheets to climb out; a second chill shocked the soles of his feet as they met the wooden floor.

He sat docile for a while yawning, allowing time for his eyes to calibrate their focus.

"Awww!" he pushed himself to his feet while running his tongue around the roof of his mouth, and then sucking his teeth he tasted a little blood which he quickly swallowed, and then dressed himself.

The water was cold from the tap, but was the cleanest he had tasted in England, it felt sharp on his face as it splashed from the tiny sink, accelerating the wake up process.

He gazed at his reflection in the small mirror, casting his eyes down towards the apex of the large black letter "A" tattooed on his chest.

"What y' gonna do when they are all dead?" whispered an aggressive mental rasp. He curled up his bottom lip and stepped into the living quarters, trying to ignore the growing provocations of his internal chatter.

"Awww!" the morning routine began with a series of circular limb rotations and stretches, closely followed by isometric tension of his abdomen, then sucking into a flat belly vacuum and holding the exhalation for as long as possible. Within five minutes his body temperature and heart rate had risen dramatically; he wiped his brow and headed towards the door.

"Morning!" April shouted from her café as he stepped into the fresh mist. "Off for your morning run?" she added.

"Aye!" he nodded as he broke from a walking pace into a steady jog.

The redundant old tracks lead him deep into the Yorkshire moors where steam engines had once run.

Astril had a system of interval sprints, with various distances marked out by the remains of old sleepers on the ground, aerobic and anaerobic *roadwork* in order to maintain explosive fitness.

His heart hit him hard and cold, right in his throat, the result of driving, pushing into a sprint, his body demanding that he back off the pace, but no, "Push, c'mon, c'mon!" in the distance, the first marker to drop the pace, he pushed hard to cross the line, then eased down.

The cold air shrank his lungs; he gasped and gulped, there seemed to be no oxygen to recover from his sprint, the slow pace jog burned his calves and thighs, his body weighed heavy.

"C'mon!" he demanded, forcing himself to override the ache and desire to halt. The medium pace continued, his lungs recovering, his heart rate steadying in readiness for the next explosive sprint.

Thirty minutes and his roadwork was finished, ending at an old empty signal box shadowed by the remains of a water tank used for the locomotives of yesteryear.

Astril had rigged up a few old tyres and chains, a makeshift gym for a dangerous killer.

His workout continued with a sickening repetition of bodyweight training, pulls and pushes, squats and lunges, followed by a combination of strikes, kicks, grabs, head butts, elbows, knees, all inflicted upon a heavy tractor tyre chained to the steel beam support structure of the water tower.

He focused with every attack, his mind visualising a real opponent.

He cycled this routine with weapons training, next time it would be knives and sticks striking hard on the old tyre and chains, keeping his skills very, very sharp, combining drills as taught to him by Miles and Filipino weapons masters. His wrist watch bleeped, calling time to end the workout, but Astril threw in a few extra rounds, the hatred driving his elbows hard into the swinging tyre. The anger finally spent its pain numbing override and destructive determination leaving him gasping and bent over, supporting himself with both hands on his thighs. The last part of the workout was to walk off the pain, to recover quickly no matter how much it hurt to breathe.

The endorphins mixed with his oxygen-rich bloodstream, flooding through his shaking muscles and penetrating his brain and mind, almost touching euphoria. As he walked back through the moors, it suddenly dawned on him that post workout comedown was the only time of the day when he was at peace, free of the ongoing mental chatter and images of either deep sadness, or extreme hatred. Sometimes when he dare look within, he hated to admit the vile truth that he actually enjoyed the kill, that brief moment when the undying quench of thirst for revenge was extinguished, and the victim had paid the price.

The self-justification of the administration of assassination.

That and the planning, the adrenalin, the payback, the victims fear, and the getting away with it. Astril knew that *the law* often thought his targets had been killed by other villains, settling scores of the underworld; thus far escape had been easy.

300 Miles south of the Yorkshire moors a long-haul aircraft was landing in London. As it touched down, Astril felt a strange tremor run through his spine, as if someone had tip-toed across his grave. He shook off the strange feeling of *something has just changed.*

He arrived at the converted train carriage where he could smell April's cooking wafting from the kitchen's extractor fan, almost directly into his nostrils.

The post-workout craving for good hot food sped him to his hot shower and straight back out to the café with hair still dripping wet.

"How was your run?"

"Same as ever – hard; and I must be strange, cos' I enjoy it!" Astril answered April.

The café was empty of other customers; Astril ordered his food and waited while April ran around her kitchen multi-tasking with her usual high speed precision.

"Do you remember that property developer who threatened me, that day I fainted when we met?" April shouted

"Ah yes, he wanted your business!"

"Yes well, he's disappeared without a trace; he never came back, maybe he's seen the light!" she added.

"Or maybe he has seen the dark!" Astril thought, remembering a late night visit he paid to the man.

CLANK. His hot plate of food landed on the table as delivered by *fast* April, but before he had time to thank her, she was back busy in the kitchen. He tucked into his breakfast greedily, washing it down with slurps of steaming, sweet tea.

He was soon finished and gazing out of the window, planning and calculating, he felt a strong pull towards Whitby, especially the Abbey, and a disturbing feeling of peace began to cloak him.

"Thanks for that!" Astril stood and walked towards the cash till and paid, leaving his usual good tip; money stolen from those who stole it from others.

Then he was out of the door and on his way to shadow Krzysztof, via the Abbey.

In a relative void……..

Leaning on the cold stone lighthouse wall, Jaden hid under his cloak, decoding Delmar's mantra,

Stop and listen to how you feel, which he did, realising that listening to his feelings had much more value than listening to the ongoing, relentless chatter of his mind, often ending in further confusion, rather than conclusion.

Your inner compass will then reveal, his inner compass, his feelings and intuition, through which the all knowing universe whispered to him, could finally be clearly heard and understood.

Your soul's desire - the truth of you, in the silence, his mental conflicts were again revealed. He desired Rebecca, but deep down he felt inadequate in some way, although his ego masked it, on the surface, he felt the tension, but dared not stop to go within, discover, accept then release the doubts, he now realised, that being true to himself, though painful, would set him free to create.

As he began to look further, he also felt the inner conflict regarding combat, and after training in various martial arts, felt he had to fight at the cause of any insult, feigning and overstressing anger, and showing offence at almost any remark or challenge; this would justify the training progress, making it all worthwhile, even though, it all felt wrong. Always ready to defend, in constant fear of loss of the fake power he thought *being good at fighting* would serve him.

And the main conflict now, was fear of not being able to escape this place, even though he had experienced surviving the beast.

To release resistance anchoring you. Having felt the inner conflicts and accepting them, Jaden felt the energies change, although he had done nothing to change or be rid of their presence, just knowing they were within and no longer hidden, allowed for their release.

Awareness was all that was required.

Accept the ghosts which haunt your mind. Jaden realised that to fight the uncontrollable thoughts of his mind, only made the overpowering thoughts stronger than ever, drawing more and more fear and insecurities in, so now, he simply allowed the Hellmakers' whispers to run their course, often agreeing with their very worst taunts regarding his self worth. Submissive as water, the negativity sank, as opposed to becoming rigid like ice, where it could rest on the surface and be seen by the worrying mind.

They may have led you to this point in time. Jaden knew now that to focus on the thoughts influenced by the field of the masses, media or dark and hateful souls, could lead him to places, outcomes and events that he would never have choose to experience.

Allow their whispers of all your fears. Jaden realised that fear has a natural use, and a healthy mind uses the feeling, in some cases to power the body.

Allow it to be.

Having survived the belly of the beast under the Sea of Blood, his fear and dread of them remained. To a certain extent he had conquered his worst nightmare, however the shadow of the former dread haunted him, but was much worse when he fought or denied it. The acceptance and admission of his own fear allowed him to conserve more soul-energy.

Focus on joy, the darkness clears. Jaden had read many books outlining methods of thoughts which may affect the energy of the world of which absolutely all things are made.

The last line of the mantra finally made sense to him. If his uncontrollable thoughts affected the outcome, then he would be at the mercy of the influence of others. It was the point at which he would choose to focus, that his energy would flow and condense. In this dark realm of fear and dread he was constantly reminded of his helpless endeavour. However, if he accepted his fear, and then allowed it to unfold, he could let it continue while he focused upon something that he loved and generated the feelings that coincide with it.

He realised that his prayers for help had been answered, he had been given a map, but the effort required to undertake the journey would be his alone; this was where he, and many others failed, the second part of co-creation.

While the loneliness of the blood-washed harbour flooded his thoughts, he gently focused upon images and memories of his family and the laughter and love they all shared, and Rebecca, how good it would feel to experience her passion again, like the first time, in the attic where she had seduced him with such ease.

His perception was focused purely on these feelings, as opposed to what he had lost, nor would ever feel again, this angle of thought was the key to his freedom.

The violent storms lashed at him through the cape, but he continued to focus on good times of the past, and more to come.

"How good it would feel to hold you again!" he whispered to Rebecca's image as she warmed his heart through his thoughts of her kiss. "I loved it when we woke like that!" he added, referring to his morning embrace of her back, spooned into his torso, his arms wrapped around her curves.

The wind continued to howl, but he remained detached from the results of the lack of change, he continued to focus within. He laughed at the memories of his colleagues at the power plant where he worked, the jokers and tricksters, the nicknames and windups. Most of them were more like talented comedians than engineers. The memory of a night out with them at a Chinese restaurant cracked more than a defiant smile. Jaden laughed out loud as he recalled his friend, *Sir Lance a Little,* a nickname branded in the communal showers, had tried to order *automatic* duck, instead of the more normal aromatic variety, as he had read the menu a little too hastily. The poor waiter had no idea why the customers who heard him laughed in hysterics.

Loving and joy-filled memories flooded his soul as blood continued to splash on the harbour, and the hateful voices whispered their hatred still.

Jaden looked out towards the dark horizon.

"May you find peace!" he whispered into the winds while pulling the cloak tightly around himself. He had finally surrendered any idea of escape. Crossed legged and still leaning on the lighthouse, he meditated, visualizing energy streaming into the illusion of his body, healing him, bringing him strength and wisdom. He smiled at the memories on which he chose to focus, breaking into a grin as it dawned on him that the harbour that he had hated for so long was all that stood between him and the Sea of Blood.

"Arghhhh!" a stabbing sensation in the crook of his right arm abruptly halted the meditation; he slipped his left hand up the sleeve of the cloak to aid with compression. His meditation had brought enough strength to allow him to finally stand; he reached forwards and retrieved the triangular key which was still on the stones before him, then he struggled and climbed to his feet.

Unsteadily, he finally limped to stand at the edge of the harbour, defiantly gazing at the gathering creatures surfacing from the Blood Sea below him.

To look upon that which brought him fear, no longer served him, and he realized this now, the creatures which hunted him still filled him with dread, but he no longer resisted, nor fought against the sickening chill that he still felt so strongly.

He turned and gazed up towards the lighthouse, wondering if he could make it to the top and maybe find some shelter inside. As he hobbled back to the stone structure he mentally forged enough determination to cut through the pain as he began to climb towards the top, with the cloak flapping in the sharp blood-tinted winds.

After many a clinching stop on the way, he finally made it over the top rail and collapsed on the watch point. He recalled his first climb when the mutant squid pursued him, but, war-torn, battered and bruised as he was, this climb was much harder.

Still fighting the bitter conditions, along with pain and weakness, he was distracted as he observed his body fading and flashing in and out of view under the cloak, as if under a strobe light.

"Am I a ghost?" he questioned, observing his hands as they appeared to flicker in and out of existence before his eyes.

"Aghhhhh!" again the pain stung his right inner arm. He sat up and observed the creatures in the dark sea below.

There was movement, vibration rattled Jaden's sitting bones; he froze, the lighthouse trembled deep to its foundations within the blood-stained harbour.

Drawing a long intake of breath, and with agonizing anticipation, he turned slowly and peered over his shoulder. To his relief, there was nothing and no one behind him. He sighed at the absence of anything unholy close by him. The tremor had disrupted the old bricks which covered the lamp lenses, debris fell onto the watch-point and over the side, crashing into the sea.

Jaden hugged and lifted a large heavy stone which had fallen from the lens and barely missed him; he cast it defiantly over the side, aiming towards the squid lurking at the base of the stone tower.

It smashed on impact on the rocks below spraying the creature with sharp heavy fragments. The creature hissed as it submerged below the blood, leaving Jaden feeling defiantly victorious, but glad to be on the high point out of reach. He wondered why it did not climb up after him as it did the first time it hunted him.

Once again he squeezed himself through the narrow entrance where the door remained jammed on its rusty weathered hinges, but rather than heading down the steps as before, he climbed a small ladder leading up into the lamp room.

At last he was out of the razor sharp winds, a sigh of relief left his aching lungs, he slid down the glass facing the old lamps, then rolled onto his side in a tight ball. The cloak wrapped him, bringing comfort and warmth at last.

A tiny flicker of light emitting from the lens caught Jaden's eye. He held his breath. The drive shaft squealed as it turned through ancient worn rusting gears, slowly, intermittently rotating the lamp clockwise in the old tower. Although the light flickered dimly, it had enough power to burn through the shadows deep within Jaden's lonely soul.

The lighthouse seemed to be operating automatically, rising from the dead ruins to give warning from this place of timeless dread.

Suddenly, without warning, silence fell as the machinery ground to a halt. Jaden paused while focusing on the lens, the faintly burning light continued to dance on the wick.

"What's happening?"

The smell of fresh air and ocean mist instantly filled his nostrils and an uneasy feeling of slowing down and rapidly gaining weight sparked a panic, he clutched his chest to steady his heart and sprang up.

"Hello............ who are you?" a young voice called from behind. Jaden held his breath and eventually turned around.

The faint outline of a boy stood before him.

"I am Jaden.......who are you?" he answered slowly and wide eyed.

The Ghost of Jaden was wondering if he was seeing a ghost of a boy who quickly vanished before his eyes.

A blinding flash from the lens exploded into his retinas causing a scream of sharp pain which coincided with sharp cutting sensations around his rib cage.

As the light faded, Jaden found himself caught between variances of two dimensions.

Beneath his feet were the moving images of the lighthouse and its gruesome surroundings; he observed the immense plane structure on which he stood, it displayed the lighthouse from afar. Slowly, he knelt to touch the surface of what seemed to him like an immense movie screen extending as far as he could see, but he touched no surface and realised that he could reach into this other dimension.

He squinted hard to focus into the pool of strange visions, but it quickly grew dark.

Above him a blur of white squares drifted past and echoing voices surrounded him. Disoriented he tilted his head to one side. Something protruded from his right arm; it led to something hanging above him.

He knew he was lying on his back and yet somehow he was moving, with faces surrounding and rushing past him.

"Where am I?" he enquired, but no reply came.

Chapter twenty-one

Astril's Ritual

December 2001.

In the recesses of the old abandoned water tower deep in the Yorkshire moors, a fire robbed a winter's night of its cold embrace. Creosote tainted the air and its hot residue seeped from the old burning sleepers stacked vertically in a large rusting barrel.

Shadows of darting rats scurried along the wall as they made their escape from the sharp eyes of a watchful owl perched high above.

Wind bellowed through the various holes in the bottom of the barrel releasing fire flies crackling into the smoky air. The rising heat expanded the ancient steel girders above, twisting them, creating moans and bangs of moving echoes all around the old tower.

After a short while, the flames lost their anger and condensed into a fierce pit of glowing, roaring embers.

In the moving shadows knelt Astril.

He shuffled as close as possible, penetrating the intense heat shield wall emanating from the barrel.

Still kneeling, he removed his sweater, placed both palms on his thighs and began to focus on the pain he endured from the heat.

The orange glow reflected from the half moon shaped blade of the kerambit which hung from a cord around his neck; a deadly weapon which could easily be concealed in the fist.

He inched a little closer, opening and drawing in pain through his third eye and guiding its energy within. The contrast of heat upon the flesh and cold concrete floor hard on his knees and shins plagued his concentration.

At last he located the deep feeling of painful compression within, begging to be relieved by killing those whom he despised. He played images of Carl and Krzysztof getting away with murder, it served to reinforce the hatred, and allow justification to make them suffer.

The memory of his tears as a young boy over the loss of his family had never faded, forever rolling through his thoughts.

"Just wait, wait till I get me hands on you!" he mouthed the empty words as he visualized closing in on Carl.

He held the feeling and released the fear of failing or being killed before revenge was served.

The close proximity of the barrel burned his flesh, and the torment of anger burned his heart. He reached out and pressed his finger tips hard against the metal, the pain increased his rage as he imagined his hands around his victim's throat. When the scum lay dead in his mind, he withdrew his hands and formed tight fists, placing his knuckles back on the barrel to forge sickening visualizations of driving a punch through the hearts of men who crossed him, Krzysztof not least among them.

Discipline to hold out against pain until the mental imaging was realized to its end was aided by ultimate desire to draw the life from his enemy.

Finally he adopted the original posture, inching closer still.

The Hellmakers influenced his thoughts, hinting at a new enemy, a name which would soon be revealed to him by an unfortunate. Dangerous gateways were in the making, and Astril was unaware of the potential consequences of this level of hate-filled visualizations.

He continued to mentally draw heat into the middle of his forehead, imagining it be stored as animal rage energy, to be later unleashed at will.

He clutched the hot blade of his knife and made two cuts diagonally across his chest, each representing a vow to kill the remaining maggots with no right to eat a good man's dinner.

Bleeding, disorientated and very unbalanced, he climbed to his feet, tied his sweatshirt around his waist, slipped on a world war two German trench coat and wandered the dark tracks across the moors back home.

The cold moon lit his way as he staggered.

The aftermath of Astril's ritual rendered him in an altered state, with visions of things which shifted between worlds, always just out of his focus. Shadows of creatures from his nightmares drifted across the tracks, with their whispers echoing through and around him.

They walked with him, accompanying him on his journey.

Before he knew it, he found himself shoulder-butting the door of his converted carriage and with each thud of his scapula his senses awoke. He paused, searched briefly and found the key to gain entry, desperate for chemical relief.

Whiskey and cigarettes, their toxins crashed into his bloodstream with a kick straight from hell; he continually charged his glass and knocked back the spirits, drawing hard on the nicotine between gulps.

The poisons finally took hold, serving to numb the pain of injured hands and to mask the mental crush of relentless hateful chatter.

With a slow discharge of smoke blowing with a hiss from tense lips, he lay diagonally back on the small bed with one leg dragging on the floor.

The whiskey tingled in his mouth and throat indicating a welcomed mental and physical numbness would soon follow.

His heel tapped the case from the small night vision binoculars beneath his bed; he reached under to retrieve them.

Moments later he was spying the night from his window. The green images in the lenses revealed no hidden strangers. He paused for a draw of nicotine then continued to scan.

The sign post reading *April's Café* creaked as it swung gently in the night winter's breeze; the frost glistened with each tilt and reflections of light was amplified by Astril's night vision binoculars. He adjusted the focus to observe movement behind the window of the left upper floor.

April came into view; her abode was above the kitchen. He lowered the instrument and squinted hard for a second, took a quick draw on his cigarette and continued to observe her action, but she soon dropped down out of sight.

"Aww!" he gasped. It wasn't long before he found himself lying flat down on the cold surface of the carriage roof in search of her image, frantically turning the lens to sharpen the view.

Sitting with her head in her hands on the edge of her bed, she appeared to be crying.

Her shaggy blonde hair draped over her face and covered her arms to the elbows; she leaned over shaking her head and occasionally drying her eyes with her forearm. Astril gazed with bated breath, his curiosity had got the better of him; although the frosty steel roof and effects of too much whisky were tormenting a full bladder, he held fast to see her next move.

His blood temperature tripled immediately as she stood up revealing her figure in nothing but underwear, she then turned and disappeared through a door out of sight.

"Damn!" he laughed to himself. "You've got a nicer ass than

Krzysztof, I'll give you that!" he joked in reference to his lenses' usual targets.

Various lights flicked on and off in the old converted station and Astril tracked her position from one room to the next as each was illuminated in turn, until finally darkness fell throughout the café.

A distant tune played mixing in with Astril's dream, he opened an eye.

"Where, where am I?" he wondered, touching hypothermia, slowly he rolled onto his back then sat up casting shadows from a winter's dawn on to the roof of his carriage. He cast about to ensure neither onlookers nor April had spotted him. Her radio blasted songs from within the café; soon she would be opening up.

He gathered his thoughts and whereabouts for a short while, feeling disgusted with himself for allowing the sight of a semi naked female figure disrupt his discipline and maybe risk his cover.

"Could have been arrested for peepin'!" he whispered as he reached to retrieve his binoculars and climbed down the end of the carriage with cold trembling bones.

The small gas fire and all the blankets he could find aided his recovery. As he wrapped up tight under the covers April wandered into his thoughts and Astril found himself smiling uncontrollably.

He grinned to himself for falling asleep on the roof in hope for another glimpse of that body.

"Will I be able to look her in the eye when I order food? Will she know what I have been up too?"

The thought of her figure led to other thoughts, feeding his imagination further still; April now appeared to him in a new light. And his hateful thoughts had been ambushed by those of passion.

"It's been a while!" he whispered forgiving himself for the late night *nature watching* incident, the thought stayed with him, accompanying him to a deep and colourful dream.

Chapter twenty-two

A Gathering of Friends and Old Enemies

December 7th 2005

Krzysztof stared wide eyed at the television. It was 11pm; he was alone in his modern flat which overlooked the castle ruins of Scarborough. The Christmas programmes rolled endlessly from one to the next, reminding him of and amplifying his loneliness. The uneasy feeling of loaning his ship to Carl and his henchmen, and the fact that his days might be numbered by a hunter killer who seemed to be drawing nearer by the hour, had kept Krzysztof in the torment of endless sleepless nights, with the anticipation of death as a constant companion.

Realizing that he could not face yet more restless hours in bed, nor listen to any more Christmas carols or repetitive songs, he pulled on his boots, grabbed his keys and headed out to his Jeep.

The dark coastal roads unwound in the headlights. Krzysztof sighed many times to the merry songs which seemed to be playing on every radio channel he tuned into. They neither lifted nor suited his mood. Unable to find a compact disc in the glove compartment while at the wheel, he flicked the off button and drove to the hum of the engine.

His thoughts plagued him, switching from the anguish of having to bear the presence of Carl and his dark deeds, and the very strong fear of assassination and how it might come.

The torment which increasingly gripped his heart was the question of how he had failed to follow his feelings, which had warned him so many times of the dangers of following Carl into the arms trade, which had also resulted in him sacrificing his bodybuilding career and his dream of owning a successful health club.

"Maybe there's no killer out there after me," he whispered to himself, "maybe it's all in my head!" His words brought him no comfort.

He sank further into his distracting thoughts which overpowered his concentration.

"Arghhhh!"

The Jeep spun one-hundred-and-eighty degrees grinding to a halt at the roadside. Krzysztof clutched the steering wheel and screamed hard, until the springs of the suspension had dampened the rocking of the chassis.

"Get a grip man!" he shouted at the eyes of his reflection in the rear view mirror. The engine had stalled, leaving nothing but the whistle of December winds.

"Must have hit some black ice!" he thought.

The Abbey was quite nearby.

"A night under the stars may clear my head!" he turned the key in the ignition, pulled back onto the road and completed his journey to Whitby, finally ending at the car park behind the Abbey.

A cold and lonely walk through the dark corridor of night echoed the feeling which he carried inside. As he sat down on the frosty bench overlooking the sea he gazed outward towards his ship anchored off the coast.

The Abbey shadowed the cemetery which in turn cloaked the bench where he sat; he paused to confirm the icy feeling of being watched as his solitude quickly evaporated. The presence he sensed of hidden unknown eyes upon him, stung at his heart.

He held his breath tight in his lungs to aid his hearing and sharpen his senses.

The shadows from the moonlit Abbey reflected his growing fear as he carefully scanned the churchyard.

The sound of the winter sea blended with that of the wind,

"No sign of anybody!" he thought.

But then, in the distance near the steps, a lone black figure seemingly awaiting observation disturbed Krzysztof deeply.

With cold watering eyes and fingers desperately clutching the weathered slats of the bench, he knew any attempt to rise and take flight would be useless; his knees would buckle even upon standing.

"It's over, that's the killer!"

Swallowing hard his mind revealed that which he was fighting and trying to deny.

The cloaked black figure stepped forward heading slowly towards Krzysztof.

"RUN!" his mind screamed at him.

"I can't!" he replied.

He looked down at his feet,

"It may be a stranger, he may pass me by!"

Krzysztof glanced to his left prompted by the crunch of footsteps breaking through the frosty cemetery grass.

All in black, with its head cloaked by a dark hood, the figure strode towards him. Krzysztof gasped and held his breath until the footsteps finally stopped, leaving him tormented in a deafening silence and anticipation of death.

"Arghhhh!" he screamed exploding from the bench in attempt to desperately fight for salvation. He blindly swung a right hook towards the stranger only to be met by a force of disproportionate magnitude that propelled Krzysztof back, almost smashing him through the bench.

He gasped for air; the impact from the heavy double palm strike had paralysed his diaphragm. The aggressor watched Krzysztof suffering lack of vital oxygen as he rolled off the bench into a gasping heap on the cold ground.

In dread of a cold bullet, Krys raised his right hand to both act as a shield and give sign of desperate submission, but pleading gestures for forgiveness gave the attacker a lever, he took Krzysztof's arm and stretched it out into a lock while simultaneously standing on his throat, thus creating a deadly choke.

Ultimate vulnerability, fear and devastation from the realization of the value of his life now at an end, submerged his mental screams for mercy and forgiveness. He struggled and writhed, a cold pounding panic drummed aggressively at his temples; and slowly, the light began to fade under the weight of the stranger's boot.

Just as his eyes began to flicker, the crush of his throat was released.

His consciousness drifted for a second to a place he often visited while dreaming. The familiar smell of an old ship and a feeling of a dry mouth from long and hard transitions displaced his fear.

He came together with a gasp.

"Where am I?"

His vision cleared, and the cold floor pulled the heat from his back.

"You are in Whitby, at the Abbey!" answered a gentle voice.

Krzysztof slowly sat up to ease the pain of heat loss that melted the ice beneath him.

Confusion and haze of the sensation of the ship still remained with him, followed by the relief of feeling his still beating heart; his lips began to form a question.

"Who are you?" he asked.

Sitting on the bench from where Krzysztof had fallen, the cloaked figure exhaled a long frosty stream of breath into the night.

"I thought you knew......., I thought that's why you attacked me, I just came....to sit on my bench!" he leaned to his left and removed a flask from his coat pocket, unscrewed the cap and took a sip, "Wow!" he muttered with a dampened cough while holding the flask out at eye level to acknowledge its contents with respect, "Neat heat!"

"I thought you had gone to New Zealand!" Krzysztof murmured as he realized that, yet again, it was Jaden who had floored him.

"The nightmares brought me back!" Jaden replied.

Krzysztof climbed onto the bench and fearfully paused before asking his burning question.

"Is it you, are you the killer of my family, and the one who killed Carl's men?"

"*So it's true!*" thought Jaden; Krzysztof's question gave cold confirmation of Jaden's ongoing nightmares. "I am no killer Krzysztof, after the trial all those years ago between me, you and Carl, I left this country and worked with Rebecca's uncle in New Zealand; this is my first and only visit since." He removed his hood and offered Krzysztof a drink from the shiny flask.

"So what brings you back?" asked the big man, hesitantly taking a sip.

"You, Carl and strange things have brought me back!" Jaden answered as he gazed out towards the cliff edge where he had touched the bones years ago. "Since I woke up on the stretcher in the hospital, after Carl stabbed me, strange things have happened to me, coincidences, bad dreams, mad dreams and great dreams. Visions, foresight and visualizations which seem to be realized!"

The whistle of Whitby's sea winds gave ease to the silent pause between the two men.

"Do you remember that twisted court case Krzysztof? I learned then how the law could be manipulated by money; Carl's father's money in fact. I also learned that the law of integrity cannot be bent in the end, by man or beast."

"Yes we all walked away!" Krzysztof replied, "So what happened............between you and Becky?"

"Although I called myself a spiritual man back then, even knowing that a part of me created our split, by my visualizations. I simply could not forgive, well, maybe I could forgive, but I could not forget. All my memories were stained by a lie, the image of you two, in that rocking chair, our rocking chair, I could no longer grasp any thoughts of our times together, they seemed to have been clouded in some way, and even this place, which I once loved so much, means nothing to me now. Does she still live around here?"

"I don't know!" Krzysztof answered uncomfortably, as memories from the dark grave of the past were resurrected by Jaden's words. "That was a one off, with me and Rebecca!"

Jaden nodded "I know, we spoke about it, in great detail, and we almost tried again, but.... anyway, I ended up in New Zealand, with Jancine, who taught me a few strange things, and her brother Dennis sorted me out with a job, until eventually I went my own way, and we all lost touch!" He looked outwards into the night sea. "I should have taken responsibility, and maybe had a little more faith, and patience, but I'm human, with a lot to learn!" Jaden whispered to himself. "But then I would never have met my love Korey!" he thought of his ex-wife, a dark-skinned mixed-raced woman. He smiled as he thought of both her inner radiance and physical beauty. "Where's Carl? And what about this killer?"

"Out there!" Krzysztof pointed into the blackness. "Carl is off-shore, hiding from a killer who almost had him, a police raid saved his ass. You see those lights far out, that's where he's hiding; there's a large replica galleon which belongs to me, and two smaller vessels, they sail back with his whores and his food n' booze. He's waiting for a large payment from one of his deals, the bald-headed little freak, then he'll be out of the country for good, and not soon enough!"

Jaden took another sip of neat heat, which was closely followed by the proverbial cough.

"So you own a ship, a galleon no less, that's intriguing. And Carl is hiding there, hasn't he considered that it's perfect for the killer?"

"Perfect, how?"

"Well he's isolated out there!" Jaden replied.

"He ain't alone, he has security, the best that money can buy, or so he preaches!" Krzysztof spat his words of malice.

"*That won't save him!*" Jaden thought, "Tell me about your ship!"

"It's a replica; it's been used in films and hired for theme weddings. I bought it with money I made from…well from this and that. I want to get into the business of hiring it out; right now it's on hire to baldy locks and the three hairs!"

"Ya' know, my intuition tells me that you ain't too keen on Carl; stop sitting on the fence and tell me how you really feel!" Jaden humoured.

Krzysztof nodded with a grin. "So what really brings you back here?" he repeated.

Jaden took yet another sip and slowly leaned forwards. His dark leather coat creaked as it tightened across his back.

"Soul division, restoration of peace and to end a conflict which has spilled blood across the last………few………centuries. That conflict being between you and me, and Carl, of course!"

Krzysztof felt an uneasy tingle of truth; his soul recognized the accurate vibration of Jaden's words of good and powerful intention and signalled this into his heart.

"It sounds almost like a ghost story, but if you are open-minded, I shall share with you what I have learned, which may save us all; that said, once you've heard it, you'll probably think I am crazy!" Jaden sighed and sank back into the cold bench. "It's not easy for me to tell you this Krzysztof; it's not easy for me to even talk to you, especially after what happened with Rebecca and all!"

"Is it about……… something about, old ships?" Krzysztof interrupted.

"It is, yes, you know then?"

Krzysztof shook his head, "No, no, I don't know, I have strange dreams and strange feelings when I see pictures of old ships, it all seems, more like a memory, but very real, and very bad!"

Jaden took a long sip of neat heat and wiped his mouth on the back of his hand. "Sometimes I question my sanity. I don't know all the answers, but I feel things are not what they seem. But if you can hold the possibility of reincarnation in your mind, then you can appreciate you have a skeleton, remains of your former self, possibly in an old cemetery somewhere!"

"But what...."

"That's not all....... maybe, if you kill someone, maybe that's not the last you will ever see of them, if you hate someone enough and vow to forever kill them, I mean, really swear that you want to hurt them, and mean it, I believe there are certain forces that will act upon such destructive desires and aid you in your quest, with no intention of releasing you from your vow....... to be stuck, forever, killing and suffering the consequences!"

"What if you swear to love someone over and over, can you return for that?"

Krzysztof's question caught Jaden off guard. He laughed at yet another one of life's little surprises; that being the reaction from an old enemy that he had not counted upon.

"I don't know; I don't have all the answers."

"How do you know all this to be true? What happened?"

"Lots of things have happened, and lots could be written off as a mad man with a wild imagination, but if anyone could explain to me how I awoke in the hospital with a strange key in my hand, made of a substance not yet known, stolen from me by the government for analysis and it's on my medical records that my bones flashed through my flesh when I woke, then I would love to hear the answer!" Jaden was abrupt "The government watch me even now, after all these years, the key they stole from me has disappeared I hear, although they deny its very existence, they think I have it!"

"A key to what?" asked Krzysztof.

"I have no idea, strange shape it was, but I think I do know of its whereabouts'!"

"Where?"

Jaden turned with a sigh of frosty breath and gazed into the eyes of the big man. Then gently turned away indicating that an answer would not be given. Krzysztof understood the message and pursued his question no further.

"I don't understand these things you say to me, you say you are here to help, how can you help? Your words are hard for me to understand."

"Long ago, a vow was made by a man named Cain, to forever kill both his foe Breaker and the Captain of an old ship. I believe I am the reincarnated soul of Cain, as you are of Breaker and Carl is that of the captain. The vow was reinforced on the harbour when I repeated the very same promise, to you both!"

"But you said you ain't the killer!" Krzysztof leaned back with a cold push of fear.

"This part of me is not the killer!" Jaden whispered, he leaned forwards and pulled up his collar to the ward off the cold creeping in. "My soul divided, leaving me weaker, and a Hellmaker was born, a killer who would rather die than lose. Hate and vengeance are his passion; he will not rest until you and Carl are dead." Jaden fought the ice tears forming with a sting. "I have nightmares, I can feel what he does but it's elusive, a blur, I can't fix upon him".

"What's soul division, how do we kill him how can we…?"

"You can try to kill him, but he uses dark meditations, and is influenced by unseen forces. He is well trained with weapons and he is single minded, full of hate, which is where he draws his power. Ending his life is not the answer. That's what the Hellmakers wish for, death, even of their own, once vengeance begins, violence gives rise to more violence, only fight I say, when cornered, if you seek to take revenge, you create more conflict. The killer who stalks you thinks he has a right to take your life, but in his wake, he leaves behind more children of murdered parents, who will seek him out, just as he seeks you. An ever-growing cycle."

"Why, why does he stalk me, and what's soul division?" he repeated, "And how do we end it?" he added.

"Psychic messages are not always clear, but I feel that Carl may have given information, which led to the destruction of his family, you are part of the organisation!"

Krzysztof dropped his head back and sighed. Although he knew nothing of any information which Carl may have passed on, he had no doubts of his capacity to squander the lives of any if it meant even the slightest gain of profit or business advancement.

"We are all made of the same substance!" Jaden interrupted Krzysztof's contemplation.

"Energy taking form in a field of the same energy. Imagine we are all icicles, floating in the sea, and being an icicle, I could melt, divide and take two or three forms from the same molecules of water or conscious energy. But having divided, I am less dense, weaker. In this case, I divided into three, but I can only feel one, the hateful one who hunts you…. and as my soul divided, I returned infertile, I cannot have children." He turned to hide his eyes from Krzysztof. "Some people would say that is my karma, my punishment, but I say to them, it's not. It's just the level of energy I needed to give up to return here to sustain this form. A matter of fact, not a matter of consequence!" he sighed from a darker memory.

Letting his wife go, so she could have children with another was a painful act of selflessness, which felt to him like punishment.

Jaden sighed again; finally the burden of knowledge had been released to a man he had sworn to kill, a man he had hated for so long. He took a long sip from the flask, swallowed hard and then took another.

Krzysztof remained silent for a moment, waiting, anticipating, and questioning his sanity; he envisioned Carl and his henchmen laughing at him for even half believing the *spooky stories* as told by Jaden.

"What's he look like? Is he big, how old?" Krzysztof enquired.

"Hmmm, I'm not sure of his age, but he's no giant, small and compact maybe, the soul division would mean a smaller physical structure to sustain, at least, I think!"

"So how do I survive this?" Krzysztof asked quickly, almost before his previous question had been answered.

Jaden replaced the hip flask into his deep pocket. "Accept the darker things you have created, take responsibility for the things you have done, accept that this may be the end for you. Accept that you are afraid, that you cannot release fear; you can however release your resistance to it. Then pray that your enemy finds peace. Even if you hate him, because once peace is found, he will be your enemy no more. No one at peace can be your enemy. The universe is like a mirror; peaceful thoughts are reflected back, and hateful ones bring more!"

"How can I pray for peace for someone I hate, or fear? Hell I don't even believe!"

"You can imagine them feeling the energy of peace, even while you are feeling hostile towards them, it's easier once you realise this is the way to truly heal the conflicts. I hated you for a long time, but I imagined you finding peace and after a while I no longer woke up with destructive thoughts against you. Until recently I had entirely forgotten about you. Taking responsibility is the discipline required, and I think, at least in part, that's what the Crucifixion was all about!"

Krzysztof absorbed Jaden's words, unsure of their validation. His ego taunted him for taking time and effort to analyze them.

"I'm not religious Krzysztof, not in the least. Faith is a personal thing!" He looked at the big man who remained silent. "But you wonder why I mentioned the Crucifixion?"

"Yes, if you are not religious, your words make no sense!"

"You can believe in God, with out embracing religion, and I confess, it's because of the way most religious people behave, that I find it hard to admit that I am a believer, I don't wish to be associated with their actions or beliefs. I believe Jesus was a master teacher, passionately giving knowledge of the universal laws, *Knock and it shall be opened unto you*, but mankind denied responsibility for his darker creations, to avoid the pain and consequences associated with truth. I think his love was so selfless, so infinite, that he took the burden, and accepted our self-denied energies which he transformed into the great pains which he endured and suffered, restoring balance, and leaving the message of life eternal.

Jaden peered at Krzysztof to check his expression as the lecture continued high upon the dark rock.

"The religionists preach that God is an unlimited power, and I agree with them. But I say an unlimited power with unlimited foresight, would know what the future holds and what any of us will do long before we do. Therefore, even though we have free will, God will still know our action before we do, before we are even born in fact, he would know those of us who make so called bad choices, before the earth was even spinning, such is the magnitude of unlimited foresight, so then, why would there be eternal punishment if we were to make a wrong choice, a sin? The same goes for prayer, God knows your words before you speak them; he never has to hear anything, I only hear your words Krzysztof, because I don't know what you will say, until you say it and it's ourselves who do not know what we shall do next, or how a certain thing feels. Doing a good deed should be a heartfelt desire to help another, not an action compelled by fear of the consequences. If you don't do the right thing, or do it only for reward, I pray through feeling, and because I wish to pray, not through fear or...."

"Ok, ok!" Krzysztof interrupted Jaden's sermon.

"All I'm saying is life is lived through us!"

"Enough!" Krzysztof repeated. "I need time to change, to learn, to try, but what of Carl?"

"I must go to him; on your ship and help him!"

"He will not listen, and there was a time when I wouldn't have either!" Krzysztof laughed. "If you go to him, he will probably have you killed; when he finally stops laughing at you!"

"That's a risk I'll have to take!" Jaden answered without hesitation.

"It's not a risk, it's a fact! You won't even make it there, and your message may not even arrive. Maybe we should phone him first, see how it goes, how he takes it!"

Jaden paused for thought. Krzysztof opened his large wallet to remove a business card.

"Phone me tomorrow. I will see what I can do, he'll be out of his skull on drugs and whores at this time of night!" he stood up and turned to Jaden. "Carl never knew what happened, you know, between me and Rebecca, it wasn't mentioned in court, we all kept it quiet, remember!"

"And you want to keep it that way!" Jaden interrupted, frowning at the card as he read the details.

"They say you were a long time dead, what was it like? What did you see?"

The December winds grew stronger, colder by the second, whilst Krzysztof awaited his answer.

"I can only remember certain things under certain conditions, in meditation or sleep, then it's gone. I know that I know, but I don't know what it is that I know!" Jaden observed Krzysztof's expression; the big man needed a more definitive answer. "I saw the light, felt peace and love beyond anything I can describe, but then I took another path, even though I was warned of its danger, although my memories of it aren't clear, I hope I never return. Although I do know that this place, the harbour, the lighthouse, is relevant!"

Krzysztof pulled up his collar and sighed, "Give me a call, I need time to think, and work things out. Call me tomorrow, ok?"

"I will call you tomorrow, but I am away after that until the end of January; I am going to see my family further south, so you'll have plenty of time to arrange the meeting with Carl and me on your ship!"

Krzysztof sighed repeatedly and rose leaving a trace of misty breath behind him as he exited the cemetery.

Left alone in the winter's night, Jaden stared towards the steps to his left. Unclear dreams and theories plagued him once more; he wished that he could be sure of his visions and rest assured that the many coincidences that he experienced were the valid signs which he often prayed for.

Krzysztof's Jeep fired up the distance. Jaden climbed to his feet while listening to the vehicle's engine fade into the distance.

He had a moment alone in the shadows of the ruined Abbey.

Time stood still as he contemplated his past.

"Alone…….. in Whitby…..again!" he said gently to himself.

With a heavy heart, he circled the church and cemetery with slow and deliberate footsteps and, while considering a method of delivering his message to Carl, he eventually found himself to be at the top of the steps.

The frosty handrail gave his palm a dull ache where he clutched it tightly during his slow descent into the town below.

The Four Masts inn cast many shadows from the yellow street light before him. Memories spilled out of its entrance washing him with nostalgic reminders. He paused to steady his thoughts. He knew that just around the corner was the old shop where Rebecca had seduced him and the cloak embraced him.

An old ghost whispered sweet nothings - and nothing sweet into his soul. A dose of adrenalin iced his veins.

"*What will you do if you see her?*" his thoughts began their dialogue, hunting for the energy of engagement.

Jaden allowed the words to roll through his mind; he knew they were a tool seeking the attention of either resistance or disagreement.

He walked through the cobbled streets counting his footsteps.

"*Hmmmm!*" he thought as he suddenly realized he had successfully defended the attack from Krzysztof. "*The Tai Chi works then!*" Jaden hid the truth of his nature very well. He knew that Krzysztof, along with many others, believed him to be a confident martial artist, a real fighter. But since the soul division, his energy was unbalanced, leaving him questioning his victories. No matter what battles and struggles he had overcome, his confidence was still in question, and he knew this.

He felt that he had lost his anger, and its absence added to its value.

He crossed the swing bridge over the river Esk to the north of the town. His way to the car park took him past the aquarium; the advertisement stopped him dead in his tracks as a large picture of a squid drew his attention.

"Hello again!" he whispered under his breath.

His presence in Whitby began to unfold some dark reminders of hidden experiences, lost in the recesses of his mind. He continued his walk to the car, his pace however had quickened.

"*Not like the old days!*" he thought, referring to the location of his lodgings, 12 miles north and well out of the town.

A few minutes later he arrived at his hire-car parked north of the harbour. He paused before climbing in and gazed across the water.

The black silhouette of the Abbey ruins reached high into the night sky. Jaden followed the jagged edge with his focus all the way across the cliffs and down into the town below. It felt hollow and loveless to him.

He shook his head slowly while pulling the car door open and climbed in.

The radio channel interrupted the silence for a moment before the engine had time to turn over and fire up.

Steam blew out of the exhaust pipe as it defrosted the condensation of a wintry night. As he left the town, he smiled as the lyrics blasted from a song on the auto-channel.

"*Remember there is nothing to remember, embrace my love it's yours if you surrender!*"

Krzysztof found himself sitting at the edge of his bed.

It was the consistent nightmares he suffered which gave validation to Jaden's words in some way.

"Old Ships!" he said to himself, as he removed his wrist watch and tossed it on the bedside cabinet.

He lay back on the bed, placed his palms behind his head and spoke into the darkness.

"I'm sorry for the things I have done, and although I am scared..........very scared – I can admit that now! I accept I'm responsible for being hunted down.... like some dog!" he ended with humour of despair.

"I hope he finds peace, whoever, whatever he is!"

A cold tingle left his spine.

Chapter twenty-three

The Unfortunate

Corpse was a medical marvel, a mystery to all of his consultants.

His foster brothers had given him the name because of his sickly appearance. His true age was difficult to determine, he might have been 15 or perhaps 25. His origin was also unknown; as a very young child, he had been found alone wandering around a small cemetery on the outskirts of Glasgow Scotland.

Very weak, with sunken eyes, Corpse suffered low energy and testosterone levels, leaving him frail and childlike.

Now and again they would let him out of the wardrobe where he was made to sleep. It lay in the depths of an old converted school, now a foster home in eastern Scotland.

It was the annual trip to York, via Whitby. Crushed under the weight of his aggressive foster brothers and carers, squeezed in the back seat, abused and repressed, Corpse gasped and fought for each breath in the converted transit van. He dared not protest, his brothers were unbeatable, "Better do as they say!"

His world was tainted by fear; dread was all that he knew, it seemed normal to him to be the test dummy in the gym boxing ring where the brothers would take bets on the number of punches required to knock him out. Then he would be made to thank them. He knew himself to be worthless, that neither he nor anyone else would ever match the strength of his undefeatable foster brothers. He had surrendered his life to the acceptance of a destiny of illness and weakness.

In his nightmares he could often hear the growling of the large black dog which slept outside of his wardrobe door.

The van skidded to a halt.

"Get out then!" scoffed the driver impatiently.

The side doors slid open and the four of them scrambled out.

The smell of food from April's café hit them sequentially. Corpse trailed behind feeling insecure about sitting in the right seat in order to avoid being shouted at again. But once inside the four men were distracted by the presence of April waiting their table. The volume of their conversation grew competitively louder in aggressive Scottish accents.

An argument was brewing between the two 18 year olds regarding the effectiveness of mixed martial arts and boxing when applied in street confrontations; both big men giving many examples of how, in the past, they had smashed or choked their enemies.

Corpse noticed a man sitting alone at a table in the far corner of the old café. He felt the urge to approach the stranger, to tell him something but the argument grew louder.

"If it goes t' ground ya boxing is ne good!" shouted Jamie pointing to the floor.

"I been on the ground many a time Boy, I still crack em out!" replied big Jon pointing at his own shaven head, "One crack on the ol' jaw and its goodnight sweetheart!"

"Not if it was a grappler down with yee!"

"Well none of yee have had the nuts to have a go yet, am still waitin!" snarled Jon giving hints of a challenge. "I knock em out before they get close enough to take me to ground! Ah can give you the names of the fools who tried me if yee wants!"

April felt uneasy by the volume and nature of her customers; she rushed the four breakfasts over to them, followed by cheese on toast for the quiet boy who looked very unwell. She ignored the nudges and winks between the men along with their disguised suggestive comments. She turned up her radio a touch and hoped that no families would come through the café doors and suffer the uneasy tension created by the small gang.

The arguments soon died down to be replaced by the sound of munching from four greedy eaters and the squeal of their knives sliding across plates.

Corpse felt the urge to speak, like he should repeat something just whispered to him from out of the air.

He felt his words may carry consequence, but his many tears in the dark wardrobe, where he heard calming voices, and saw strange faces and figures, had reached critical mass, he was about to induce a change in the direction of many lives.

He stared into the centre of the table.

"If you only fight untrained men and drunks, you're a coward really, a bully!"

Words of truth even if spoken from the weakest of souls, may cause pain in those who resist them the most.

His sentence fell on deaf ears as the four stared at the plates from which they continued to greedily devour their food.

Corpse looked over at the lonely man in the corner. The urge to speak was still strong.

"I saw the ghost of Jaden!" he called out. As the name was given, a connection was energised, and a common path was now accessible for three lost souls.

No response.

The four men looked over to observe who Corpse had spoken too.

"Ain't yee forgot about that yet?" said Jamie.

"Aye I remember that," grinned Jon, "when he was a wee nipper a few years back, in the lighthouse, everyone ran out shouting *Ghost!*"

"Aye but Corpse stayed in for a chat, hey, I bet the spook was more afraid of our Corpse than he was of the Ghost eh? Ha a ha ha ha!"

"Corpse, didn't your ma tell you not to talk to strangers?" sniggered Jon, "Who is he anyway?"

"Keep talkin'. I'll let ya know!" the stranger thought as he reached down under the table, appearing to scratch his ankle.

A rock song began playing on the radio, the lyrics giving warnings of strangers. The words played unnoticed.

"EEE, ya gonna answer the boy?" Jamie called out to the man

No response.

"I dunno some folk have ne manners have they Jon?"

Corpse felt immediately submerged in guilt and sorrow. If only he had not spoken to the poor man, now it looked like *the fearsome four* were about to spread their reputation even further.

"You three go teach him some manners while I finish me tea!" Jon ordered.

The three men grinned as their chairs slid away with a screech and they collectively stood to attention.

Jamie quickly led their march over towards the man and placed both of his hands on the table to take his weight; he leaned in to deliver his threat verbally.

Response.

The stranger interrupted the flow with a pre-emptive strike.

Jamie shared the mindset of many over-confident aggressors and complacency was his downfall. He intended to use words of fright followed by fists of might, but just at the point of inhaling before speaking, the stranger exploded out of his chair and plunged a large diver's knife into Jamie's load bearing hand. The blade cut all the way though the bone and protruded out through the bottom of the table.

The shock of ambush discharged its disturbing energy into to the unprepared two, who stood frozen either side of their screaming comrade.

Corpse dropped his glass of water as he witnessed the blinding speed of violence unfolding before his eyes.

The stranger continued his counter attack; he used the edge of his tray and jabbed hard into the throat of the man to his right, then smashed it hard over the head of the second man to his left. Jamie remained crying in agony, his hand pinned to the table which the stranger kicked over to cause further injury and suffering.

April observed the revelation of the true nature of a man whom she had thought she knew.

Astril grabbed the chair from which he had sprung to do some *real damage* to his stunned and off balance victims.

The wooden structure shattered under the pounding of endless and systematic scattered blows delivered to the three would-be attackers.

By the time Jon realised that the screams were those of his brothers, the damage which was not in his favour, had already been done.

Astril gazed down.

"It's a good job I'm in a fuckin' good mood!" he grunted sadistically in reference to sparing them their lives.

"There maybe trouble ahead..... so there'll be glass fights and smashed spines and flesh bites!" Astril whispered his twisted version of an old classic.

The desire to slaughter all of them was almost irresistible.

Migration of dark energies enlarged his pupils empowering a

dehumanising cold stare from the depths of an unforgiving soulless killer.

"Put ye hands up n' fight like a man!" Jon scoffed hoping Astril would not use the remains of the chair against him. "Fight fair!" he added while raising his fists. "C'mon!"

Astril spoke into empty space dead ahead of him, Jon was not yet worthy of a glace. "Don't…. make…. me…..laugh, don't quote fair when you've just sent these three pre-pubescent girls over to try n' rough me up!"

Jon's arrogance blinded him. "Fight me!" he growled. "Put down the wood n' fight!"

Astril turned his head to scowl at the man, "No, I don't want to fight you!" he then turned square-on.

"Fight!" the Scottish accent boomed aggressively.

"You don't understand," Astril replied, "I don't want to fight you the way you're used to, things are gonna get bad for you…….. really bad, no referee, no eight count, no tap outs, no one to save you, y' see, I'm not going to fight you……….. I'm going to kill you!"

Pushing the table aside, Jon strode across the room, his eyes fixed on the expressionless man who stood before his fallen brothers.

Astril's fingers curled about the simple, turned leg of the chair; the rest lay on the floor at his feet. He studied the man approaching him, his fists clenched, his face a mask of hatred. This was a man who lived through fear, a man who knew how to use violence to enforce his will.

Jon knew that any man who could take out three others so quickly must be dangerous, but he had never been beaten, so he attacked, intent on teaching the stranger a lesson he would never forget. He planted his feet and twisted slightly to his left, winding his body tightly. He launched his left fist, knowing that its sickening impact would be followed by his right.

Astril watched the man's preparations. He held his own weight evenly on his feet and began to shift slightly, stepping forward and sweeping the thick piece of wood across himself, shielding his face and connecting with the other man's wrist, feeling a satisfying crunch as the radius shattered. Astril countered with a jab of his own, breaking his assailant's nose and then brought the chair leg down on his clavicle, smashing bone and cartilage. He raised the club again, but the other man fell, overtaken by a wave of pain.

Astril stood over him, unforgiving; the chair leg rose again and again, as both it and his boots were used as primary weapons to finish the man who lay broken on the floor.

A crucial and defining contrast between the two men was Astril's insatiable desire to fulfil a deed of revenge, versus Jon's lust for the image of himself as a fighting hard man.

The power of standing strong, feared, and victorious satisfied his ego.

"Unbeatable! Look at the scum; their expressions soon change when they know they're goin' down!" he whispered.

His anger was self perpetuating, powered by the resistance of having to spare them

Only to avoid attracting any attention from the law, he intended to stay at April's until Krzysztof's termination, however, a strong mental influence gave order to commit a vile deed.

"Kill the boy, kill the boy, kill the boy, kill the boy!" it repeated.

Astril dropped the blood soaked and splintered chair remains on Jon's battered body and removed the half moon shaped knife which hung around his neck hidden under his sweatshirt.

Four men lay writhing in pain before him. He accepted that he would have to kill them along with April once the job had been done to make it look like a violent incident between her and the gang; then go after Krzysztof straight away.

He turned to focus on the terrified boy who crouched trembling in the corner.

"DO IT NOW, DO IT NOW, DO IT NOW!"

The desire felt to him like self harm, however, he trusted the Hellmakers influent energy without question, unaware that this termination would make him theirs forever.

He stepped forward, the knife held lightly in his fingers. It would be a simple act to wedge the blade in the side of his neck from behind his head and slicing forwards to cut the arteries and throat.

Darkness immediately engulfed him.

His eyes flickered open to observe the twitching fingers of his right hand inches away from his knife which lay on the floor in front of him.

He realised that he was lying face down but was unsure of the how of it.

His fingertips began to crawl, walking his hand to reach the weapon.

"GET UP!" His willpower blasted the order within.

The hatred offset the pain from a deep cut in the crown of his head; he was unaware of the blow which he had suffered only moments before.

The café appeared to be empty; he climbed to his feet and held still for a moment to gain focus. The wrecked chair legs lay on the floor to his right soaked in blood; his eyes followed the red trail leading out of the door.

He did not recall granting his victims permission to leave, their absence outraged him, the hatred fired adrenalin through his blood stream to try and overcome a decreasing ability to focus and balance, he staggered towards the door still clutching the knife.

The van doors slammed shut and the vehicle rocked as the engine misfired. Astril scowled realising his victims were trying to escape.

Black smoke belched out of the exhaust pipe filling the car- park with fumes, the van jumped forwards and stalled. The frantic whirring of the starter motor began once more. Astril staggered towards the van, his balance was disturbed and his vision was becoming increasingly blurred. A woman he remembered as April came into view; although she had been beside the van all along, his realisation of her had only just transpired. She hurried past him and out of sight.

He paused for a second, the van would be locked. He needed to act fast; his guns were locked away and hidden, there was no time to fetch them. The engine fired up but stalled yet again. Astril squinted towards his railway carriage; he hurried over and reached underneath to grab the petrol cans he stored there to keep the fumes out of his car.

The injured men in the van watched him walking towards them. Corpse was in the driving seat for the first time in his life. He desperately tried the ignition again; Jon was still unconscious in the back seat and the other three were screaming desperately for him to get the van started.

Petrol splashed over the windscreen and a horrific anticipation of death unified the fearful screams within.

Astril reached into his pocket for a lighter to ignite the petrol drenched van without regard of his close proximity to the potential combustion, he began to strike up a flame while gazing emotionlessly into the side-window at Corpse.

Corpse paused for a moment, silence fell in the van as he slowly turned and gazed into the dark dehumanizing eyes of Astril who stood outside holding a lighter, a flame danced around the open shiny steel cap. Corpse gently closed his eyes and shook his head twice, as he opened them to refocus, the flame of the lighter faded out. He then turned the keys and the engine fired up.

Astril began to try and relight but darkness, resulting from yet another unseen blow, sent him once again to the floor.

As he came to he observed the van erratically leaving the car-park, "NO!" he shouted while desperately crawling after it. Fear of loss enraged him; his muscles soaked all of the energy from his system as he crawled on all fours on the cold wintery ground.

His strength was fading fast. "C'mon!" he demanded his system to release more adrenalin, "C'mon" he repeated furiously. His mantra powered him breathless to the exit near the roadside where he collapsed exhausted leaving his soul out of anger, and his body drained and injured.

In a spiritual game of chess played between the energy of a vow now owned by Hellmaker energy, verses Jaden and Krzysztof's influence of the field via peaceful visualisations, the hatred of Astril's ritual had just been prematurely spent.

The weak repressed young boy had just saved all of his foster brothers, and now their egos would have to come to terms with the undeniable truth.

The following night April soaked her aching muscles in a hot bath. She had strained her back dragging Astril's unconscious form up her stairs to take care of him and then cleaning the blood stains from the café's wooden floor. She wondered if he would be angry with her for knocking him down twice with her heavy rolling pin, but she felt that she had needed to save the men from Astril and Astril from himself.

He lay in her spare bedroom to the rear of the building, still unconscious and murmuring strange and unpleasant sounding chants in a language not spoken on earth.

The following morning Astril awoke to find someone sitting at the end of his bed chatting with him. Her words meant nothing to him, nor did his surroundings. He sat up leaning against a pillow simply breathing.

After an hour or so, his awareness slipped suddenly back into his body, like a hand sliding into a glove.

"What's happening? Where am I?" he asked.

April swallowed hard and carefully explained how she had sneaked up and hit him twice with her rolling pin, once in the café and then again outside. She emphasised how her actions had only been intended to stop the violence.

She stuttered a little and repeated herself to fill the awkward silences and blank expressions radiating from Astril's face.

"It was you, you brought me down?" he asked, needing confirmation.

"Yes!" she whispered.

Astril looked down, his eyebrows raised slightly and the corners of his mouth began to twitch, he raised his hand to cover his face with open fingers.

"Are you ok?" April asked him.

Astril nodded; he tried, he fought bravely, but he could no longer contain himself, the irony of living a life on the edge only to be brought down by a lady with a rolling pin infected him with uncontrollable laughter.

"What's so funny?" April giggled, she felt relieved.

"If only you knew!" Astril gasped.

"It's winter alright!" Astril pointed to snow gathering outside on the corner of the window frames while wiping his eyes from laughter. "What day is it, how long have I been here?"

"A few days that's all. Are you hungry?"

"Very!"

"I'll get you some breakfast!" April stood up.

"You don't have to look after me!" Astril smiled.

"I know, but you did get those thugs out of my café, even if you did get a little carried away!"

"A little carried away alright!" Astril thought, as April's words may have qualified for this year's understatement if she knew of his true intentions.

Although April feared the man in her spare bed, she felt safe with him around, and suspected that the land developers may be leaving her alone due to his presence. If she had known the degree of Astril's interference in this matter a few months ago, the reality of his nature would be devastating to her.

The smell of a cooked breakfast from downstairs pulled Astril out of bed. He realised that he was only wearing boxer shorts and smiled at the thought of being stripped by April while he had been unconscious. He wondered if she had seen him completely naked at some stage, as she wrestled his clothes off him.

He found his combat trousers folded on the wooden cabinet at the bedside; he pulled them on releasing a clean and fresh aroma. "She's washed my clothes!" he whispered to himself.

Still feeling weak and slightly unbalanced he pulled on his sweatshirt and carefully made his way downstairs following the music from a small radio, which led him to the kitchen.

Moments later and they were both sitting at a little wooden table engaged in small talk; they avoided the subject of the violence which had brought them together in the present circumstances.

Astril greedily scoffed his breakfast.

"Sorry, I am ravenous!" he confessed while mopping his plate with bread.

"You always are; I cook for you pretty often remember?"

"Anyway, how did I end up almost naked?" Astril asked sternly; he smiled to express the true nature of his enquiry.

"I thought you would be more comfortable and your clothes were covered in blood and petrol and dirt from the road!" she replied with a blush.

"Yeah, yeah! That's a lame excuse, admit it, you just wanted to check my ……..!" he joked over his mug of tea.

"Well you can undress me next time I pass out!" April replied, "But remember, you have to wash and iron my clothes!"

"The last time I ironed I burned my right ear!" Astril said gently, then sipped his beverage.

"What, how did you manage that?"

"The phone rang!" he answered laughing at the punch line, "The old ones are the best!" he added.

"Awww that's poor!" she laughed. "Any more of those and I will have to hit you with the rolling pin again!"

"So you can strip me again! Ha ha ha! I know your game!"

"I better not tell you about the bath I gave you!" April laughed.

"Ughh?"

"Well….. you will never know, will you?" April smiled.

"I feel abused, violated; have you done this kind of thing to tenants before? Maybe there is a help group, the April aftershock group, for those who've been unconsciously exposed!" Astril laughed out loud and then shook his head, "Brought down by a rolling pin, then stripped! What will become of my street cred?"

"Don't mess with us girls, we play rough, and we get what we want!" April replied as she put the kettle on the small stove to make more tea.

As the week unfolded, Astril assisted April with small repairs in her café. She decided to close to the public during the final weeks leading up to Christmas.

Other than a quick trip to pick up some fresh clothes, Astril never made it back to his sleeper car; he lodged in the spare bedroom at the back of the building.

Early morning starts and long days of hard graft left the café gleaming with new coats of paint, a few new light fittings, repaired tables, new menus and a general new ambience as designed by April.

It was 8 o'clock on Saturday evening; Astril was sweeping up paint chippings from his repairs to the inner windowsills near the café entrance. His converted train carriage outside in the wintery dusk caught his eye. It reminded him the weapons hidden away inside; suddenly he realised that the diver's knife from his ankle holster and the kerambit blade which normally hung around his neck were no longer present.

It felt strange to him that it had taken him so long to notice the weapons were gone and his obsession also seemed to have evaporated almost without a trace.

"How am I going to ask April what's she's done with 'em?" he thought.

An immediate dull pain of anxiety weighed heavily across his brow; he dropped the brush and pressed his forefinger and thumb into his closed eyes, then pinched the bridge of his nose with a sigh.

The plaguing vow to kill his enemies had remained silent for days. During its short absence, Astril had experienced the feelings of peace, along with the company of a strong little soul who had succeeded where many had failed; she had brought him down physically and lifted his soul spiritually.

He now had relativity, as opposed to one dimensional perception.

Intellectually he knew that to love someone could lead him to the pain of loss, a potential bargaining tool or vengeful paybacks to hurt him should ruthless enemies discover someone close to him. Subconsciously, he knew that to be a killer at his level meant that his enemies had already won. Fear of loss had stolen his freedom to ever fall in love. He felt this, but had not dared look within to dismantle the source of this vibration. To face the truth of this could be his undoing. The current of his soul was constant, but blocked by the ego which was influenced by the Hellmakers. One day however, he might just catch the message, he may have to listen.

"Astril, I am going get a shower then make us some food!" April shouted from upstairs.

"Oh...ok!" he answered, trying to disguise his voice to seem cheerful.

He completed the task at hand; tidying up served as a distraction from his conflicting thoughts; he placed the tools neatly in a corner then headed to his bedroom.

Music blasted from April's bedroom; she had turned the volume high, so that she could sing along to her favourite tunes while in the shower.

Astril smiled in reaction to the inconsistent melody from behind the bathroom door.

"Thought you'd know the words to this one by now!" he laughed, "We only hear it about a hundred times a day!" The harmonies suggested a rhythmic tap of the foot, but Astril resisted.

After a short while, April's singing from behind the bathroom door became clear, no longer drowned by the rush of water; the sliding sound of the shower door indicated that she had finished. Astril scanned around his bedroom for his graders to trim his hair short. "Where are they?" he thought as he rubbed the back of his neck and head. "Ouch!" the cut from April's assault with the rolling pin stung. "Maybe I'll let my hair grow a little!" he grinned.

His bones felt heavy and he was becoming aware of a dull ache throughout his body. The lack of adrenalin and stress was allowing his bio-feedback system to highlight injuries and internal damage inflicted over the years caused by anger, hard training and a hateful attitude. The subtle warning signals of his nervous system were no longer inhibited by toxic chemicals brought on by vile images in his mind, the demand for deep rest and recovery overwhelmed him.

He sat on the bed, with his elbows resting on his thighs. April streaked across the landing past his door.

"All yours!" she shouted referring to the bathroom being free.

"Ok!" Astril felt lifeless; he sat up, stretched his arms and yawned.

April turned her music off, dried her hair and quickly got dressed; she noticed Astril had not yet made it to the bathroom.

"Are you ok?" she asked, peering into his room. She smiled on discovering a half undressed Astril sprawled across the bed and sleeping heavily.

The sound of the shower disturbed Astril,

"Awww" he sighed, pulling the covers over his head. "It's still dark, why is she having another one?" he thought, "I know why her mum named her April now. April showers, she's always in there!" He smiled and congratulated himself on the creation of a new joke.

He pulled himself up feeling hollow, "I'm ravenous!" he thought. The rumble from his belly agreed with him.

The lock clicked and the bathroom door sprang open.

He called out to April, to intercept her quick dash across the landing.

"How come you've had another shower?"

April popped her head around the door, "Ah, so you're alive then, I thought all the work we've done had finished you off. Can't you keep up with a girl?"

Astril expressed confusion.

"You have been asleep for two days, I had to put you to bed again and yes, I did undress you, AGAIN!"

"I'm starving!" he replied.

"Get a shower then I'll see you downstairs; we'll get something to eat!"

"April showers!" Astril laughed gently.

"Pardon?" she enquired.

"I'll tell ya later!" he grinned.

Astril left nothing, his plate was clean; the salmon and pasta was delicious.

"I'd better pay you extra rent for all you are doing for me!" he said.

"Yes, I agree, you should!" April smiled, "but you've helped me with the repairs, so we'll call it even; would you like some wine?" she asked.

"Not for me thanks, though, I do have some vodka in my carriage, do you fancy a glass? Its good stuff, the real deal, might be too strong for you though!"

"Too strong!" she frowned, "bring it on!" she nodded.

Astril unbolted the front door of the café and stepped out into the cold midnight air.

A few minutes later both of them had settled down at a table to share a bottle of Astril's favourite spirit, however, after one glass, April found she preferred her usual drink, so she indulged in a bottle of her favourite red wine. She maintained the easy flow of chat; sensing it to be wise to avoid asking Astril about his history. She observed him through a series of glances, his serious demeanour, short hair and closed aura was still present even though the conversation was light and playful. She found his age hard to pin down.

Astril was also paying close attention to his hostess; she often tilted her head slightly when she gave a wide smile which lifted her bright blue almond shaped eyes.

Her figure was athletic, carved from a hard fast work ethic and lifestyle.

Time ran away with them, April called time at 3:00am and, feeling intoxicated, they staggered upstairs to their bedrooms, each bidding the other goodnight.

Each of them lay in their own bed staring into the darkness, both realizing that there was a slight attraction and both wondering if the other felt the same. Their ears rang with increased blood flow from a fast heartbeat, driven by a combination of sexual anticipation and alcohol.

April stared at her door wondering if Astril might perhaps knock or walk in. Astril listened carefully for any sign of movement from the next bedroom, a creaky floor board maybe. The hours unfolded and neither of them made any advances to the other, eventually the warmth of the beds seduced them into a deep, intoxicated sleep.

It was ecstasy to wake up holding someone close; the feeling of body-heat radiating from her back into his chest was comforting. The bed was soft, and the heavy covers pushed their bodies into the mattress.

Astril surfaced from a dreamy state of mind, he held still while searching his memory to make sense of his situation.

April rubbed his left thigh with her left palm as they lay together embraced on their right sides.

Still he had no recollection of how they came to be together. The bed felt different, he realised he was not in his own room. The central heating hummed in the distance making it hard to concentrate and stay awake; his head was still spinning from the vodka that he had drunk earlier and his mouth felt very dry. With a sigh he pulled April tighter in to his chest and closed his eyes and despite the mystery of how this may have happened, he felt so naturally peaceful and drifted back into a deep sleep.

Alcohol continued to course through them both, washing out the normal mental processes, leaving the primal brain and basic instincts influencing their moods in their dreamy embrace.

The intermittent gentle rhythm of April's rear caused Astril to stir. "Is that deliberate?" he wondered.

Her grinding motion grew stronger and more frequent.

Astril's heart rushed, the heat from the rapid beat quickly spread throughout his body. The fire of burning desires raised their temperatures to a level of perspiration. Hot and wet, with steamy alcohol tainted sweat, they clung tightly spooned together.

April reached further behind Astril's rear and pulled him closer, she could feel his contours pressing into her body; his rhythm matched hers as she led the erotic motion which had lifted both of them out of their dreamy slumber.

Gently the hip grinding eased down, finally becoming still, leaving them both exposed to an intense wave of each others body heat. Both could hear their increasing hearts being driven by anticipation.

April grabbed Astril's forearms and pulled gently requesting him to loosen his grip, as he did so she turned into him. Their breath intertwined as they settled into each other, both lying on their sides. April rubbed against his lips with her nose which he kissed gently, she released a sigh and tightened her grasp around his torso. Astril was high on the smell of her hair resting across his face; he cupped her head to lead her lips towards his.

Their first kiss was born.

Astril's right arm slipped under April's waist, the gasps between their passionate kissing gave them both small pauses to absorb the intensity of the moment. His knee and inside thigh slid under her light frame, gently he rolled onto his back using his leg and arm to pull her on top of him.

Her kisses grew wild in response; Astril ran his hands down her back and slid his fingers under the elastic of her underwear to feel her rear. April pushed her posture hard into him, tilting her pelvis while rising up slightly onto her knees, forming a small arch in her back. His fingers extended further, deeply probing and exploring her; little by little he inched closer until he finally touched her centre.

April continued to gasp in between the heavy kisses which she laid upon his face and lips. Astril gently teased and stroked her lightly using two fingers of his right hand, while his left palm cupped her rear.

April felt too wild for oral foreplay, she explosively placed both hands on his chest and bolted up high. She tore off both of their underwear and slid onto him, gently to begin with, but her hip grind quickly increased in rhythm.

Astril felt the power of April's little soul. In their short time together she had knocked him out, looked after him, made him laugh and was now taking the lead in the bedroom.

He observed her silhouette riding him in the darkness, both of them moaning with ecstasy with each drive of her pelvis, the excitement of the first time, and its unexpectedness, held their focus in the moment.

Astril placed both hands on her hips to guide and drive harder, faster, more; the alcohol still present helped him delay his orgasm.

April finally slowed the pace and lay flat on his chest; her wet brow met the sweat running off his body and she could hear the pounding of his heart under the deep rise and fall of his rib cage.

Still inside, Astril turned her to her back, now he was on top, he scooped both of her legs high using his inner arms behind her knees, then grabbed her wrists to pin her gently but firmly. April gasped in anticipation, the position felt forceful, slightly out of her control, with the fear of danger of no escape.

Astril began to thrust and circle his hips, mixing up the intensity, sometimes just pushing in and holding the deep position, other times driving hard, fast strokes.

April was out of control, high on her new experience of being taken, almost without choice. She felt that Astril would never hurt her, even though he was indeed a dangerous man, but the fantasy of being desired so badly unified her mind to physical joy which led her to quickly climax.

"Don't you dare stop!" she moaned repeatedly.

Astril thrust harder and faster, but the orgasm felt to be in the distance from him; he paused to catch his breath and released April's legs.

"Are you ok?" she whispered but Astril gave no reply.

He drew back slightly to rest.

"Yeah," he finally answered, "I'm ok!"

April placed both of her feet gently on his chest and playfully grabbed his flesh by pinching with her toes.

She then sat up and kicked her legs over to turn to all fours and began to tease Astril with an erotic pose as she looked at him over her shoulder.

"She knows what she's doing alright!" it struck Astril.

His blood boiled as he slid into her without haste.

He pulled hard onto her hips; his heart was in his throat and his body felt charged and in desperate need of relief.

"I'm gonna…arghh!" he cried with joy as he climaxed hot and hard into her.

Together they fell in a heap; the bed slats creaked from bouncing bodies on its mattress.

When he finally caught his breath Astril asked, "How did I end up in your bed?"

"You went to the bathroom and came into my room after. Don't you remember?"

"No I don't, maybe you spiked my drink!" he joked.

"No, not at all, you came in because you wanted to. You know you did!" she replied, as sharp as ever.

Astril spooned her up again and smiled, "I'm gonna keep a close eye on you!"

"Good!" replied April immediately, having the last word as usual.

Over the following few weeks April and Astril could not keep their hands off each other. They spent Christmas and New Year celebrations together and at the end of January the café reopened for business.

Astril absorbed every second of this new experience with gratitude. The presence of April had displaced his drive to take revenge. However, the Hellmakers continued to whisper of the vow to kill Krzysztof, but its power had begun to grow weak and was diminishing.

Something had to be done.

In the early hours of a cold winter's morning, Astril lay with April in her big wooden bed; he was wide awake and lost in a tormenting cycle of thoughts. He was an illegal-alien in England who had slipped into the country on a fake passport, just as Miles had taught him.

A killing ghost, taking revenge with an alibi of not even being in the country of his victims.

He knew that he would have to disappear at some point and then maybe return legally if he wanted to be with April long term.

Deep within he felt that with great effort, he may be able to give up his quest to kill Krzysztof, which may have been the effect of an unseen current projected by Krzysztof's visualizations. However Astril knew that no matter how much he may love April, it would be impossible for him with his present depth of hatred, to give up the hunt for Carl Carlyle.

April had stolen his focus, ambushed him; he had simply not been prepared for the effect she would have on him when he had drawn up his plans.

His conclusion was to avoid looking down the corridor of his mind which led to the chamber of horrors of his past. He knew that was where the chain reaction of hatred always began to fuel his anger. For the first time ever, he was going to let life unfold in front of him and see what may come his way.

Chapter twenty-four

Hellmakers and Fearbreakers

Early February had brought Krzysztof the welcome news that his ship would soon be returned to him. Carl, who was hiding on board just off shore, had received the substantial payment that he had been waiting for; to Kryz, it had seemed a long time coming.

The post workout shower felt better than ever and Krzysztof soaked up his endorphins all the way out of the gym and to his Jeep.

He threw his kit bag onto the passenger seat and retrieved his mobile phone from the glove box. It indicated 3 missed calls from a local number. Just as he was about to dial it, his phone began ringing from the same number.

"Hello Kryz, it's me, Jaden, I'm back in Whitby, are you busy? Can we meet up?"

Krzysztof paused for a few seconds before replying, "Yes okay, where?"

"Is the café near the harbour okay, say about an hour?"

"Okay," Krzysztof replied; he knew that Jaden would be back as promised, but he was caught off guard. He promised himself that this was not going to spoil his mood, all seemed to be finally going well and he was soon to be rid of Carl and be back in possession of his ship.

The hour quickly passed and both men sat in the café where Jaden had sat with Rebecca and her dog many years ago. The tension was easing slightly with small talk until Jaden mentioned Carl.

"He won't meet you. I asked him and he just laughed, I did tell him all that you said, and he was curious but only because he thought you may know who the assassin was!" Krzysztof said firmly.

"But he won't meet me?" Jaden asked

"No!" came the immediate reply.

Jaden paused for thought; he looked around the old café his mind awash with associated memories.

"May I ask one last favour Krzysztof?"

"Go on!"

"May I speak to Carl on your phone?"

Krzysztof sighed; he stared into his large mug of tea, "If I do that, will that be an end to it all, no more of this?"

"All I wanna do is give him my message, then I will be out of here!"

"But I already told him!" Krzysztof insisted.

"I know, but it's important to me that I try!" replied Jaden.

"Okay then, we had better get my phone; it's in my Jeep. Let's do it now and get it over with."

Both men exited the café and headed to the car park. The winter chill hurried them along to Krzysztof's Jeep; they climbed in and fired up the engine to provide some warmth from the vents.

Both men gazed out to sea from the windscreen observing the replica galleon that was just visible on the horizon. Krzysztof removed his phone from his bag that was now on the back seat and began to dial.

He adjusted the mode to loud speaker so Jaden could hear.

An interactional link between three old souls was about to be connected once again.

"What now?" Carl scoffed as he answered the phone.

Krzysztof replied immediately with a barrage of insults before finally informing him that Jaden was with him and had a message.

There was a short pause of silence.

"The killer that hunts you cannot be avoided unless you visualize that he finds peace!" Jaden announced, "In fact, that's the best way to deal with anyone who means you harm!" he added.

"Judas!" came the reply from the phone.

"Think he means me!" Krzysztof whispered.

"Listen to me you bible punching freak, I don't want my enemies to find peace, I WANT THEM TO FIND PAIN!"

The hateful intent of Carl's words released an energy spark which drifted across the Yorkshire moors and settled as an idea in Astril's aura field.

"I think I will shadow Krzysztof for one last time, to see how I feel," Astril thought. An idea from nowhere it seemed. He continued his run through the moors.

The explosive and aggressive battle of words between Carl and Krzysztof continued over the phone.

Jaden felt increasingly uncomfortable as he witnessed their hostile language of threats and insults. Just as the blue veins in Krzysztof's blood-red neck began to bulge under the pressure of high discharging deafening blasts of rage, Jaden clicked the door open.

"I'm going back in the café!" he said calmly during the brief silence of Krzysztof's sharp intake of breath.

Krzysztof acknowledged him with a nod and started the engine before Jaden had even had time to close the door; his Jeep screeched out of the car-park and was soon racing down the roads to Scarborough.

Krzysztof eventually hung up on Carl, cutting him off in mid-sentence; his Jeep pulled hard onto the drive of his home. "Not long now...........not long now!" The thought of Carl going into hiding somewhere far away almost left him feeling a sense of gratitude towards the unknown killer for scaring him away.

He gathered his phone and gym bag and entered his house.

The strawberry flavour protein drink was not in the pint glass for long, an evidential red line stained Krzysztof's upper lip from where he had poured it almost straight down his throat. It was soon cleared off by a long wipe of his forearm.

Jaden and Carl's words cycled uncontrollably through his thoughts, taking over and disturbing his afternoon's business contemplations.

He gave up and rested in a large leather chair, staring into space with an empty expression.

A neutral point in an unseen game of spiritual chess had been reached.

Astril's hatred towards Krzysztof was fading.

Carl had been given a method by Jaden to release an attractor field which would bring him harm. If he had had the foresight to wish the man who stalked him to release the pain that drove the hatred, he might just have found peace, thus calling an end to the hunt.

Jaden had visualized those who caused him pain to be at peace. And although he found it very difficult return to Whitby, let alone pass on his spiritual truths to men who had caused him such heartbreak and pain, almost ending his life, his discipline was strong enough to find the angle of thought and physical effort required to overcome the stress and obstacles put his way so that he might finally end the vow made by Cain.

Perception is everything; potential is nothing more than potential-until it is affected by the energy of perception.

After a few hours of staring at a blank wall, Krzysztof felt the urge to drive his Jeep aimlessly along the coast and enjoy the radio.

Three hours of road therapy calmed his mood and on his return journey, he decided to pull into Whitby Abbey.

He soon found himself sitting on a bench in front of the old church looking out to sea.

Just as he had begun to wonder where his day had gone, he noticed that his ship seemed to be a little further out to sea.

Krzysztof felt confused, Carl and his men had neither the ability nor permission to sail the vessel. He stood up and squinted, the security boat which normally shadowed the replica galleon was no longer present. Something felt wrong.

His phone was still in his pocket, so he quickly dialled Carl on board, as he stared at the silhouette of his ship sinking below the horizon.

Carl finally answered the call, "What?" he said abruptly.

"Carl, where the hell are you taking my ship? Who the hell do you think you are?" Krzysztof blasted.

"We're playin' pirates!" Carl replied. "Told ya he'd call!" Krzysztof heard Carl's voice fade slightly as he informed someone on board of the call.

"Carl, get the ship back to anchor point, NOW!"

"As soon as your little maggot friend has walked the plank far out to sea, we will be back, nice and safe. Don't you go worrying now will ya!" Carl replied with sarcasm.

"What!"

"We nabbed Jaden from the café. We can't go leaving loose ends now can we, he may be the killer disguised as a geeky religious nut!"

Krzysztof paused for a brief moment. "You got Jaden, on board?"

"Yes on board, but not for long, right, got to go, I have a beating to watch, then I have to play Captain Carl, I never made anyone walk the plank before, I'm quite looking forward to it, see you soon, bye, bye!"

"Carl......Carl, don't hang up, Carl, get the ship and Jaden back here now, Carl!" Krzysztof repeatedly blasted, but he had been cut off. He slammed the phone hard onto the back of the bench almost smashing it; his head was swimming. He grabbed the keys from his pocket and ran back to his Jeep, distracted by anger and fear. The stranger close by remained unnoticed. The secret of Carl's location had just been revealed by a simple, angry phone call.

Blood dripped onto the boards of the dark hull of the ship. A bucket of ice cold water brought Jaden back to consciousness.

"Ya better get used to the cold water ya squirming little maggot!"

Jaden choked for air. He hoped desperately that it was all just a nightmare, but the horrendous pain in both hands from the 8 inch nails pinning him to the chair delivered him back into the hull of pain where he had been brutally beaten and then nailed to his seat.

"I wanted to break your legs, but Carl wants you to walk the plank! You'll be dancing on that plank when I've finished with ya!"

Jaden peered through tears of pain at his two tormentors who seemed to take great pleasure in dispensing agony to anyone who dared cross them.

"Let me introduce you to my good friend, mentor and bodyguard Mr Griffin. He's going to find out everything you know about this assassin and even if you know nothing, we'll have a ball anyway!" Carl laughed.

Mr Griffin grinned at Carl before his head swivelled on a giant neck to stare hard into the soul of Jaden. He wore a long beard which was somehow at odds with his shiny bald head.

He leaned forwards to rest his weight on Jaden's bleeding hands.

"It's not often I get to kill a straight!" he shouted over Jaden's scream. He released the pressure and headed towards the tool chest that was kept at the rear of the hull. The ship was still being refurbished so lots of hardware had been stored until completion. "Looks like I will have to improvise mate, but don't you worry, I am sure I'll find something especially for you!" he said as he began sorting through various items.

Carl sat on a stool and made himself comfortable to observe his old enemy's suffering. He lit a large cigar and blew the smoke towards Jaden.

"In a previous life you threatened to throw me overboard, I don't think it worked then and I don't think it will work now!" Jaden said nervously.

"Believe me, you are goin' overboard........eventually!" Carl replied.

The dimly lit hull had been abused by Carl and his men as they partied between the large galleon and the security ship which often shuttled men, women, food and drugs to and from the mainland.

His henchmen had no respect for the vessel as highlighted by the two dart boards nailed to the vertical timber structures, empty beer cans and bottles piled under the steps leading from the deck and the smell of stale smoke from the many cigarettes burned during all night gambling sessions.

Other than Jaden there were only three men on board- Carl, Mr Griffin and a hired gun, who was presently on deck steering the vessel. The security had come to the end of their contract and Carl intended to be out of England in less than forty eight hours now that he had finally received a large and long-awaited payment.

"We'll see what we can do with these!" Mr Griffin said as he threw an assortment of tools at Jaden's feet, "Like I said," he grinned, "it's not often I get to do a straight!"

"You'd be nothing without us straights!" Jaden whimpered.

BANG!

A heavy blow from the handle of an adjustable spanner exploded on the side of Jaden's jaw releasing a thick fountain of blood which scattered cracked teeth across the wooden boards.

"Did I......did I say you could speak?" Mr Griffin shouted.

Carl laughed but also grimaced with anticipation of the pain that Jaden was suffering.

"Let him have his say mate, I do find his lectures entertaining!" Carl requested. "You were saying?" he added.

"Cons!" Jaden coughed, "you cons need us straights, you need us, but straights don't need you!" Jaden raised his head and stared deep into the eyes of Carl, "When one of your gang members gets shot or you or a family member is unwell, you go to the hospital and probably get treated by someone you would call a geek and would probably have bullied at school for being smart. That geek became a doctor and saved your worthless life, in a hospital funded by straights paying tax. Without them there would be nothing. The list goes on. You are the bile that no fucker needs, a minority draining all that is good, eating a fucking good man's dinner. Despite this fact, and even though you are scum, and I hate you both, I still hope that you find peace!"

Mr Griffin turned and faced Carl with laughter, "I see what you mean, he's good!" He turned back to face Jaden and shouted "We don't want to find peace, we love the violence!"

Jaden started to speak, but stopped to spit out blood and a tooth, then began once more, "When you stabbed me at the harbour, and I vowed to kill you, my soul divided. That's who's after you, and let me tell you, you are only playing at violence; he'll show you the real thing!" Jaden warned Carl.

Mr Griffin grunted, taking offence at Jaden's comment regarding violence.

"The only thing that divided was your sanity, you should have died there and then, to save yourself the pain of a long night," Carl sneered. He turned to Mr Griffin, "Shut him up, I'm sick of his lectures!"

"Thought you said he was entertaining!" replied the bearded man as he taped over Jaden's blood drenched mouth. "Time to get serious!" he added as he lit the flame of a small blow torch used on the ship to heat bitumen. "You know, I have made people choose which member of their family I am gonna kill in front of em, boy or girl I said, and I made 'em choose, so think of the night me and you are gonna have!"

"Think I'll get a little closer, I don't want to miss anything now do I?" The pair gathered around the blood drenched chair which imprisoned their victim. Mr Griffin raised the blow torch and Jaden raised his head, he was terrified and in dreadful pain, but he felt a current of calm energy dampening his fear. For a second he thought he saw movement in the shadows from behind the two men. It came from near the steps leading from the deck of the ship.

"Burn his eyes out!" sneered Carl

"I intend to!"

"Let me do it!" Carl grinned. He took the blow torch from Mr Griffin and held it high to antagonize Jaden's mental state further still; he then began to bring the flame slowly towards the face area. Jaden buckled fighting the pain of shredded flesh and split bones from the nails holding him in the chair. He could smell the gas from the searing heat.

A deafening series of screams filled every dark void of the ship; the release however was not enough to ease the magnitude of pain felt by the victim.

Jaden gasped as he opened his eyes to reveal who was screaming and why.

Carl fell onto the boards clutching his armpit, the handle of a small knife protruding from under his arm.

Mr Griffin spun around in haste; an up-thrusting razor sharp diver's knife met him as he turned and plunged through his jaw, slicing through his tongue smashing out his front teeth.

He was held there, high on his toes, impaled, as the attacker extended the weapon inflicting immediate agony. Mr Griffin choked and coughed on streams of his blood cascading down his throat. The weapon was retracted sharply and the bleeding victim collapsed in front of the chair.

Astril and Jaden's eyes met for the very first time.

Earlier that day Astril had felt an inspiration to follow Krzysztof for one last time. The chain of events had unfolded and Carl's location had finally been revealed as Astril had overheard the phone conversation which had taken place at the Abbey. He had responded immediately, sprinting down the steps to the harbour and hijacking a small fishing boat at knife point.

They had caught up with The Sea Dog and Astril had climbed aboard the moving vessel after giving serious warnings to the fisherman. Once on board he had quickly killed the man at the helm, before venturing slowly down the steps to the hull.

Astril paused, his pupils expanded from the influence of energy from a dark vow made long ago. He clutched the knife in his right hand; blood ran down the blade and dripped onto the toe of his boot.

Mr Griffin lay writhing in agony at his feet. The inhuman gurgling cries of pain and shock served as a sickening confirmation for Jaden who realized that his nightmares and visions of Astril were true.

"Hmmmmphh, Hmmmph!" Jaden protested through the tape still covering his mouth.

Astril slid the knife into his belt then bent over and picked up the hammer that had been used to knock the nails into Jaden's hands.

Jaden felt the non forgiving saturation of Astril's presence at this proximity. The pain in his hands diminished for a moment as he fearfully observed the dark creature slowly stand up with its eyes fixed on the hammer gripped tightly in its hand.

Mr Griffin had begun crawling towards the steps; inch by blood-soaked inch he struggled on. Astril checked to see if Carl was anywhere near a weapon; he remained a whimpering, curled up ball tending his injury and trying to remove Astril's half moon shaped knife from his arm pit.

Jaden could only look on as the creature stepped over Mr Griffin, "You!" the creature called out in a gruff voice. His prey froze on all fours; he knew now the dread of his many victims as he turned his head, whimpering like a child. His eyes met the impassive stare of the figure standing over him and he watched as the hammer rose slowly, deliberately above the other's head.

Astril threw his weight and all of his hate behind a powerful downward smash into Mr Griffin's skull. The impact smashed bone with enough shock to burst the half slaughtered man's eye out of its socket.

Astril regained his feet intent on striking once more, but the job was done.

"Babb a bab maa ba bab," Mr Griffin lay murmuring a brain damaged song of the dying. His eye lay exposed on the boards, still connected through ruined veins and nerves.

Astril raised his boot and stamped down hard.

POP.

The tiny sphere exploded under his foot.

Jaden fought hard to prevent himself from vomiting; he knew he would choke due to his mouth being taped up.

"Aye eye captain!" Astril said with a mixture of hatred and sarcasm.

He turned to his next victim, the one whom he most hated.

The blow torch which Carl had dropped from the attack was still burning; its circular gas cylinder had allowed it to roll to the back of the hull, its flame pointed towards a coiled length of old thick rope.

Carl sensed Astril's eyes upon him from the far end of the hull. He climbed to his feet, exaggerating his pain in hope of mercy.

"Who ordered the hit? I can buy the contract, I have money, listen, listen, there is a case full of cash upstairs, it's yours, and plenty more where that came from, who are you? Who ordered the hit?" Carl repeated himself over and over, but Astril gave no reaction, he remained motionless, his stare icy cold, unreadable.

After what felt like an age to Jaden, Carl finally stopped pleading. The hum of the engines below, mixed with the murmur of the remains of Mr Griffin's brain-dead chant.

The ship creaked as it sailed freely, no one at the helm.

Astril dropped the hammer, pulled the knife from his belt and walked past Jaden towards Carl.

"No, no NO NO NO NO!" Carl cried as he dropped submissively to a kneeling position. He knew with absolute certainty that he had no chance of overcoming his assailant.

"I am no assassin!" Astril spoke in a lowered tone. "Because of you, my family are dead!" he added.

"But I don't even know you!" cried Carl

"You found my family's location and informed the Dombrowskis; their little killing team massacred everyone but me!"

"Are you the one who killed Krzysztof's family?" Carl swallowed hard.

Astril nodded very slowly wearing a blank expression. "Yes, and I saved the worst............ 'til last!"

"C'mon man, it's not like I pulled the trigger or nothing and it was the bloody Poles that financed it. C'mon man, they always put out jobs like this to Franz Schlachter. Him and his boys did it." Carl relaxed, he looked up and smiled, "C'mon man, let's work something out."

Jaden witnessed the beating; long, furious, merciless. Again and again Astril's knee thundered into Carl's face, his hands holding firm on his victim's head, until Carl's nose was smashed, a flattened, ruined, bloody mess.

"Ahey!" Astril bellowed as he threw the bleeding villain hard to the boards.

The rope finally began burning from the heat of the blow torch. Astril noticed it as he stalked the crawling and desperate Carl Carlyle.

A kick hyper-extended the victim's elbow; it cracked backwards causing Jaden to look away, the burst of screams making him retch as he fought back the sickness.

Astril marched past Jaden, he seemed to be looking for something, and he soon found it; he snatched the blood stained hammer from beside Mr Griffin, who was still slurring an unrecognisable dead man's dialogue.

He then approached Jaden, still appearing to be searching for something, he scanned around the chair. A series of screams and pleas for his life was made by Carl as he lay writhing in a pool of blood near the growing flames at the rear of the hull.

Astril reached behind the chair, Jaden fearfully leaned over to try and catch a glimpse, but the searing pain in both hands restricted him. The chair had been nailed down, it would not budge.

Astril stood back up with the box of nails which had been used to pin Jaden to the chair. Jaden's dread of Astril's next evil deed far outweighed the morbid curiosity to watch. He turned his head, and wished only that he could cover his ears.

"No, no please no, arghhhhh, no, arghhh, no!" Carl's high pitched cries seemed endless. Bang bang bang bang, the hammer fell on nails which cracked and squelched as they were driven through flesh and bone.

Jaden knew that he had just escaped a horrific death from the hands of Carl and Mr Griffin, despite this however he would never wish this magnitude of pain and suffering on the two gangsters. He rubbed his jaw against his shoulder to try and release the tape over his mouth.

Astril stood above Carl who lay face up, spread out, hands and ankles nailed to the blood red boards.

He dehumanised Carl. The writhing scum at his feet had killed his family and was probably responsible for the suffering of many more. As far as Astril was concerned, these worthless-eaters had done it to themselves and they should experience that which they had given. He was still improvising and struggling to contain his rage, he wanted to kill him with his bare hands, a personal termination. The fire to his right was growing in strength; the light from the flames revealed a hand-held, battery powered circular saw by the tool chest.

The images of the funeral of his loved ones from long ago, along with the loneliness and identity change for protection, fuelled his hatred.

The differing perspective of Jaden and Astril was relative to their experience of life so far.

Carl watched crying with dread as Astril picked up the circular saw; he then set the blade depth to half an inch and pulled the trigger. The motor powered through its tiny gears with high pitch squeal. The power tool was brought close to his Carl's face in order to antagonize him even more.

"How dare this filth plead for his life...........it has no right!" Astril raged. "Scared are ya? Well my family were all scared, thought you could get away with it didn't ya? Well guess a–fuckin-gain!" he screamed.

Jaden watched in horror as the dark killer became possessed and consumed by pure rage.

Astril knelt over and stretched Carl's body on the boards by pushing hard against his throat with his left hand, his right hand then sank the sharp blade into Carl's solar plexus. The teeth roared through the flesh and bone of the semi slaughtered villain. The steel was not deep enough to cut into any vital organs as it tore into the victim's chest spraying blood and splinters of bone.

Astril threw the saw to one side; even at this stage of extreme violence his rage had not subsided.

Carl lay barely alive, a trembling mess of near-dead flesh nailed to the boards.

Jaden's eyes flooded with tears as he witness Astril kneel over the man's chest and rip open the rib cage with his bare hands, slavering with desperation of reaching in and tearing the heart from its cavity before the victim died. It was important that he felt the agony of his termination.

The sound of chokes and grisly, snapping squelches sickened Jaden as much as the sight of the horrific murder before him.

Although Carl lay dead, Astril's rage intensified further still; he gripped the warm shredded heart in his right hand and smashed it repeatedly in Carl's terror stricken, soulless face.

When there was nothing left but mashed valves, he reached for the power tool and continually pounded Carl's skull into fragments until the motor housing of the circular saw finally smashed from the endless high-velocity impacts.

Astril climbed to his feet breathing heavily. He paused for a brief moment then released his firm grip on the remains of the saw. It thumped on the boards.

Jaden's continuous rubbing finally released the tape from his mouth.

At last he could spit out the blood which poured from his broken teeth. He felt like he had swallowed a gallon. Astril pulled the half-moon shaped kerambit from Carl's armpit, then turned to face Jaden.

Both men were drenched in blood; Jaden in his own, Astril in that of three others.

Their eyes met.

"You will pay for what you've done; we both will!" Jaden croaked.

Astril was still breathing heavily after the extreme effort in fulfilling a long awaited desire.

"Oh my self-righteous little friend.... I think....that you'll find, that I have in fact....already paid!"

Jaden was searching for words to inform Astril how their souls were linked.

"I wish I could do that again!" Astril pointed at Carl's corpse, he felt unsatisfied, and the desire to kill Carl again, even now, seemed insatiable.

"Careful what you wish for!" Jaden thought.

Astril wiped the blood from the half-moon blade on his sleeve. He approached Jaden.

"I'm sorry but there can't be any witnesses," he whispered, "I'll make it quick."

Despite staring death in the face Jaden felt a calm energy about him.

"I have survived a far less forgiving and far more ferocious beast than you will ever be!" Jaden said as he saw his reflection on the blade of the oncoming knife.

Chapter twenty-five

Vows Unlimited-Step into the Darkness

A heavy rumble of thunder cascaded through the distant clouds.

The Eroda continued to sail her voyage across the dark and lonely Atlantic Ocean.

Most of the crew had disappeared below deck leaving only the sound of creaking timbers above.

A storm was brewing, rough seas lay ahead of the old ship, but she was weathered and had survived many hostile conditions before.

Breaker sought comfort within the captain's quarters at the ship's stern. Blood streamed out of his mouth from a broken jaw and smashed teeth and he was wracked with the agony of his brutally damaged knee.

The shock from Cain's intense and violent attack had wrecked the man both mentally and physically.

The captain sat with his head tilted back to aid his bleeding nose which had been broken by Cain's hard kick in the face.

The ship's surgeon tapped at the door and let himself in; he struggled down the short and narrow corridor carrying towels, a bowl of warm water, bandages and splints.

He knew that he had to restore both the captain's and Breaker's health because there was no further chain of command; the rest had died on the treacherous return voyage. The doctor knew that the captain would be incapable of keeping order by himself, so he tended their wounds carefully.

Breaker had finally tasted the fear and pain that he had prescribed to his many poor victims over the years; he had never expected that anyone of them would ever stand against him, he thought himself to be unbeatable, and the agony of defeat was unbearable. Violence was all that he had.

"What will the men think of me now? Does this mean more men will beat me? Will there be more pain and fear to come?" The uncontrollable negative voices within him chanted his fears relentlessly and he realised that his size was no longer a weapon he could rely on.

The captain observed the broken man; Breaker's expressions had given away his fear to all on board. Voices echoed around the ship out of the darkness and the captain felt an icy cold fear threatening his safety.

A body fell past the window and splashed into the cold sea.

"There goes Cain!" said the surgeon as he tightened a splint to Breaker's leg.

"And not a moment too soon, they took their time to chain him up and carry out my orders, the crew are slack, I will deal with them later, see if I can speed them up a little!" the captain growled; he then ordered the surgeon out of the cabin, even though his work on the two men was unfinished. The captain needed time alone with his bodyguard.

The door creaked shut leaving both men alone in the silence, the captain searched his shallow soul, but he could not even find a few simple words of comfort required for his cousin. A man of no compassion, the captain's only true concern was his profits and safe arrival home.

Breaker's eyes followed the captain as he unlocked a small cabinet holding the rum.

He charged two glasses and placed one in Breaker's trembling hand.

"We'll be home very soon, you did well, it's not easy keeping order on a ship loaded with scum!"

Breaker remained silent; he sipped the rum just handed to him. He felt alone with his self-destructive thoughts as he gazed out of the window and into the black night. *"Time for change"* A comforting feeling washed over him. But it didn't last.

"What?...This is your ship, you keep order, you beat Cain, you alone stopped him!" His ego was creating inner conflicts. Breaker stared into his rum; maybe the answer lay somewhere in the bottom of the glass. The conflict grew rapidly; it was beginning to feel almost as painful as the fight.

"You beat him!" his ego continued.

"No, not really, he could have finished you while you were counting your teeth on the deck!" replied the truth from his heart.

"I don't think so...... I am not going to give up over one close defeat, I wasn't ready, it won't happen again."

"You are brave now he has gone, but remember his vow to kill you, how it made you feel. It's time to give it up; if you continue down this path, it will take you to a dark place," his heart laid down the truth once again.

"Really....where is he now, where? I am going to become twice as strong, and twice as mean, no one but no one will ever cross me again!"

The ego stirred Breaker's anger; he began nodding to himself as he felt the power of adrenalin squeeze into his blood stream from the glands above his kidneys.

"Careful!" his heart warned him.

"Careful.........of who, where is Cain now?"

"How's the rum?" the captain interrupted the inner dialogue.

"The rum is fine!" replied Breaker, holding up the glass and peering through the liquor at the tainted lamp light.

"You're lookin' a lot like ya ol' self again. Feel strong enough to keep order? How's ya leg?"

Breaker nodded, his jaw was swelling and the pain from broken molars prevented him from speaking too much. He pressed the cold water soaked bandage against his face to dampen the agony. Another sip of rum eased the shakes.

"I'm gonna assemble the crew on deck and brief them. You stay here, enjoy your drink!" the captain smiled and squeezed the big man's shoulder as his confidence in Breaker's recovery increased.

Moments later and all hands were on deck under orders of the captain. It was beginning to rain and the crew braced themselves as the Eroda creaked and rolled on the rise and fall of growing waves. The wind howled through the masts, bringing cold sea spray on deck.

The Captain stepped out of his cabin; it was located at the stern of the vessel and stood slightly higher than deck level. Breaker followed close behind, pain still evident in his face. At both port and starboard were steps leading to the higher deck where the helm was situated.

"I hope all of you now can appreciate, just how hard it is to keep order on this ship, and the sacrifices my cousin has to make to protect you all from trouble makers like Cain!" The captain's voice croaked as he attempted be heard, but the winds carried his voice out to sea. He drew a large intake of breath: "You all know I am a fair and compassionate man and my crew always come first and foremost. That includes every single one of you, and I think, so far, you'll all agree, that I have been lenient!"

He paused and drew another breath while grabbing the double breasts of his uniform. He nodded his head and scanned the men for eye contact. "But I will tolerate no more!" he blasted, "Anyone who steps an inch out of line, will suffer Cain's fate, and will soon join him......... overboard. Do I make myself clear?"

"Aye captain!" muttered a collective reply.

"It's been a hard crossing....we've lost a lot of men, let's not lose any more!" the captain added.

The flickering lights which radiated from the captain's cabin became eclipsed by Breaker's large frame as he shuffled forwards to join the captain. He kept a stern expression in an attempt to mask his pain

"Looks like a storm is ahead of us, prepare the ship!" ordered the captain. The crew responded and took action under the watchful eyes of the command.

The captain turned to face Breaker, "Maybe we should have made Cain suffer badly rather than just chaining him up and throwing him over board......... would have been a good example to educate the crew!" he scoffed.

"The men have seen enough violence, I'm sure they're clear!" Breaker muttered. It seemed that he had finally had his fill of blood, pain and endless cries of agony aboard this ship.

"Hmmmm, maybe we should throw a man overboard, put a little fear back into the men!" the captain muttered as he scanned the deck.

Breaker shook his head, "I haven't the strength, maybe tomorrow!"

Obsessed with revenge, the captain looked about himself in search of a victim; anyone of whom he could make an example, his desire to be feared was his becoming a passion.

"I wish that troublemaker Cain was back here, I'd............." the captain froze mid sentence.

"You would what?" Breaker asked, but the captain was wearing a confused expression which rapidly developed into a look of sheer terror as he gazed over Breaker's shoulder. "What is it?" Breaker dared not turn to look for fear of what he might find behind him.

A smashing blow exploded through Breaker's skull; once again he fell hard onto the deck. The impact was delivered with a heavy and powerful solid force.

Emergency adrenalin pumped hard to override the injuries and escape. *"What's happening, what's happening, what's happening?"* his fearful ego was begging for answers. He opened his eyes to try and focus. As he came to, the ringing in his ears was quickly displaced by a terrible sound of dreadful screams. His cheek pressed against the cold wood, his head felt heavy and he dared not move for fear his skull would crack and fall apart such was the magnitude of his pain. But the agonizing plea close by demanded that he roll over to see who was in peril.

A cloaked figure sat high on the captain's chest pinning him hard by the throat against the deck with one hand whilst simultaneously hammering his face and skull with a large link of chain clasped in the other.

Fountains of blood spewed from the captain's head as the hateful onslaught continued.

The crew observed hatred like never before. It was clear that the stranger had an evil and merciless desire to inflict serious pain and suffering on the captain and Breaker.

"Arghhhh!" growled the cloaked figure with the driving force of rage as he repeatedly rained down blows with the heavy metal ring. The crew did indeed hate the captain, but the magnitude of violence behind this attack sickened them, the energy of this killer was felt by all and tears welled in the eyes of some of the helpless sailors.

The screams from the victim died down as unconsciousness was reached. The hooded killer dropped his improvised knuckle duster; it clanked onto the deck and bounced into the blood pool scattering droplets across the already red-drenched boards. He drew the sword from the murmuring, beaten captain and climbed to his feet.

"Up close............... and personal!" whispered the stranger to himself.

The crew were exhausted; weak, hungry and repressed from the long, torturous voyage; even collectively they remained too afraid to rush the violent stranger.

He turned to face them.

Breaker lay broken to his left and the captain lay before him, gurgling through his blood filled throat, his life spared simply that he might absorb more pain and suffering.

Clutching the captain's sword, the cloaked figure took a step forward out of the shadows cast by the timber structures; as one, the crew maintained a healthy distance and simultaneously took a step back.

The lamp light revealed the cloak to be nothing more than a dark blanket wrapped around his body and held in place by rope.

"Who......who are you?" came a nervous request from one of the crew.

The wind rushed through the vessel raising haunting cries from the rigging and sails.

THUD.

The sword was thrust into the boards and the stranger took another step forward.

As one, the crew watched as he removed the hooded cloth and turned his head towards Breaker.

Moonlight broke through the drifting night skies and fell across Cain's profile as he gazed upon the crew once more. His eyes appeared inhuman, large and black like a killer shark. His intense and hateful expression served as a warning to any crew member who may be considering saving the lives of the captain or Breaker.

The body which had been cast overboard was that of the sailor who had been sent to throw Cain into the ocean.

"Cain?" a crew member whispered in question from behind the mid-mast.

"Not Cain...........Not this time!" his voice carried the vibration of a cold and calculating killer.

"Look.....it's Cain, I knew it!" gasped one of the sailors to a shipmate.

"Not Cain!" growled the man. "ASTRIL.....I am Astril!" he added as he admired the destructive introduction that he had inflicted upon Breaker and the captain thus far.

He turned his focus inwards to whisper to Cain and Jaden's essence.

"Sometimes all you need..... is a weapon." He preached to them of their failures against their enemies. "I said I wanted to kill Carl again. Be thankful for what you wish for!" Astril's knowledge and memories blended with those of Jaden and Cain, and from whence he had just arrived.

Although the captain and Breaker lay bleeding before him, (Astril-Jaden-Cain) felt the soul presence of Carl Carlyle and Krzysztof, there within them somewhere.

Breaker's physical agony was overshadowed by fear and confusion upon recognising his attacker; the man who he had thought to be well below the ocean by now. His heart cried out to him as he observed Cain, "You should have listened to me!"

"Yes, you should have listened, you caused this!" agreed his terrified ego which always stood ready to take credit for a win, but would never take any responsibility for loss or failure. The adrenalin increased his strength; he rolled onto his side desperately seeking composure.

(Astril-Jaden-Cain) stepped towards the whimpering captain who was now conscious and trying to crawl away, desperate to seek refuge somewhere, though the steaming blood trail left a path that even a blind man could follow.

"What have I become?" a vibration from the essence of Cain arose as he observed the bloody mess.

"Your vow brought me here," Astril answered internally.

"You must stop this," Jaden's vibration was now also whispering to (Astril-Cain)

"It's too late for that.........and your vow also brought me here," Astril growled internally, "As did your failures!" he added.

Astril read Cain's memory further, he recalled images of the captain's joyful expression as he inflicted pain, death and long drawn out suffering of the men, women and children during the many transitions.

"Now I know why I am here!" Astril felt the beginning of a vengeful wave which he was very familiar with and he knew how to ride and harness its power.

He exploded into a rapid repetition of brutally powerful kicks which hammered into the captain's ribs, the impact splattered blood droplets across the faces of several crew members; they winced and scattered across deck, diving for shelter.

After an eternity of merciless, crippling blows, the savage attack ceased, leaving the captain writhing in pain, bathing in yet more of his blood, tears and waste.

(Astril-Jaden-Cain) gasped for air from the intense energy spent in the destruction of his former captain's rib cage. He drew a large intake of breath and raised his booted foot. He drove his foot down mercilessly, smashing the captain's ankle bone. The deafening snap echoed around the deck and the horrific screams and cries from the victim caused Breaker to vomit in the pool of his blood in which he lay.

(Astril-Jaden-Cain) reached for the sword, pinned the captain under foot and tilted the blade to reflect the moonlight into his victim's eyes.

"Oh no!" a crew member gasped.

The cutting of flesh and bone from the diagonal swinging slashes took the crew to a new depth of fear and darkness as they witnessed their captain slowly being slaughtered by his own sword.

The killer sliced shallow depths, intentionally missing the vital organs so he could prolong the agony. A kick would interrupt the pace now and then to allow Astril to catch Cain's breath, and to turn over the captain's body. The pause was also to keep check on Breaker or any potential attackers from the crew.

Breaker covered his ears and began to cry from the dread of being carved into little pieces. The long tormenting screams made him realise that Astril was taking his time to make the captain suffer. It seemed to be lasting a lifetime.

"I'm sorry, I'm sorry, I'm sorry!" he repeated "If you spare me I will make good all the suffering I have caused, I will find a way," Breaker cried into the night seeking the presence of a higher power.

The terror was choking his every cell, the sounds of cutting and screaming from the captain's slaughter continued and the realisation of no escape finally overwhelmed him. The magnitude of mental hell forced him to accept that he was a coward at heart; it sickened him that he had taken pleasure in causing the pain and dread in others that he was now experiencing himself.

He pleaded for forgiveness, his realisation empowered his perception.

A surge from deep within his heart expelled his fear for a second; a memory of a kiss on his cheek from his sister before he left home warmed him.

The feeling of her love for him eased him further, her kiss would *keep him safe* she would say.

His eyes flickered closed as his beaten head thudded onto the boards.

As he faded out, his bones felt as if they had been crushed, and for a second, he thought he saw a flash of green light from somewhere deep behind his very own eyes.

Battered and cut to shreds, with smashed bones and wrecked joints, the barely alive captain's screams faded as yet more of his blood washed the boards red.

The crew continued to fearfully observe the slow destruction of a man who had once commanded life and death of all on board.

He was truly suffering a slow and painful fate that many of the crew thought was richly deserved.

(Astril-Cain) dropped the sword and knelt over his victim; the hatred continued to course though his veins, boiling his blood, commanding his actions and influencing his motivations.

His hands clutched the captain's throat with a crushing grip; he would periodically release the pressure to allow him to regain consciousness and realisation of his last moments on earth.

"I told you I would kill you over and over didn't I..........Didn't I?" (Astril-Cain) said sternly with a low-toned rough voice.

The final crush of the captain's throat was witnessed by all. The killer slammed hard with the choke, bouncing the head of his prey against the boards over and over.

After an eternity of violence, (Astril-Cain) hatred was at last spent; he released the very dead captain's body, reached for the sword and sucked in air as he climbed to his feet.

The crew backed off slightly as his large dark eyes gazed back at them.

He appeared inhuman.

The crew parted as he focused towards the mid mast.

Breaker sat leaning his battered body against the large timber.

Upon seeing him, (Astril-Cain's) hatred became strong again, fuelling his anger and dark intentions; he stepped forwards with all eyes upon him.

Breaker appeared calm despite the extreme danger he was facing.

"Do you ever dream of a large black dog, scratching in the darkness?" Breaker asked.

(Astril-Cain) froze.

The crew witnessed the effect of Breaker's words, they seemed have stunned him.

"People like me create people like you and people like you create more people like you; for when you kill in revenge, you leave behind those who would seek to kill you in revenge. The children of men you have slaughtered!"

Breaker felt compelled to utter the words that had come to him - from where he did not know. They felt right to him, an immediate knowing. "Go home to April...... before it's too late!" he added.

(Astril-Cain) felt a timeless memory flood through his soul, immediately dampening the anger.

"April!" he whispered to himself.

"There's someone in the water!" a crew member shouted, "over there look!"

A few men gathered portside. The ocean was illuminated by sheet lightning from the low black clouds. The light not only revealed a man swimming frantically towards the vessel, but a gruesome squid-like creature pursuing him.

"What's that?" came a cry from high in the rigging, "there's something huge in the water. Move yourself, come on man get out!" The sailors began to call to each other and point, urging him to swim.

(Astril-Cain) took his eyes off Breaker, the focus of the crew drew his attention along with theirs out to sea. He took a step towards portside and gazed into the flashing void as sheet lightning continued to illuminate the dry, stormy night.

He observed a massive black shadow just beneath the distant waves. Its presence immediately opened an inter-dimensional memory. To this point Astril had accepted his unknown arrival, but the squid-like creature in the water aligned a regressive memory. (Astril- Jaden- Cain) stood balanced and in full realisation of the presence of each other within as they witnessed Jaden, the ghost of himself, in peril.

Broken spiritual laws created by the passionate vow of a simple soul out for justice, further influenced and compounded by dark forces, allowed (Astril-Jaden-Cain) along with the crew, to experience a blend of time-bending dimensional crossovers.

The crew called out to the man, urging him, beckoning him to cross the distance and make it to the ship.

(Astril-Jaden-Cain) held a steady posture; his breathing was heavy, as he replenished the oxygen spent in slaughtering the captain.

He looked down and observed blood dripping off the blade of the sword and onto his boot, reminding Astril of a job unfinished; he turned slightly to gaze at Breaker.

Panic stricken by the sight of the creature, the crew continued to urge the man to swim for safety aboard the Eroda.

(Astril-Jaden-Cain) stepped closer to edge of the deck in order to better observe events in the sea below. The inner essence of Jaden was aware of this nightmare and the defiant essence of Astril felt an immediate rage, he threw the sword hard into the water in an attempt to bleed the creature. He cursed as it fell short of the intended target.

The holographic nature of the universe decoded the illusions of time under influence of various visualisations and vows.

(Astril-Jaden-Cain) was able to observe a fragment of his soul - Jaden as he swam, aided by the powerful cloak which had helped him shift between dimensions.

The sacred quantum energy of which all things are made is capable of being in two places or dimensions at once. (Astril-Jaden-Cain) was allowed to gaze upon the ghost of himself, just as the ghost of Jaden was allowed to sense and see his physical self in the form of Cain, on the ship.

The high winds tore a black garment from the man in the water. Hidden by the darkness, it tumbled across the surface of the ocean waves towards the Eroda.

Startled by the black shadow heading speedily towards him, (Astril-Jaden-Cain) failed to react quickly enough.

The crew observed a bursting flash of red and green light emanating from the cloak as it wrapped around Cain, sweeping him off his feet and throwing him across the deck, almost dropping him overboard.

The energy essence of Astril and Jaden immediately diminished leaving Cain writhing under the cloak, stained with the memories of his future soul-divided self. The consequences of his hateful vow to kill over and over were revealed to him. He gasped as he fought his way back to his feet, clinging to the mysterious garment. It felt warm and dry despite having blown in from across the ocean.

The crew waited in silence. None of them had the will or the courage to approach and investigate Cain as he struggled to wrap himself in the cloak. He never questioned its origin; it felt so natural and familiar to wear it.

Superstitious whispers and warnings began to generate even stronger fear among the men. The creature, the cloak, the flashes of light and the presence of Astril's extreme violent energy along with his slaughter of the captain led their anticipation to dark imaginings of the possible outcomes.

Cain observed the fear in their eyes. The men watched him, the same look in their eyes that they had once given Breaker. He felt sickened by how he made them feel; he had become that which he most hated.

He looked at Breaker who lay unattended and bleeding on the boards. He recalled suddenly why he had been made to suffer the beating to begin with. He had been caught giving water to a female prisoner being held below deck. No one aboard but the captain and Breaker knew who she was or why she was being held captive.

"The prisoner below..........let her go, bring her up on deck!" Cain ordered.

Two crew members followed his command without question and disappeared below.

From shipmate to commander, Cain realised the power of fear, and how it defeated those who used it against others. He sensed that if he remained in charge by harnessing this power, the cycle of violence would take him down also.

He observed the bloody mess of the captain who lay dead on the blood drenched deck.

"Overboard, throw it overboard!" he ordered, pointing at the remains of the most hated corpse on deck. Again the men followed his command.

The consequence of the extreme give - and - take of violence began to rise throughout various injuries throughout his body as the adrenalin and extra soul energy began to fade.

He fought against the pain as he tried to come together physically, spiritually and mentally.

The Eroda dipped in the dark ocean waves, her lights around various points on deck flickered through a fading misty fog.

The dreadful creature and the man it had pursued had both disappeared below the dark surface of ocean.

Cain ordered the ship's surgeon to aid Breaker.

He reflected while the crew organised themselves: "My hateful vow caused all of this!"

"You aided a prisoner, as you related to the torments of repressed freedom within yourself, and then suffered unjust consequence. Forgive yourself for your reaction, for its source was your sense to your God given right to overcome repression and be free of violence," the answer came to him through immediate knowing.

"But with Jaden's essence came knowledge: "I could have taught people to write, and after I hurt Breaker I also could have stopped, but I continued the violence!" Cain answered the knowledge within. "Will I be forgiven?" he asked in reference to his new perception of a higher consciousness.

"You have evolved through your pain, and so has Breaker. Unlimited consciousness has unlimited foresight and knew even before you were born, where, why and how you would relatively fail to evolve. Forgiveness is unnecessary; you cannot surprise the universe. To credit yourself with this power to offend that which created you, demonstrates your lack of understanding of the true nature of your unbreakable connection with the energy from which you are made and from whence you came."

Cain turned and gazed out to sea, he pondered the finest of lines between self defence and violent rage, which so often spilt into an unstoppable force which he had experienced first hand.

"Having fought back, it was more than I could do to stop!" he thought, "Surely there must be another way!" he added.

Footsteps approached him from behind; he turned to observe the female prisoner being escorted towards him.

"Let her go!" he blasted.

The two shipmates released her and disappeared on deck.

He immediately saw terror in her eyes as she observed the bloodstained dark-cloaked man before her.

Cain observed as she began to tremble and shake, he felt sick to his soul that yet another seemed to fear him.

"It's me Cain.........I gave you water, do you not remember me?"

She stepped closer wide eyed. "What......what happened to you?"

whispered an Irish accent.

Cain immediately recognised her soul.

"April, you are April!" he gasped.

"No, I am Neasa!" she replied.

The whirlpool of Cain's soul still held the combination of Astril's present and future vibration, Cain received a strange blend of feelings from various points in time.

"April, I'm so sorry for the things I will do, and what I have become!" he croaked.

"Neasa, my name is Neasa..........although, I do understand, partly.... I think!"

Cain led her towards the captain's quarters. She was unsteady due to the cramped conditions below and limped painfully across the deck.

"Are you alright?" he asked.

"Yes, I haven't walked or stood up straight for a long while, nor breathed such clear air!" she paused to inhale the ocean spray. "May I stay here a while, in the open?"

"Of course, you are free to do as you choose!" Cain replied "Why are you captive?" he asked as they both leaned on the starboard timbers and gazed into the break of dawn.

Neasa turned to observe Breaker who lay battered on the deck under aid of the surgeon. Avoiding having to answer Cain's question she asked "What happened to him, where's the captain?"

Cain stared sternly dead ahead. He gave no answer. He felt Neasa lean on the timbers beside him.

"Can you help me?" she whispered "I need to get off this ship?" Her words revealed cold and dark realisations of the consequences of his actions, he realised that he too needed to escape the vessel on which he had killed the captain.

"Land on portside!" blasted a cry from the crow's nest high above.

Their spines tingled simultaneously in acknowledgment of their personal thoughts of escape coinciding with the call signalling land close by.

"We must be slightly off course, that'll be Ireland, the south!" Cain said as he crossed the deck to portside.

The crew still feared him and followed his orders. He made arrangements to set a course towards the distant land breaking into view on the horizon; he felt the men's relief when they realised that he intended to leave to vessel.

By mid morning the Eroda was anchored off the coast of southern Ireland. A small rowing boat of four passengers made its way through the calm waters towards the shore. Cain gazed at the rhythmic rise and fall of the oars cutting through the water laboured by two crew members sitting behind him. He reached overboard to dip his hand into the blue ocean. The cold water washed through his fingers, the current gently massaging them.

He gazed past Neasa sitting before him. The Eroda's three masts loomed in the distance, casting sinister shadows upon the waters. He shook his head slowly in reaction of the torments which he recalled as prompted by the overpowering image of the floating slaughterhouse. The suffering and bloodshed that he had witnessed in others and experienced himself, only then to become as violent as his persecutors, made him question the origin of the dark vessel, it appeared evil to him.

"Who is April?" Neasa asked.

Cain pulled his hand from the sea and pressed it against his ribs; the cool water eased his pain slightly.

He gazed at Neasa. Although she was dressed in the ragged remains of a man's clothes, Cain caught the hidden beauty which shone from her bright green eyes.

She parted her wild, long, dark hair and tucked it behind her ears while gazing at Cain and waiting for an answer.

Although the energy of Jaden and Astril had left Cain, he still had a fading echo of memories and insight from both of them. He connected to the knowing within.

"April is a lady who a splintered part of my soul, called Astril, could fall in love with......... she is a natural seer. In fact.......she is the future you!" Cain smiled,

"You are gifted too are you not? You see things, sense things," he added.

"A gift you say, more like a curse, it brings me nothing but trouble!" she answered.

"Who is Astril?" she asked.

Cain linked in with Astril who would give nothing away, but could be described through Jaden's creative energy.

"Astril is unique, his strength lies in his ability to harness and contain his rage forging himself into a cold and patient calculating killer. He uses dark meditations, rituals and visualisations, before he attacks he accepts that he may already be dead himself. And he knows that no matter how much a man is feared, he will always bleed and is as mortal as the next man."

"How is it you see the future so clearly?" Neasa asked.

Cain sighed, "A hateful vow links me there, and it caused soul division, twice I have felt an influx of power."

Neasa shook her head and gazed into Cain's eyes searching for further answers.

"I have memories which are not my own, and they are fading fast. A man called Jaden touched…." Cain paused

"What?" asked Neasa. The two crew members eased off the oars in order to listen.

"Jaden touched the bones of this body, my body," he said, drawing his hand across his chest, "drawn by a vow I made, a vow to kill. Its power unfolded throughout time to make that happen. Then again on a ship, I see Jaden in trouble, badly beaten and tied to a chair, Astril is close by with a knife, he steps forwards to kill Jaden, but as they make contact……..there is a flash……their energies come together, darkness falls in both of them, that's when Astril came here and killed the captain, and almost killed Breaker."

"Whispers from the future into the past, forever the effect of the words shall last," Neasa whispered.

The boat hit bottom and ground to a halt; both oarsmen jumped out and pulled the small vessel from the currents to rest on the sandy shore.

Cain climbed out and turned to help Neasa but she was already in the water. Both of them splashed through the small breaking waves and made for the shore.

The ecstasy of feeling land beneath their feet caused them both to sigh in synchronicity. Cain turned to observe the two crew men pushing the boat back into deeper waters.

"Tell Breaker I'll see him at the abbey!" he shouted.

Neasa blew the hair from her face. "What abbey? Why have you betrayed yourself so? You are on the run now, are you and Breaker not enemies?"

Cain shook his head then turned back to gaze in her eyes. "Something happened on the ship, Breaker's bones flashed through his flesh; somehow, deep within me, I know that somewhere in his future his bones are to be uncovered by his future soul....... Somewhere there is an abbey I must find...and meet him there!" he turned his head and nodded towards the boat fading out in the distance heading towards the Eroda. "Did you see the fear in those men's eyes? It sickens me. They were once my shipmates, now they cannot bear to even look at me!"

"It's the cloak you wear, it gives off an air which most men dread........for it is the cloak of the Reaper" Neasa informed Cain as she sensed the origin of the powerful garment. "With it comes a key to allow you to pass to the other side without first having to die" she added.

"I am not sure I am ready for this!" Cain said while removing it and sitting down on the sand. Her words brought him discomfort; he sensed that she may have revealed a terrible truth.

"It'll not be in this life time!" Neasa answered quickly as she sat beside him.

Cain looked over his shoulder, "We're in Ireland!" he said.

"I know, it's where I was born... where I am from!" Neasa replied as she too turned to look out across the green hills leading from the beach.

Cain propped his head on clasped hands with his knees supporting his elbows and gazed out to the Eroda.

He watched for a while until the anchor was finally weighed and the ship began to sail towards England.

He gently closed his eyes to try and bridge a conscious connection between his present focus and his relative future soul. Although the power which enabled him to previously do this was rapidly fading he felt the vibration of Jaden.

He felt the tilt of Krzysztof's ship, and saw visions of a growing fire close by. Still nailed to a chair, Jaden was drifting in and out of consciousness. The foremost thought and vibration that Jaden was generating was to visualise peace rather than seek revenge upon those who would harm him.

The energy then shifted to Astril lying on the boards beside Jaden.

The contact between the two had caused a surge of soul charge and exchange of power which had rendered them both unconscious.

The contrast between the two souls was extreme, Jaden humming a song of peace but the tune of violence was never loud enough for Astril.

A breaking wave brought Cain back to the shores of Ireland.

Neasa lay exhausted beside him.

As he became present he contemplated his vow and Jaden's visualisation. He realised in both cases, it felt as though their efforts at the time would have no affect on their outcome.

But he began to see how powerfully the feelings he had deliberately generated had influenced the unseen currents of energy which had affected his outcome.

He realised that if he had known the power at the time then he might perhaps have been more at peace.

"It never feels like its working at the time!" he whispered "I wonder if that's what they mean by faith," he added. "Maybe I can have faith in something.... Something wonderful...... without having any interference from the religious preachers."

Neasa raised her torso and leaned her elbows in the sand; Cain turned, he could see the reflection of the sea in her eyes.

Together they watched the Eroda sail out of view, its departure bringing relief to their hearts as the ship finally faded from sight. They then gently climbed to their feet and disappeared inland and into Ireland's green hills in search of a new and peaceful life...............that is........if their vows would allow them to.

Disharmonising vibrations sourced from the stored energy of many meditations of escape disrupted a dark soul causing him to wake. Astril's vision cleared as he lay face down in a pool of mixed blood in the burning ships hull.

He felt, and trusted a feeling of... "Cut yourself where the wounds may be seen." And so, he reached for the knife.